BY:_____

MISS WILTON'S

Waltz

NO LONGER PROPERTY
SEATTLE PUBLIC LIBRARY

RECEIVED
APR - - 2018

OTHER PROPER ROMANCES
BY JOSI S. KILPACK

A Heart Revealed

Lord Fenton's Folly

Forever and Forever

A Lady's Favor (eBook only)

The Lady of the Lakes

The Vicar's Daughter

All That Makes Life Bright

OTHER TITLES BY JOSI S. KILPACK

The Sadie Hoffmiller
Culinary Mystery Series:
*Lemon Tart, English Trifle, Devil's Food Cake, Key Lime Pie,
Blackberry Crumble, Pumpkin Roll, Banana Split,
Tres Leches Cupcakes, Baked Alaska, Rocky Road, Fortune Cookie,
Wedding Cake, Sadie's Little Black Recipe Book*

MISS WILTON'S *Waltz*

PROPER ROMANCE®

JOSI S. KILPACK

SHADOW
MOUNTAIN

© 2018 Josi S. Kilpack

All rights reserved. No part of this book may be reproduced in any form or by any means without permission in writing from the publisher, Shadow Mountain®, at permissions@ shadowmountain.com. The views expressed herein are the responsibility of the author and do not necessarily represent the position of Shadow Mountain.

Visit us at ShadowMountain.com

This is a work of fiction. Characters and events in this book are products of the author's imagination or are represented fictitiously.

PROPER ROMANCE is a registered trademark.

Library of Congress Cataloging-in-Publication Data

Names: Kilpack, Josi S., author. | Sequel to: Kilpack, Josi S. Vicar's daughter.
Title: Miss Wilton's waltz / Josi S. Kilpack.
Description: Salt Lake City, Utah : Shadow Mountain, [2018]
Identifiers: LCCN 2017037099 | ISBN 9781629724133 (paperbound)
Subjects: LCSH: Music teachers—England—Bath—Fiction. | Man-woman
    relationships—Fiction. | Bath (England), setting. | GSAFD: Regency fiction. |
    LCGFT: Romance fiction. | Novels.
Classification: LCC PS3561.I412 M57 2018 | DDC 813/.54—dc23
LC record available at https://lccn.loc.gov/2017037099

Printed in the United States of America
PubLitho, Draper, UT

10 9 8 7 6 5 4 3 2 1

Prologue

As a vicar's daughter, Lenora knew that doing the right thing was not always easy, in fact it was rarely so. It was *right* that Evan Glenside had broken his engagement to Lenora after realizing he'd fallen in love with her sister Cassie. It was *right* that Lenora had stood up to her parents after they had forbidden Cassie and Evan from seeing each other. It was *right* that tomorrow morning Cassie and Evan would marry in Father's church and begin their lives together. There was comfort in having been an essential part of so much rightness, but it was *not* easy.

All her life, Lenora had been known in Leagrave as the shy Wilton girl. The daughter of the vicar who struggled to maintain eye contact, who kept to herself, and whose only friends were her five sisters. Lenora was used to that, but the number of consoling looks sent in her direction since the broken engagement and the whispered gossip made it impossible for her to stay here.

"Poor girl," the neighbors were surely saying in piteous tones. "Such a strange little thing."

And Lenora just kept playing the pianoforte, providing background music to everyone's life while hiding behind her instrument.

The guests were slowly leaving the informal gathering on the eve of the wedding, and Lenora kept her eyes on the music as her fingers moved over the keys with tender exactness. There were still a few people in the room—mostly extended family who had come for the wedding—when Mother put her hand on Lenora's shoulder, her way of saying that Lenora could stop after this piece.

Once she'd finished, Lenora attempted to slide out of the room before anyone drew her into conversation. More often than not, when people addressed her, she would stare at the floor, fidget like a child, and make everyone uncomfortable.

Two more days, she told herself, and her stomach filled with butterflies—some fluttering due to nerves, but some due to excitement and relief.

Lenora was nearly out of the drawing room when Cassie took her arm. She'd thought her younger sister was still making sparkling conversation with their guests. Sometimes Lenora felt like Cassie had received Lenora's portion of social graces, as though such abilities were slices of cake. "Two for Cassie and—I'm sorry, Lenora, there's none left for you." But then maybe Lenora got Cassie's musical portion. She didn't mind too much because, given the choice, Lenora preferred music and her own company. And yet, that was changing too. At least it had been in Bath, where she'd escaped for a little while. Then she'd come back home to Leagrave and picked up the role she'd always played—the shy prodigy.

"Walk with me in the yard?" Cassie whispered.

Lenora wished she could object, but she didn't know when she would come back to Leagrave. This might be the last time she and Cassie talked privately for a long time.

"Please," Cassie added, apparently sensing Lenora's hesitation.

They left the vicarage by the back entrance and stepped into the quiet yard. The night was cool, and Lenora looked around at the familiar landscape, bathed in silver from the half-moon. She would miss this. She would miss *them*, and yet she was ready. She could feel it in a way she'd never felt before. Her future would be in Bath; her past would remain in Leagrave.

"Are you all right?" Cassie asked amid the sound of night birds and crickets.

The concern in Cassie's voice was sincere, reminding Lenora that although she often felt separate from her family, she *was* a part of them. She took comfort in knowing that she would always be a part of them, even if she was not *with* them. "I am." Lenora patted her younger sister's hand and gave her a reassuring smile she hoped would help prove her words.

"But you would not tell me if you weren't," Cassie said, a note of regret in her tone. "In fact, no one would be able to tell because you keep your thoughts so very much to yourself."

"That I keep my thoughts to myself does not mean I am not all right." Lenora faced Cassie, gathering her courage in hopes that her sister would hear her sincerity. "I have no regrets of what has happened, and I *truly* want you and Evan to be happy. Please do not let assumptions of my feelings detract you."

Cassie paused, her face relaxing. "I don't doubt that you want us to be happy—that is what is so remarkable."

"It is not so remarkable," Lenora said, shaking off the compliment. She was not distraught over the broken engagement or that Evan had fallen in love with Cassie. Lenora had not loved him, she'd simply seen him as the solution to the awkwardness of her social position. Being a man's wife—any man's wife—would give her a place, allow her parents to breathe a sigh of relief, and secure her future. It was all she'd ever wanted, and Evan's brief courtship was the closest she'd ever been to attaining that goal. But now that was over, and her goals were different. "This is right, and my knowing it gives me peace." She hoped Cassie would believe her.

Cassie cocked her head to the side as she regarded her older sister as though seeing her differently. The idea increased Lenora's confidence even more. If someone else recognized the changes that had been taking place within Lenora these last months, then the change was not a figment of her imagination. "And what shall you do, now?" Cassie asked. "What will your future hold?"

Lenora looked away, but the temptation to tell Cassie was nearly overpowering. *Two more days*, she told herself. That was when she would tell her parents. But what if she told Cassie *now*? Would it be wisdom or folly? Lenora stepped away and crossed her arms over her chest as she looked across the yard.

Cassie allowed the silence for a moment, but she'd never been one to wait very long. "I have sensed that you do not plan to stay in Leagrave once the wedding is over."

Lenora looked at her with sharp surprise, then turned back to the trees. The desire to share her plans increased now that Cassie suspected something. "I do not want to detract from the wedding."

When Cassie spoke, her voice was soft. "So you will not stay?"

"Aunt Gwen left me with an open invitation to return to Bath and . . . I am different there."

"You mentioned that when you spoke to Papa."

And yet no one has asked me what I meant by it, Lenora thought, then shook off the criticism. Being one of eight children meant that you were heard when you spoke up and demanded attention. Lenora demanded nothing. But now Cassie was asking, and Lenora was ready to answer.

"I attend Aunt Gwen, and rather than speaking around me, she pulls me in to conversations and forces me to share my opinions. It was overwhelming in the beginning, but in time I realized that I was capable." She turned and met her sister's eyes. "It began with your advice to smile and focus on my breathing, and then, though it was ill-fated, my time with Mr. Glenside forced me to step further out of the circle of my comfort. I thought any progress to be worthless when I left for Bath, but in fact that became a starting point." Lenora was still uncomfortable in a crowd, but she was getting better at meeting people and being seen as her own person rather than one of the vicar's daughters, and the shy and awkward one at that.

"And so you will seek your future in Bath?" Cassie asked.

"For now," Lenora said, unsure what her long-term plans might be. Four months ago, she would never have imagined *this* change, and it was oddly scintillating to not know where this new journey would take her. Cassie had always been the adventurous one, the sister who took her own path and never allowed herself to be overlooked. Lenora would never be Cassie, but recently she'd found more strength than anyone knew she had and there were times when she imagined that she might discover even more hidden aspects of her character. It was exciting to feel as though she were getting to know herself the same way she was getting to know other people.

Cassie was still waiting for an answer.

"I have no regrets of what has happened, Cassie. I see the place it has taken each of us, but I hear the whispers too. I feel the pity. It will take time for the gossip to settle, I think, and perhaps even longer for Papa to fully agree that this was the right choice." She smiled but then shrugged, belying the seriousness of what she would say next. "Beyond that, I have come to realize that I was raised with one expectation for my future—a husband and children. I never doubted it would happen or that it was the only path for happiness. I am twenty-three years old, and I have had one man cry off from his engagement and marry my younger sister. My prospects are poor."

Cassie winced.

Lenora put her hand on her sister's arm and smiled sympathetically. "I have *no* regrets, but society will keep its score. For so long I have lived amid panic that if I do not marry, I shall have no joy or purpose at all. I no longer feel that way, Cassie. I have seen another side."

Cassie did not seem to understand. "What side?"

"One of independence, confidence, and comfort in my own company." She'd said it—out loud! Speaking the words confirmed the truth of them to Lenora even more.

Cassie gasped. "You are not spurning marriage?"

"I am no longer *expecting* marriage to define my future. In fact," she paused, then rushed forward, invigorated by sharing confidences, "I have looked into a position as a music teacher at a girl's school in Bath. Aunt Gwen has been helping me. We met with the headmistress just before I left."

Cassie's mouth fell open, but no words came out.

Lenora felt an unexpected deliciousness at having surprised her sister. Lenora never surprised anyone.

Finally, Cassie spoke. "Mama and Papa will not be pleased."

"No, they will not," Lenora said, her smile falling as she considered the very real pain this would cause her parents. "Which is why I will wait until after the wedding to tell them." Her plans were already in motion, however, with the help of Aunt Gwen, who seemed to understand, without Lenora having to explain it, how much she needed a different life. Lenora did not want to hurt anyone by her choices, but she would not sacrifice her happiness either. "I hope to return to Bath by September so I might be situated at the school in time for the new semester."

"But if you become an independent woman . . ." Cassie trailed off, as though unsure how to complete her sentence without giving offense.

"I may never marry," Lenora finished for her. Men sought out young women in drawing rooms not classrooms. "I know that, and I am at peace with it."

"Are you truly?" Cassie sounded stunned. If her reaction was this strong, how on earth would their parents react?

Lenora took both of Cassie's hands and smiled. "Truly. I have come to realize that if I cannot be pleased with myself, I cannot be pleased with anyone else. A husband cannot make me whole. I must do that for myself." Bath had shown her the potential of finding that wholeness, and she would make any sacrifice necessary to be comfortable in her own skin.

"And you think teaching is the answer to finding that wholeness?"

"I do," Lenora said, then added, "for now."

Cassie blinked back tears. "I feel responsible for this."

Lenora smiled. "Then I hope you take pride in that responsibility because I have never been more excited about my future. I get to fill my days with music and make my own way in the world. I want you to be happy for me." Lenora rarely felt like the older sister, but at that moment, she did.

Cassie paused, and then pulled her shoulders back and lifted her chin. "Then I shall be. I feel that after spending our entire lives together I am only just now beginning to know you."

Lenora laughed. "I feel the same." She took Cassie's arm and turned her back toward the house. "I do hope amid your wedded bliss that you will find time to write to me so we might become the sisters we ought to have been."

"I shall write to you every week."

They walked in silence until they reached the back door of the house, then Cassie turned to face Lenora one last time. "I can never thank you enough for forgiving me and giving me the chance to be with Evan. It would not have happened without you."

Her gratitude warmed Lenora's heart. "You can thank me by soaking up every bit of happiness you can."

Cassie shook her head. "You are too good, Lenora. What else can I do? Surely there is something else."

Lenora paused a moment. "You can pray for me, Cassie. Pray that I find the same happiness you have found, one way or another."

"I shall do so every day."

Lenora gave Cassie's hand a final squeeze. "Then be happy. It is everything I want for you and Evan both."

The sisters shared an embrace and went inside.

Because of their houseguests, Lenora and Cassie were sharing Cassie's room, but Lenora could not sleep. Long after Cassie's breathing had evened out, Lenora slipped out of bed, into her dressing gown, down the stairs, into the boots she always left by the back door, and outside into the night.

She had started her Night Walks, as she called them, a few years earlier on a night where she felt fit to burst with anxiety after enduring a disastrous social event where she'd done everything wrong, as usual. The soft sound of the stream behind their home had always soothed her, but that had been the first time she'd gone at night. Once at the stream, she appreciated the increased stillness she found there, and the bindings in her chest loosened until the emotion released itself. She had cried into her hands, mourning everything that was wrong about herself.

She'd returned to the river at least a dozen times since then, always on the heels of something overwhelming, when she needed to express what she could not at home. Tonight, she did not need to cry, she just needed the peace and comfort the river gave her as she prepared to leave Leagrave, likely forever.

Two more days, and she would leave the pity behind. Two more days, and she would not be known as the vicar's daughter who must watch her every step. Two more days, and she would be *free*.

Chapter One

Two Years Later

The third button on Mr. Harpshod's waistcoat was of a different design than the other four. Lenora wondered if the man's valet had sewn it on prior to tonight's dinner party without time to find a better match. She imagined Mr. Harpshod putting on this favorite vest—silver filigree upon black silk—realizing the button was missing, and bellowing for help. She imagined him huffing and grubbing and running his fingers through his thinning hair while saying things like "Would you look at the time?" and "I've half a mind to turn you out completely, Justin." Or David or maybe Bartholomew. Did valets have names such as Bartholomew? Would they be called by their surname? As a vicar in a small hamlet, Lenora's father had never had a valet.

"Don't you agree, Lenora?" Aunt Gwen asked.

"Oh, yes," Lenora said, an expert at keeping half an ear to conversation while still absorbing the details around her.

"The lemon macarons are my particular favorite," Aunt Gwen added.

Lenora opened her mouth to share her opinion of the delectable cookies—her personal vice—but Mr. Harpshod spoke before she'd managed to utter a sound.

"Oh, yes, indeed." Mr. Harpshod went on to say that while Hoopers' macarons were very good, they were nothing compared to the macarons he'd had from a confectionary in Portsmouth a few summers ago. He had a house in that city, you know. Left to him by his mother's uncle.

Lenora wasn't offended by his interruption and maintained a polite expression; she never minded being on the listening side of any conversation. She looked at the mismatched button on Mr. Harpshod's vest again and imagined another scenario in which he was not as well-heeled as he professed to be and could not afford a new waistcoat, therefore he had to make whatever repairs necessary to continue the farce of his wealth until he could land some windfall investment or procure a rich wife. The house in Portsmouth was decrepit and mortgaged. Perhaps he'd come to Bath in time to be settled for the winter season where he would meet the heiresses on display while they waited for the London Season to resume in the early spring.

Her polite smile did not shift as her mind wandered, and when Mr. and Mrs. Grovesford announced that they had to be on their way, she lifted her eyebrows in the universal expression of "So sorry this lovely evening must come to an end." And it had been a lovely evening. Aunt Gwen had allowed her to play the pianoforte in the too-warm room during much of the drawing room socializing, and when Lenora had finally joined the conversation, the guests had been gracious and witty, and she'd conversed easily.

Even Mr. Harpshod was not objectionable, but there was nothing particularly endearing about him either. His sister—a quiet thing of eighteen years—rose when he did. As did Mr. and Mrs. Shelby, who were speaking with Mr. Johnstone on the other side of the room.

Aunt Gwen loved to entertain on Sunday evenings, and the company was always good, but Lenora was not sad to see the dinner guests leave. Sunday evenings were for Aunt Gwen, but once the house was still and the moon was high, the night was Lenora's. She'd become quite comfortable in Bath, though no one would ever guess just how comfortable. She was very different from the woman she'd been in Leagrave.

"What an enjoyable evening," Aunt Gwen said once the guests had been shown out. Her terrace house boasted four levels, with a large bay window in the front parlor that overlooked Gay Street. Aunt Gwen nodded to the footman standing near the door, and he left the room. She had a secret fancy for whiskey, but never indulged when she had guests. That she didn't consider Lenora a guest was something Lenora took rather a lot of pride in.

"It *was* an enjoyable evening," Lenora agreed. "The chocolate custard was especially good. I'm glad you allowed Cook to experiment on a company night."

"Oh, I am, too," Aunt Gwen said with a nod. "I shall have Cook put it on regular rotation."

"An excellent idea."

The footman returned with a tray holding a single glass of whiskey.

"You are sure you won't join me?" Aunt Gwen said as she took the glass.

Lenora answered with a laugh; Aunt Gwen made the same offer every evening. "Yes, Auntie, I am sure." The smell of whiskey was enough to put her off the foul drink; she was not one for liquor.

"I would not tell your father," Aunt Gwen added conspiratorially, pressing harder than usual.

Lenora shook her head. "You would not have to. He would smell it on my breath when I see him at Christmas in three months' time." She winked, and Aunt Gwen laughed. Lenora of Leagrave never winked. Lenora of Bath only winked when funning her aunt, but it was yet another change she could credit to the city.

Aunt Gwen took a long swallow and melted against the cushions of the settee with a sigh. "Does that mean you will go to Leagrave for Christmas, then? You've made up your mind?"

Mother's invitation had arrived the middle of August—a full fortnight ago and months ahead of necessity. She would be soon following up on why Lenora had not yet answered.

"In all honesty, I would refuse Christmas if I felt I could do so without infuriating my mother." Lenora hadn't been to Leagrave since Cassie's wedding.

"I think you mean breaking her heart."

Lenora wrinkled her nose as though considering Aunt

Gwen's concern. Her parents did not seem particularly *hurt* by her having missed two years' worth of holiday celebrations, just embarrassed that they could not boast that all six of their perfectly traditional daughters were mothering and homemaking the way God intended for women. Spending Christmas at the vicarage would likely include a few sermons on marriage and family and how the roles were key components of God's plan for all women. Lenora did not look forward to that, and yet she *did* look forward to seeing her family, including Cassie and Evan's new daughter.

Aunt Gwen finished her whiskey. "They worry about you, Lenora, that is all."

"I know." Lenora did not want to think on the topic any longer. It was late enough in the evening for her to excuse herself. There was a new moon tonight; her favorite nights were the dark ones.

"And your thoughts on Mr. Harpshod?"

Lenora looked up in surprise, took in the slightly shamed look on her aunt's face, and reviewed the evening in the space of a blink. Mr. Harpshod was a single man invited to a dinner party with exactly one unmarried woman, who was not his sister, present. Lenora had noted his buttons and his thinning hair and yet entirely missed that he was . . . eligible. "Aunt Gwen!"

Aunt Gwen avoided Lenora's eyes as she beckoned the footman to fetch her empty glass.

"You of all people?" Lenora continued, frowning. "And him of all men?" She struck a thoughtful pose and put a finger and thumb to her chin for effect. "I would suggest a chiseled jawline, enchanting eyes, and perhaps broad shoulders next time. Yes, definitely shoulders." She couldn't actually remember Mr. Harpshod's shoulders, which meant they must not have been anything remarkable.

Aunt Gwen narrowed her eyes, joining in the spirit of playfulness. "I had no idea you had such physical expectations."

"I have *no* expectations," Lenora clarified with a laugh. "But if you are playing matchmaker, at least make it a game worth playing on my part." Lucky for her, there were very few men of such description in Bath, which had transitioned thirty years ago from a resort of fashion, pedigree, and wealth to a lovely town of cures, comfort, and a decidedly gray-haired population. Few people kept their own carriages, and those who did not walk everywhere were carried to and fro on sedan chairs, like royalty.

"What a shameless thing for a vicar's daughter to say," Aunt Gwen said, but her smile was encouraging.

"Well, as I've said before, I am different in—"

"—Bath, I know," Aunt Gwen finished. "You *should* go home for Christmas and let your family see what a saucy girl you've turned into."

"If that is not the pot and the kettle, I don't know what is, Auntie." Lenora was afraid that when she returned to Leagrave, she would retreat behind the piano, move quietly from one task to another, and spend the majority of her time listening to conversation swirl around her while entertaining her sisters' children. That's what spinster sisters were for, after all, and she suspected her sisters all felt a bit put out that she did not travel from one household to another to help each time someone was ill or had a new baby. "I enjoy my independence in Bath, that is all, and that is what I shall tell them. The *sauce* will not come with me."

Lenora glanced at the clock—quarter after ten. She stood and crossed the room to give her aunt a kiss on the cheek.

"So, no to Mr. Harpshod?" Aunt Gwen asked as Lenora pulled back.

"No to Mr. Harpshod." Lenora put her hands on her hips. "I must say I'm surprised that you of all people would do such a thing."

Aunt Gwen's marriage as a young woman had not been a love match and had produced no children. When her husband died unexpectedly, Aunt Gwen invested her inheritance and purchased a terrace house, living a gentlewoman's life without needing to marry again. Aunt Gwen had never goaded Lenora regarding marriage, which Lenora assumed meant that Aunt Gwen approved of Lenora's choosing against the institution she herself had not found overly enjoyable. The footman arrived with an additional glass of whiskey. Good. Aunt Gwen would be asleep by eleven.

Once the footman had left, Lenora spoke again. "Who put you up to it—my mother?"

Aunt Gwen shifted, looking everywhere but at her niece.

"My father?"

"Victoria," Aunt Gwen finally said, placing the blame squarely on the most meddling of Lenora's older sisters. "She wrote to me and asked that I please help you find a husband, that your parents and sisters are distressed. I thought I would create this one event so I could tell her I'd done as she asked."

"Because I can never be happy without a husband?"

Aunt Gwen looked at the floor. Contrition did not suit her.

Lenora sighed and sat down next to Aunt Gwen on the plum-colored settee. "I am not angry with you."

Aunt Gwen met her eye, repentant and oddly insecure. "Are you sure?"

"I could never be angry with you after all you've done for me, but . . . do not do this." She held her aunt's gaze to be sure that she was understood. Lenora's stomach tightened at giving her aunt an order, but she had spent the last two years teaching obstinate fifteen-year-old girls to play *Für Elise*. She could stand up to her aunt. "If I have to look out for prospects when I stay with you, I'll stay at the school on the weekends. I cannot make room for considering marriage again. I wasted twenty-three years of my life on that plan. Let me have the freedom to pursue my own course. Please." Lenora was impressed with how steady her voice was and how practiced the words felt despite never having articulated them before.

"Very well, but living alone becomes lonely over time. I have friends and I enjoy my independence, but the evenings are long, and I have no children to comfort me as I grow older. I wonder if I was too determined in not attempting to find love when I had the chance."

"I will remember that you told me as much," Lenora said obediently, but her decision had been made two years ago. "Good night."

Lenora placed a second kiss on her aunt's soft cheek before making her way to the bedchamber Aunt Gwen had given her when she'd arrived in Bath the first time. The school term was starting tomorrow, so Lenora would move back to live in the staff apartments during the week. Her trunk was half-packed; she'd finish in the morning.

Lenora's stomach fluttered with nerves until she thought of the river waiting for her in the dark night. She rang for the maid who would help her out of her dress and take down her hair. At the school, Lenora wore plain dresses that she could manage on her own and pulled her hair back in a simple knot at the base of her head. But Aunt Gwen required full evening dress that necessitated assistance. It was like living two lives in Bath—three, if she counted who she became for the river.

"Thank you, Dorothea," Lenora said when she was in her dressing gown and her long blonde hair hung down her back. She gathered the tresses and began plaiting them as though it was her final task before bed.

"G'night, miss," Dorothea said before closing the door behind her.

Lenora completed her plait, but then used half a dozen pins to secure it in a flat spiral on the back of her head. She crossed the room and locked the bedroom door before going to her wardrobe and removing the hatbox from the back corner. Inside were a pair of men's trousers, a linen shirt, a knit cap, and a long, but thin, black coat. Perfect for roaming the streets of Bath and looking to any casual bystander like she was a young man walking off his worries. She wore her own sensible boots.

She'd promised herself she would not resurrect her Night Walks in Bath, and for the first ten months or so she had contented herself with walking during daylight. But Aunt Gwen often accompanied her, and once Lenora began serving as the pianist at the Pump Rooms every other Saturday, she met so many people that it seemed she was continually stopped for conversation during her walks. Her meditation of the river had become lost in the society of this city of pedestrians. And so, she'd developed a plan.

Chapter Two

The early September night was crisp as Lenora made her way toward her favorite spot on the River Avon. There were men on the street, but she'd expected that and did not lift her head as she casually crossed to one side of the street or the other to avoid them. She pulled her cap down to cover any bit of exposed hair, shoved her hands deeper into her coat pockets, and kept her chin against her chest. She turned the corner at Walcot, glancing around the darker street without slowing her pace.

A hundred yards later, she ducked between two shops, stepped behind a pile of crates, and climbed over the waist-high brick wall into which was set a sagging wrought-iron gate, chained shut. Once over the wall, she stepped over the crumbled top step, and then walked lightly down the remaining stone steps that led to the exposed section of shoreline she thought of as her sanctuary.

This little spot was some distance north of Pultney Bridge—the side that did not boast the lovely architecture and façade—and no one came there at night. It was a utilitarian area, free of benches or footpaths, but with a large walnut tree and a small wooden dock with a winch to assist in drawing water, though there was no bucket. The rope was brittle and frayed, attesting to its disuse. Lenora liked to think that no one knew of this place anymore but herself, and the fact that she'd never met another person here made it an easy enough fantasy to believe.

She'd thought about telling Cassie about her river walks in one of her monthly letters to her sister. She was fairly confident Cassie would laugh over it and even approve of Lenora's secret independence. As young girls, their differing temperaments had not been well-matched, leading to frustration on Cassie's part and insecurity on Lenora's. Maybe as they got older, they were becoming more similar: Lenora more outgoing, though quietly, and Cassie more mild now that she had a family that needed her attention. Or perhaps living apart helped them to better appreciate the other, and, in Lenora's case, emulate her younger sister. Often when her anxiety began climbing up her chest like a spider, she would think of what Cassie would do and be able to face a particularly overwhelming situation.

Lenora brushed the surface of the short stone wall beneath the walnut tree with the sleeve of her coat before she sat and pulled her knees to her chest. She watched the dim light weave through the city buildings and reflect off the black water of the river. She let out a breath. Her classes would start tomorrow, and the inevitable energy of her new students would leave her exhausted that first week. The advanced courses were delightful as they were made up of girls who were proficient and eager to perfect their skills. It was the Introduction to Music class that made Lenora's anxieties rise.

Mrs. Henry required all new students to take music in one form or another. If they already played an instrument or sang, they took an advanced performance class. If they did not, it was Lenora's responsibility to teach them notes and composers well enough that they could at least follow a conversation on the topic. Unfortunately, Lenora had found that if a girl had no musical basis by the time she came to school, she had little interest in the topic.

Lenora had taken to teaching far easier than anyone had expected—including herself. When she'd revealed her plans following Cassie's wedding, her parents had told her she would not last a full term. But with music as the subject, and small classes respecting her knowledge, Lenora had found her place. The first term had been fraught with anxiety and stammered lessons, but in time she'd learned to lose herself in the instruction, gained respect of the other teachers, and exceeded all expectations.

Now seasoned and confident, she looked forward to seeing her favorite students again and was excited to try something new with her beginning students. She had prepared a one-handed ditty they could learn to play as proof that everyone had some musical ability. Lenora hoped the activity would work better than her opening lectures of the past had, but it was a risk, and risks always made her nervous. Well, except for her walks to the river at night wearing men's clothing. She hugged her knees tighter and began mentally composing a letter of confession to Cassie—wouldn't she be shocked!

When Lenora smelled pipe smoke in the air, her body and mind froze. All the lightness and calm she'd been basking in was sucked away, leaving cold dread in its place.

She was not alone.

In all the months she'd been coming here, Lenora had never encountered another person. She swallowed, her mouth dry as she tried not to imagine what would happen if someone discovered she was *not* a young man walking through his worries.

The smoke was coming from the right—on the other side of the wall from the stairs which were her only escape. She stuffed her rising fear away; she had no time for it and must keep her thoughts clear. Carefully, Lenora lowered her knees from her chest and put her feet on the ground beside the wall, grateful that summer had not yet given way to fallen autumn leaves that could crunch beneath her boots. She stood slowly, wondering how she had ever found this subterfuge exciting. The prospect of being caught wiped away all sense of freedom she'd come to take for granted. She took a step toward the stairs. And another.

"You there."

She ran, her thin black coat billowing out behind her like a cape and her heart nearly beating out of her chest. Her foot was on the bottom step when her coat was caught from behind. She swallowed the scream that shot up her throat, aware even in her panic that her voice would give away her secret. Even her *ability* to scream was quickly quashed, however, when she hit the ground, every bit of air pushed out of her lungs, leaving her gasping. She had never thought to bind her chest when she went out at night, never expected anyone to get close enough to notice. She could see nothing through the darkness surrounding her except the pinpricks of light popping in her peripheral vision.

The severity of her situation weighed on her as she realized how vulnerable she was, how badly this could end. She tried to think of what Cassie would do, but panic overwhelmed the clarity she so desperately needed.

The man leaned down, grabbed her collar, and lifted her to her feet. She pulled free, but the man stood between her and the stairs. She rounded her shoulders forward to hide her chest and reached up to pull her cap down over her forehead. Her hand touched hair; the cap was gone.

"I didn't mean to pull you off your feet. What are you doing here so late?" the voice asked her, low and gruff.

She'd only heard one voice, which meant he was alone. Not that she felt much relief. She finally took a full breath, then lowered her voice to answer. "Walkin'." She must have lost the cap when he pulled her to the ground. Had she truly been *pulled to the ground*? Had he noticed the plait pinned at the back of her head? This was bad. Very, very bad.

She stepped away from him, glancing at the stairs that she now had a clear path to; they were only four or five feet away. Could she make another run and be successful this time? He took a large step to the side, matching her positioning and blocking her view of the stairs. He folded his arms over his chest, making him even more imposing. She did not look up.

"On the river at midnight? What's your name?"

"Christopher," she grumbled, giving her brother's name as though she had planned it, as though she had done anything like this in her life.

"Do your parents know you are out? How old are you?"

She tried to step around him. "Gotta get home."

The man stepped to block her a second time. Lenora couldn't lower her chin any further without exposing the plait pinned at the back of her head. She still hoped the dark night would conceal her. The man took her chin in one hand and raised her face toward his.

She saw longish dark hair free of a hat, dark eyes, and a square jaw peppered with a day's growth of beard. The cut of his coat testified that he was gentry, but his class only gave her mild relief. He might not be as prone to hurting or robbing her as some ruffian might, but he could ruin her reputation if he realized who she was. She could see the question in his eyes; he knew something was not right. Her instinct to get away took hold. She'd watched her brothers squabble in the yard for years—one could learn a great deal through observation.

She only had one chance. Fast and sure, she leaned into him rather than pulling back, throwing him off balance just enough to allow her to bring her knee up and then jab the heel of her boot onto the top of his foot as hard as she could. At the same time, she pushed both hands against his shoulders. He hadn't been expecting the attack and crumpled to the side.

Lenora took the stairs three at a time, mentally chanting *Don't trip, don't trip, don't trip!* If she fell, he would be waiting for her at the bottom of the stairs and the life she'd built here would be destroyed. She could feel her plait pull loose from the pins, bouncing on her back as she ran. She didn't dare look over her shoulder, didn't dare risk losing her focus.

She jumped over the crumbling top step, then leaped onto the top of the wall, but lost her balance and fell on the other side. She scrambled to her feet, hearing pounding on the steps behind her and a voice though the words were lost in the pulsing heartbeat sounding in her ears. She skirted the crates and ran through the alleyway. She had never run so hard in her life and was unsure how long she could sustain it. Her lungs were bursting, struggling to draw a full breath.

To Milsom Street—turn right, she told herself. She heard a voice curse behind her. She rounded the corner on Milsom Street and nearly collided with a group of men. She spun around one of them, whipping him with her plait in the process.

"A chit!" he called.

She put her head down as hot tears rose to her eyes. She had never been so terrified in her life, and the terror kept her moving forward. She heard footsteps behind her and headed into a park, through trees, around the pond. There was a fence along the back, surely there was a gate somewhere close . . . there—

She darted through it, and then ducked behind the next shop she passed. She collapsed in the shadows, a hand over her mouth to try to hide the sound of sucking for breath. Her hands shook, and her brain felt like mush. What had she done? She pulled further into the shadows, listening for footsteps but unable to hear anything over the pounding pulse in her ears.

He didn't catch me, she tried to reassure herself. But what if he had? She imagined being pulled to her feet, being identified and—what? Taken to the constable? Forced to beg for release? It seemed more likely that she would die on the spot, her heart giving out completely.

How could she have ever felt safe playing such a stupid game? She was twenty-six years old, respectable, well-bred. She was a teacher for heaven's sake, and the daughter of a vicar raised to always choose the proper course in any situation. If she *were* caught, it was nothing less than what she deserved.

She didn't know how long she crouched in the corner like a child—half an hour, perhaps longer. No one passed her hiding place, but it still took several minutes before she could gather enough courage to stand. She had to get back to Aunt Gwen's house before the panic she felt exploded out of her chest and left her to bleed to death in this alley.

She tucked her plait into the back of the coat and turned up the collar to conceal it as best she could. She headed toward the street, pausing between each tentative step to listen closely. She was on the north end of Milsom Street. If she could reach Quiet Street, she could cut across to Queen Square, then follow it up to Gay Street. Ten minutes. Fifteen at most, and then she would be safe in her room.

She reached the edge of the shadows; she heard nothing other than the expected night sounds. She took a step, cautious and ready to run if anyone confronted her. No one was there. She took another step into the darkness, looked both ways, and headed for the nearest corner.

She walked as fast as she could without running, afraid it would make her too conspicuous or that she'd collapse in the street from the exertion or that her plait would come loose again. When she heard the laughter of a group of men coming the other direction, she entered an alley and went around a row of shops. Her heart nearly stopped when a cat leaped across her path.

Soon enough she was on Gay Street—Aunt Gwen's house in view—and she felt as though she could finally draw a full breath. She went through the gate and took hold of the metal trellis with shaky hands, all the time half-expecting the pipe-smoking man to step out of the shadows.

Had she truly gotten away from him? Was he terribly hurt? She closed her eyes, stunned that she had acted so quickly, disgusted with herself for having possibly hurt him, and yet a tiny bit impressed that she'd gotten away. She—Lenora Wilton, who had hid behind a pianoforte most of her life—had bested a grown man. She shook her head, refusing to take any pride in the actions of the night.

She slid through the bedroom window and closed it quietly behind her. Only then did she allow her knees to give out. She huddled on the floor and cried with fear and relief. *You're safe*, she told herself. But she didn't *feel* safe. She felt vulnerable and foolish. Tomorrow was the first day of the new term. She would take her trunk back to Mrs. Henry's Female Institute on Chilton Road in the morning and stand before the young women she was charged to serve as an example for. There was the parents' tea tomorrow afternoon. Would she still be shaking when she had to make polite conversation with the parents who were responsible for her salary and believed she lived a life above reproach? What would they say if they knew? How would she get through it?

She wrapped her arms around herself and closed her eyes, trying to calm herself and ironically wishing the river were there to help her.

Chapter Three

Lenora slept—praise the heavens. When Dorothea woke her at eight o'clock, Lenora sat up, rubbed her eyes, and told herself that everything that had happened the night before had been a dream. The memory caused her heart to race, however, and she knew she'd never succeed in talking herself out of what had happened.

Daylight restored some of her security. She hadn't been found out. She hadn't been hurt. The night had been dark, the man who'd blocked her path was a stranger and, since she would *never* go out at night again, she had no fear of encountering him or the other men on the street she had bumped into ever again. She'd learned a powerful lesson—she would not waste the education.

When she arrived at the school, the houseman took her trunk up to the room she'd be sharing with another teacher on the third level. The evening dresses, opera gown, pearls, and headpieces Aunt Gwen had deemed absolutely necessary stayed at the terrace house awaiting Lenora's weekend visits. Her serviceable day dresses, practical shoes, and reading glasses would remain at the school with her music and her students.

Lenora went straight from the foyer to the music room, which served as both classroom and recital hall. The term schedule was on her desk, and she was relieved to see that her advanced classes were first and the Introduction to Music class was at the end of the afternoon.

Mrs. Henry's institute was a modest school, without fine furnishings or highly-pedigreed students, but it offered a solid education in those subjects necessary for young women preparing to enter society. Lenora was fortunate to have this position, and after last night's escapade, she was more determined than ever to be worthy of Mrs. Henry's trust in having hired her. She'd had no experience and stammered through the first interview, but Mrs. Henry had been impressed by Lenora's musical ability and was willing to take a chance.

Lenora spent fifteen minutes setting out her music sheets, arranging the chairs, and trying *not* to think about last night, which of course meant she thought about little else. The feeling of hitting the ground. The way her ribs and shoulder ached today. What if her head had struck a rock? What if the man had noticed she was a woman when he'd pulled her to her feet? What if he'd kissed her like some debaucherously wicked hero in a Gothic novel? That thought made her cheeks flush with heat. Where had such a thought come from?

Her cheeks had barely started to cool when someone entered the room a few minutes before her first class was to start.

Summoning what she hoped looked like an authentic smile, she turned and felt the smile soften quite naturally.

"Emmeline," she said, clasping her hands in front of her and allowing the girl to make her way across the room.

"Good afternoon, Miss Wilton," Emmeline said, holding out a box as she curtsied slightly. "My mother asked me to give you these caramels as a back-to-school gift."

The day was off to an excellent start, and Lenora pushed last night further to the deepest corner of her mind. And her father may have been right about reading novels—something she'd only taken up after coming to Bath. Apparently, they did fill her mind with wicked, horrible thoughts. If only she could blame the river walks on the stories, but she'd started them long before she'd ever pulled the first novel from Aunt Gwen's collection.

Performance Level Three was delightful. All four students were returning ones and had kept up their practice during their summer holiday. In addition to Emmeline's caramels, Regina's mother had sent a length of Italian lace, a luxurious item Lenora was humbled to receive. She planned to use it on a dress she kept at Aunt Gwen's.

The level two class had two new students, one of whom played the flute, bringing the total of that class to six. Lenora had never taught such a large class that relied primarily on instrument work. There were only three pianofortes, so she'd have to come up with the best way to give each girl the attention and practice time she needed. She'd had flute students in the past, however, so she felt confident she could make it work.

Advanced Music was made up of five students who had experience with either the pianoforte or singing and who wanted to improve their skills to performance level. This was an optional class, which meant each girl wanted to be here. Lenora reviewed what the girls could expect during the term and explained when they would have access to the music room for practice. Each class had an allotted hour each day through which the girls would rotate. Four hours on Saturday were open to any of the girls so long as they signed up in advance. Lenora would also be available on Monday and Wednesday afternoons for additional tutoring in half-hour sessions, as needed.

The girls were attentive, and one of them stayed after to tell Lenora that she had come to Mrs. Henry's school specifically because of the music program, which she had heard of from her cousin who was currently one of Lenora's level-three students. Lenora was beyond pleased at such a compliment, and she told the girl how excited she was to have her as a student.

The day had gone so smoothly that Lenora had forgotten to be anxious about the introductory class, and she was able to welcome the new girls quite naturally as they came in. All twelve of them were first-time students at the school and ranged in age from twelve to fourteen.

It was a large class, but Lenora knew a few of the girls would be respectful, shy away from trouble, and try to do their best— girls who would rather go unnoticed than cause the least bit of discomfort to anyone. Lenora related best to that type since she had much the same temperament. Then there would be a group of girls who were looking to be led. And then there would be the third group: the leaders who the first group would respect but avoid, and who the second group would follow. Lenora had seen any number of confident, kind, and determined girls take on the role of leader.

But not every natural leader was on her side, and within two minutes of orientation, Lenora knew Catherine Manch was going to be the type of leader Lenora dreaded. At twelve years old, she was one of the youngest girls in the class, but she was outspokenly defiant.

Miss Manch kept turning around to face the other students instead of Lenora. All eyes went to her as though the girls could not help themselves. They laughed at her interruptions and comments, and Lenora had started to sweat by the time she finished introducing herself and her musical experience. She moved on to talk about what the girls could expect from the class, fearing that last night's horrible encounter had left her more sensitive to this student's behavior than she would have been otherwise.

Lenora focused on keeping her voice steady and maintained a level louder than normal in hopes of keeping the students focused on her. "By the end of this week, you will know your solfège for pitch and sight reading—"

"And then you shall reward us with sweets?" Miss Manch interrupted, her eyebrows high on her forehead as she looked at Lenora with doe-eyed interest. She was a pretty girl with curly brown hair, hazel eyes that reflected a keen mind, and a slender build since her body had not yet transitioned into a woman's shape. "I prefer orange custard to raspberry and chocolate biscuits to shortbread. I detest treacle." She said the last with a dramatic flourish of her hand and a scowl that made some of the other girls laugh.

Lenora smiled tightly but could feel her anxiety increasing. *I'm just shaken from last night. Everything seems worse than it really is.* She chose to ignore the interruption in hopes that by not responding, she would not play into the antics. "And then we shall continue learning the notes of the staff. My goal by the end of the first month is that you know your notes and where to find them both on a written measure and on the pianoforte. Then we shall—"

"Dance a jig and parade through the Circus?" The same innocent expression reflected back to Lenora. The followers tittered; the quiet girls had wide eyes and flushed cheeks.

"I would ask that you please not interrupt, Miss Manch," Lenora said with what she hoped was the right balance of authority and patience, though she could feel a flush creeping up her neck. "Once we get through my introduction, I will teach each of you how to play the single hand of a little ditty called—"

Miss Manch stood. "Oh, I can play already. Both hands."

Lenora's smile tightened, but she kept it in place. Of course, the girl could play. Why else would she be taking the most basic music class geared for girls without any musical education? "No interruptions, please. Sit down, Miss Manch."

Miss Manch did not sit. Instead, she gave Lenora a challenging look, turned sharply, and moved toward one of three pianofortes, sitting down at the center instrument.

Lenora moved toward her, wondering if she should send for Mrs. Henry to help get this girl in line. She'd had to do that on one occasion during her first year. *Be strong. You are the teacher.*

"Students are not allowed on the instruments without permission and orientation, Miss Manch."

Catherine sat up straight, put her fingers on the keys, and began playing *Greensleeves*. Lenora stopped halfway across the room in surprise. The other girls in the room were as stunned as she was. Even in their ignorance, they could tell a proficient hand when they heard one. Why on earth was Catherine Manch taking an introductory course if she could already play?

Miss Manch was looking at her with an expression of clear defiance, as though confirming that she'd won this match. The expression unstuck Lenora's feet from the floor. She crossed to stand in front of Miss Manch with her hands on her hips, glad that in the girl's seated position Lenora was taller. Miss Manch didn't stop playing; she didn't even stumble over a note.

"Return to your seat, Miss Manch."

"Oh, I'm fine right here, thank you," the girl said sweetly, still holding Lenora's eyes as she played. Her fingers fairly flew across the keys.

"You are never to touch an instrument without permission. Return to your seat." How Lenora wished her heart was not racing and her mouth did not feel so dry. She could feel heat in her cheeks. She was being made to look like a fool before her students who were whispering from behind.

Miss Manch switched mid-measure to the second part of *Rondo Alla Turca*, slamming the keys for the harsher chords.

Lenora raised her voice to be heard over the music. "I will give you one more chance to do as I ask, Miss Manch. Return to your seat."

Miss Manch said nothing, her upper body assisting her in the playing. She missed a note and pulled her eyebrows together, focusing more intently on her hands.

Lenora took hold of the girl's upper arm. Everything changed in an instant.

Miss Manch slammed her hands onto the keys, causing a discordant cacophony of notes, then screamed and threw herself off the bench. "She hurt me!" Miss Manch cried, holding her arm.

Lenora stumbled back a few steps while the other students gasped in surprise. She stared at the girl writhing on the floor and felt her thoughts cracking like hard candy. The screaming continued. Seconds ticked by, and Lenora could do nothing but stare. Last night she'd reacted on instinct and done exactly what she'd needed to get away. Today she was unable to do anything at all.

"Miss Wilton!"

Mrs. Henry's voice broke through her scrambled senses, and Lenora spun away from the drama in front of her to see the headmistress storming across the room. "What on earth is going on here?"

"She threw me to the floor!" Miss Manch said, moving to a seated position on the floor but keeping hold of her arm.

"I . . . I . . ." Lenora stammered. She needed time to align her thoughts so that she could explain. She needed the river. She had neither.

"Gracious," Mrs. Henry said as she stooped and helped the girl up.

Miss Manch gave the headmistress a grateful look, her chin still quivering. There were no tears, Lenora noted, though Miss Manch sniffled and took gulping breaths. Mrs. Henry put a hand around Miss Manch's back and escorted her to her seat where the girl curled into her chair, the perfect display of a wounded creature. The other girls were completely stunned. Lenora was certain that, like her, they had never seen such a scene before. Did they know Lenora had not thrown her to the floor? Could they tell the girl was putting on some sort of depraved show?

Mrs. Henry turned her steel-gray eyes to Lenora, a hundred unasked questions showing in her expression. "You've ten minutes left in class, Miss Wilton. I shall stay to observe."

Lenora nodded dumbly and returned to the front of the room. She could not remember what she'd already said. Her heart was beating fast even though she'd done nothing to exert herself. She had been reduced to the Lenora of her youth—the nervous, protected, incapable girl whose thoughts were thick. The girl she thought she'd outgrown since coming to Bath.

Thirteen faces looked up at her: eleven with various shades of uncertainty. Mrs. Henry's expression was a mixture of anger and concern. Miss Manch maintained her beaten posture. Lenora did not look at her.

She swallowed, and took hold of the first thing she could think of to say. "My hope is that within the f-first week you will know your solfège, which is primarily concerned with notes and pitch." She'd said that already.

One of the girls, not Miss Manch, twittered. At the back of the room Mrs. Henry stamped her foot, and the girl fell silent.

"And b-by the end of the month you will know every note on the . . . pianoforte."

It went downhill from there.

Twenty minutes later, Lenora was alone in the music room, her elbows on her desk and her face in her hands as she willed herself not to cry. After class had been dismissed, Lenora had tried to explain to Mrs. Henry what had happened, but it hadn't come out right since Lenora's thoughts were still skittering about. Tears of frustration filled her eyes and made her feel pathetic. She focused on her breathing in hopes of centering her thoughts. She had half a dozen small exercises she went through when she needed to overcome her nerves. Early on she'd had to center herself several times a day; now it was intermittent. At social events, usually, but seldom at school, which had been a safe place. Until now.

Lenora finally asked if she and Mrs. Henry could talk about it later, once Lenora could line up her thoughts. The look the headmistress had given her showed concern. Why would a teacher need time to formulate the truth? But Lenora was not herself, or, rather, was not her *Bath* self. Her thoughts were scattered about like dried corn in the chicken yard.

"Parents' tea is starting in the company parlor, Miss Wilton."

Lenora looked up at Miss Carlyle, another third-year teacher, though a decade older. She taught needlework, something she'd become proficient at through her years of nursing her mother through ailing health. "Is everything all right, Miss Wilton?"

Lenora smiled and smoothed her hair, hating that she might look as undone as she felt. "Yes, I'll be there in a few moments."

"The first day of the new term is always daunting," Miss Carlyle said with a smile that brought out the two dimples in her round face. "I'll see you in the parlor."

Lenora spent two minutes taking deep breaths, trying to push away the extreme emotions of the last several hours. She needed to breathe and smile—as Cassie had taught her to do years ago when she was uncomfortable in company—and resume a confident demeanor for the parents of her students.

She remembered another exercise she hadn't used recently—*find three things you can see, two things you can touch, and one thing you can smell.* She looked at the clock, the window, and the door, then touched the desk and the chair, then inhaled the scent of the lemon oil used on the pianofortes. Her thoughts settled, and by the time Lenora reached the parlor, she felt more capable of managing the hour.

The first familiar face she saw was Regina's mother, Mrs. Cotswold, who was chatting with another teacher near the doorway. Mrs. Cotswold immediately invited Lenora to join their conversation. Lenora was grateful to be included, but wished she could hide behind the pianoforte instead of behind the mask she pulled out for social occasions such as this.

She kept count of how many people were in the room—

another calming exercise she hadn't used for some time. Thirty-four to start, then two left, four came in, another one left, two more entered. She chatted a few minutes, listening mostly, moving from one group to another every few minutes as expected. If she spent an average of four minutes with each small group, she could finish the room by the end of the hour and escape.

She was halfway around the room when a man entered and walked directly to Mrs. Henry, who was a few feet away from Lenora's conversation with another set of parents. Lenora took note of the man's limp but barely glanced his direction since she was listening to Lizzy Bradshaw's parents discuss the Austrian piano tutor they had hired on for the summer.

Lenora split her attention as she often did, keeping one ear on the conversation she was engaged in and the other tuned to the discussion taking place behind her while she also watched the door for more exits and entrances. She would likely end up in conversation with this man before the afternoon was out, and it would be wise to glean a bit of information that would make more comfortable conversation.

"My apologies for my tardiness," the man said in a low voice to Mrs. Henry.

"I am glad you were able to attend, Mr. Asher. I would like to speak with you afterward. There was . . . an incident."

Lenora felt a fizz of anxiety move through her. Certainly there had not been two separate incidents on the first day of the term. But Mrs. Henry had called him Mr. Asher, not Mr. Manch. Lenora wondered if he could be Catherine's stepfather.

An uncle, perhaps? A guardian chosen by her parents when they realized their daughter was incorrigible?

"I will stay after, then." His words were clipped.

"Very good," Mrs. Henry said.

As he moved toward the refreshment table, she turned to get a look. If she were going to be pulled into the private meeting Mrs. Henry had requested—teachers often were in order to testify of a student's poor behavior—she wanted to know who she would be facing. Would she be able to explain what happened more clearly to him than she'd managed to explain it to Mrs. Henry? Blocks of anxiety stacked up in her chest at the imagined scene of facing a man with his hands on his hips and fury in his eyes. She blinked away the image and took the man's measure as he walked away from her. He was tall with dark hair and broad shoulders and a definite limp—a war injury, perhaps? She watched him load his plate with the tarts and miniature sausages set out on the sideboard. Then he turned to face the room.

Lenora nearly dropped her cup of tea. It was the man who had accosted her on the bank of the river. The man she'd attacked in exchange for her freedom. His eyes slid past her, looking over the other attendees, and she was able to breathe. *He didn't recognize me.* He limped toward the punch bowl, and she remembered jamming the heel of her shoe on the top of his foot with all her weight and all her strength. He limped because of her!

"Miss Wilton?"

Lenora looked at the concerned expression on Mrs. Bradshaw's face. "Are you all right? You look rather pale."

"Yes, thank you, but . . . No, actually, I think I need a bit of air."

Her companions shared their sympathies as she set her cup and saucer on the sideboard and moved toward the door. She risked a glance at Mr. Asher. Maybe she was wrong, and her mind was playing tricks after the anxieties of the day, but he glanced at her over the rim of his teacup. She couldn't look away, and he held her eyes a moment before his eyebrows came together slightly. She disappeared through the doorway.

Chapter Four

L enora was lying on her narrow bed, one arm thrown over her eyes, when she heard a rapping at the door. She sat up while inviting whoever was there to come in, thinking it was the upstairs maid with terrible timing. It was Mrs. Henry. Lenora stood quickly as the headmistress closed the door behind her.

"You left the tea."

"I . . . I had a sudden headache."

"No one leaves the parents' tea, Miss Wilton. I believe I have made this clear to all my teachers."

"Yes, you have, I'm sorry." Lenora tried to smooth back the wayward strands of hair that had come loose. Her repose had not been nearly as effective in stilling her nerves as she'd needed it to be. Mrs. Henry seemed to be waiting for Lenora to say something, but Lenora had no words. She certainly couldn't explain why she'd left—aside from the false headache she'd already cited.

Mrs. Henry let out a breath. "I need to talk to you about Miss Manch."

"I did not hurt her, Mrs. Henry," Lenora said as the words she had been searching for filled her mind. "I asked her three times to return to her seat. She would not do it, and so I took hold of her arm—not violently—so as to lead her from the piano stool. She threw herself to the floor and staged the display you came upon." Why hadn't she been able to explain it so concisely the first time she'd had the chance? Blast her addled nerves which led to an addled brain. She could not allow herself to fall back into that smallness, no matter how tempting. She would not be that girl!

Mrs. Henry clasped her hands in front of her. "I was afraid of that." She pulled her eyebrows together. "Miss Manch is a special case for us." She walked to the small window that overlooked the shops of Chilton Road. It was not a view worth contemplating, except if you were trying to avoid someone's eyes. "She's had difficulties at other schools."

Lenora wasn't surprised after what she'd seen today, but Mrs. Henry's Female Institute was for upper-class young women preparing to make their debut, not troubled girls. "Her uncle is wealthy," Mrs. Henry said when Lenora did not comment. Her words were followed with a sigh, long and drawn out and . . . ashamed?

Uncle, Lenora repeated. Hence the differing last names. "With all due respect, Mrs. Henry, most of our students' parents are wealthy." Mrs. Henry had never spoken to her so casually, and she wanted to be careful in how she handled the conversation. Something about it felt fragile, and Lenora feared she was treading on thin ice.

"Mr. Asher is *very* wealthy," Mrs. Henry said, turning to face Lenora. "And very generous. He offered a sizable donation to the school in exchange for us overlooking his niece's past behavior at other schools and enrolling her without the usual references. It was an offer I could not resist, Miss Wilton. The dormitories are in need of repair, the parlor furnishings need replacing, and the rugs in the teaching wing are nearly threadbare. I trust you will not judge me too harshly for my decision."

Lenora knew there had been past discussions regarding what repairs had to be made, and which ones could wait. Donations to the school were not uncommon, but usually made in ten- or twenty-pound increments. Based on what Mrs. Henry had said, Lenora imagined Mr. Asher had offered far more than that, which meant more could be done than mending a cracked windowpane or ordering a new mattress tick to replace a worn one. Then her focus latched onto something else—had Mrs. Henry said *schools*? Miss Manch had been kicked out of more than one? She was only twelve years old, an age when many girls experienced their *first* school away from their family.

Mrs. Henry continued. "I had hoped—well, her uncle had hoped—that a new city and a new school would be a fresh start and put her on her best behavior." She squared her shoulders. "I am still hopeful that her outburst today was brought on by the stress of a new place. She has not had the benefit of stability most of our girls can take for granted. Her parents are dead, and she spent years moving from one family member to another until her uncle took charge of her care. She needs routine and order, and we are a school devoted to those things."

Lenora said nothing. Miss Manch needed more than routine and order. She needed . . . what? Lenora didn't know. It was impossible to believe that in a few years' time, the girl would be fit to enter society when she could not sit through the first ten minutes of an introductory music class.

Mrs. Henry let out a breath full of the burden of her responsibility. "I may have been hasty in allowing her to enroll, only her uncle seems so devoted to her. He's taken a house near Laura Place for the year to support us however he can and to allow her to stay with him on weekends, but he is desperate for her to be successful here, and the school could use his donation."

"The other girls follow her," Lenora said, testing the range of her comments. "If her behavior continues as it is now, we will lose the loyalty of other students." To say nothing of the fact that Mr. Asher was the man she'd encountered at the river last night. Lenora wanted him and his niece as far from her world as possible. She felt selfish for her thoughts, which spurred her to say something nice about the girl. "Though, she is a gifted musician," Lenora said, almost in defeat.

Mrs. Henry pulled her eyebrows together, then shook her head as though confused.

She didn't know? "Easily as talented as my level-two students, perhaps as good as level three, though I would need to do a proper assessment to know for certain."

Mrs. Henry's eyebrows remained stuck in the middle of her wrinkled forehead. "If that were true, she would have requested the advanced music courses. Neither she nor her uncle said anything about her musical ability, and she seemed particularly put out to be required to take an introductory course."

"I don't understand why she wouldn't be forthcoming about her talent, but she is very good." The musician side of Lenora wanted to explore the girl's ability and add to what she'd already been taught, steering her toward a proficiency that would be possible with Miss Manch's type of natural talent. Every other part of Lenora wanted nothing to do with this girl's education.

Mrs. Henry turned back to the window. "She was disruptive in other classes too," she finally admitted, "but not to the extent of her behavior in yours. Yet I feel compelled to give her another chance, not only because of her uncle's support but because I do not know of another school that would accept her."

Mrs. Henry glanced at the clock on Lenora's wall. "We need to remove to my office; Mr. Asher is probably already waiting for us. I spoke with him at the parents' tea and told him we would be meeting at precisely 4:30 to discuss the incident. I had wanted to give you a bit more information so you would understand my hope that we can give this girl another chance."

"Are you certain I should attend?" Lenora said as panic rose up like the River Avon after a storm. It wasn't unusual for a teacher to be part of such a meeting, but this would be Lenora's first parent's council. And for it to be with the man from the river made it difficult for her to breathe. The butterflies in her stomach were strangling her.

"I shall need your account of what happened, and your support. I would also like your opinion of Mr. Asher—if you think him as devoted to Miss Manch's success as I do. Your opinion will be valuable to me in my assessment and my decision on how best to move forward."

As Lenora followed Mrs. Henry down the stairs, she tried to calm her nerves. She was going to be brought face-to-face with the man from last night, who was also the uncle of the worst student Lenora had ever had. She could not think of any person in the entire world she would like to see *less*. It took everything she had not to run back to her room. *Cassie would face him*, she told herself. But would she? She couldn't imagine anyone in her position not feeling the horror she was feeling now.

Lenora's heart thrummed in her chest when they entered Mrs. Henry's office. Mr. Asher stood, his gaze moving past Lenora, which allowed her to take a deeper breath than she'd managed since leaving her room. If he knew she was the person he'd met on the riverbank, he'd have kept his eyes on hers longer, wouldn't he? Instead, he gave her no special attention as he waited for the women to sit—Mrs. Henry behind her walnut desk and Lenora on the chair furthest from his own—before resuming his seat.

"What happened?" he asked, both eager and hesitant.

Lenora did not to look at him.

Mrs. Henry summarized Miss Manch's misbehaviors in the other classes, then asked Lenora to explain what had occurred in hers, as it was the most extreme. Lenora recounted the experience as objectively as possible, glad Mr. Asher did not seem any more attentive to her face than was to be expected. Near the end of her recounting, he dropped his head into his hands.

When she finished, Mr. Asher apologized to her directly, though he did not meet her eye. She nodded an acceptance, but reminded herself that he'd thrown her to the ground the night before.

"I know I've no right to ask, but can you please give her another chance?" Mr. Asher turned pleading eyes to Mrs. Henry. "I truly believe if she can find a place of comfort and safety, she can improve her behavior. Your school came highly recommended not only as an institution of excellent education but also one with a nurturing atmosphere that I feel Catherine needs above all else."

"I am pleased to hear we have such a recommendable reputation, but that is also dependent on our students. One difficult girl can fracture the respect necessary to teach all of our students. The first week of a new term is important in establishing teacher-student relationships, and Miss Manch has affected every girl in Miss Wilton's class already."

Mr. Asher turned to Lenora, startling her as she had nearly forgotten she was a participant in the conversation. She'd been seeing three things, touching two, and smelling one in order to keep herself calm. When she met his eyes, her heart raced all over again.

"You say she plays the pianoforte?" he asked.

He didn't know either? Oddly enough, that calmed her, increasing her curiosity while diminishing her anxiety enough that she could answer. "Quite well."

"Then perhaps she needs a more advanced class." He sounded desperate and turned to Mrs. Henry. "Catherine is exceptionally bright, and she *can* behave better than she has shown. When I first took over her care, she was defiant and difficult, but the two of us have established a rapport since then, and we are much improved. Change is difficult for her, but I truly believe she can settle and benefit from everything you offer your students." He turned back to Lenora. "Please allow her another chance. I will talk with her and help her understand how important it is that she not repeat the actions of today."

"You have not helped her understand as much already?" It took a moment for Lenora to realize she'd spoken the words out loud. She felt her cheeks heat up and lowered her gaze to the carpet. *I will not be a simpering girl,* she told herself. She looked at him and straightened her posture, hoping it wouldn't be obvious she was coaching herself through this process. She could do little about the flush in her cheeks, however, and so she ignored it in hopes Mr. Asher and Mrs. Henry would do the same. She focused on her breathing: four counts in, four counts out.

"I have, of course, pressed upon her the importance of behaving well," Mr. Asher said, turning to look at Mrs. Henry. Lenora slumped slightly in relief before catching herself and forcing the improved posture in case he looked at her. "Perhaps if she knows she is about to be turned out, she will settle in better. Perhaps she is testing all of us to see where our boundaries are."

The three of them sat in silence, all waiting for someone else to speak. Despite herself, Lenora better understood why the headmistress agreed to accept Miss Manch in the first place. Mr. Asher *did* seem devoted to his niece and truly concerned for her education and improvement. He had not threatened to withdraw his donation nor had he attempted to excuse her behavior or place blame on Lenora or the school. Rather he seemed to ache for his niece's success and was willing to humble himself in front of two women, no less, in order to ensure it.

Do the right thing, she told herself and suddenly, doing so felt like penance. As if, through this act, she could erase last night from having happened. Lenora took a breath. "I would be willing to advance Miss Manch to the next-level class if you are willing to grant her another chance, Mrs. Henry. Perhaps she will rise to the occasion if she is challenged. She *is* very bright, and we have seen before how highly intelligent students need higher levels of instruction in order to keep their focus." She'd done it. Said all the words. Sacrificed for someone else's benefit. Her clergyman father would have been proud of her, if she could ever confess why she'd needed to do the right thing in the first place.

Both Mrs. Henry and Mr. Asher dropped their shoulders in relief, further assuring Lenora that this was exactly what she should have done. She'd made everyone happy. Except herself, but she would settle for less self-flagellation.

"Thank you, Miss Wilton," Mr. Asher said. His smile was quite lovely. Not that it mattered, since she would be avoiding him as much as possible in the future. She nodded and looked at the floor. She feared that the longer they looked at one another, the more at risk she was for him to recognize her. "I'm certain she can improve. A challenge and higher expectations will surely be just the thing she needs to have a turnaround."

He apologized again, then stood and left the room.

Lenora and Mrs. Henry spoke a few moments longer, and then Lenora was dismissed. The girls ate dinner every night together in the dining room, with two teachers on rotation to help supervise. It was not Lenora's night, thank goodness, so she could dine an hour later with the other teachers. She needed to lie down and make sense of all that had happened. She was exhausted but felt sure an evening to herself and a good night's sleep would put her back to sorts by morning. All was well.

"Miss Wilton?"

Lenora turned to face a maid who was holding out a box about six-inches square. "A parent left this for you on his way out a few minutes ago."

His way out? Lenora accepted the box and continued to her room, a feeling of trepidation overtaking her. Once in her room, she sat in the single chair positioned below the small window between the two beds. She placed the box in her lap and paused before lifting the lid. Inside was the black knit cap she'd lost at the river the night before. On top was a folded square of paper, and when she could catch her breath, she picked it up with trembling hands.

> *Miss Wilton,*
> *Meet me at the river at 6:00. I am certain you know precisely where.*
> *A. Asher*

Chapter Five

L enora stopped at the wall separating her from the back of
the shop and the crumbling stairs. She'd never been to this
spot on the river in daylight, and the disrepair that somehow
seemed romantic in the darkness was only testimony of neglect
in the sunlight. She put her hands to her stomach, wishing she
could stop the churning she felt. Why had she come? She should
have ignored him—what would he have done then? Gone to
Mrs. Henry? Perhaps.

She could go to Mrs. Henry, confess herself, and ask for the
woman's understanding. But the risk was too great. Not that this
meeting wasn't a risk, but she *knew* what would happen if she
divulged her river walking to the headmistress: dismissal. Aunt
Gwen would learn what she'd done. Her students would learn
of it. Lenora of Bath would be reduced to Lenora of Leagrave
with even more gossip to trail behind her. The consideration of

potential repercussions made the ground shift beneath her feet, and she opened her eyes to reorient herself.

She blinked back the tears that had formed. She was overwhelmed and frightened, and yet she could not stay on this side of the wall. She was already a quarter of an hour late. *What does he want from me?*

There was only one way to find out.

Navigating the wall in a dress and petticoats and stockings was humiliating, even if no one saw her. *Oh, please, let no one have seen me!* She took the stairs slowly, lifting her skirts and wishing she were wearing trousers, which were surprisingly comfortable as well as functional. She smelled Mr. Asher's pipe smoke before she saw him standing at the edge of the river, looking over the greenish-brown water with his back to her. She hadn't realized how soundlessly she'd moved until a fallen walnut crunched beneath her foot. She froze as he spun around, his pipe held as though he might throw it at her. She stumbled, biting back an apology and reminding herself that she owed him nothing.

They held one another's gaze, then he adopted a more casual pose, though his tension continued to radiate. He walked to the low stone wall Lenora had sat upon last night, turned over his pipe, and tapped out the ashes. He slid the pipe into the inside pocket of his coat and turned to face her.

"I thought it odd that you brushed off the stones before sitting down last night. After you ran off, I better understood why that action had stood out. A young man would not bother to preserve the seat of his trousers."

Lenora did not look at him as he spoke, but kept her gaze focused on the ground and her hands clasped behind her back. *He watched me from the first moment I arrived!* Which meant he'd already been there. Which meant he'd lit his pipe both without her notice and with full awareness that she *would* eventually notice. She felt taunted and trapped.

"I had meant to offer you an escort home, but then you sprang up like a cat and made a run for it," he continued.

She huffed without meaning to, eyes still on the dirt at her feet and her face on fire. He'd seen her in *trousers!* He was likely right now comparing the young woman standing before him to the hoodlum of last night.

"You don't believe me?" he asked.

Lenora lifted her eyes, swallowed, and summoned the confident manner she'd learned since coming to Bath. "You knew I was a woman and yet still pulled me to the ground?"

"I feared for your safety as a *young man*, more so when I realized the truth. There is a reason women are to be chaperoned in a city like this. I meant it when I apologized for pulling as sharply as I did; I expected a bit more resistance." He smiled as though to apologize again. She did not acknowledge the attempt.

"You threw me to the ground like a sack of grain," she reminded him. She'd never been treated like that in her life, not even from her brothers in play when they were young. Cassie would wrestle with them, but never Lenora.

"And you went on to attack me quite ruthlessly—shall we speak of that?"

She felt her cheeks heat up again and shook her head. She did *not* want to speak of that. Seeing him now in the clear sunlight made it all the more astounding that she'd gotten away the night before. He was tall and strong and yet she'd bested him? The spark of pride she felt only testified of what a wild woman she'd become.

Mr. Asher continued. "I must say I had a bit more confidence in your ability to defend yourself once I could walk." He grinned.

She did not smile back and had to look at the ground again. There was kindness in that smile, as if he wanted them to be comfortable with one another. Yet he had forced her to come, and she sensed the lingering air of a threat between them. She wanted him to get to the point, and then again, she did not want that in the slightest. What would Cassie do in this situation? She hadn't a clue.

"You know your way around Bath at night, which means you've made your walks a habit."

Lenora continued to stare at the ground. This man was not someone she was going to trust with her secrets, and she did not need his accusatory tone in order to regret what she'd done.

"I will not reveal you."

She looked up. His eyes were darker than his niece's, almost black, and his skin brown enough to attest to his having spent time in warmer climates than this. He was handsome, in a rugged way, but still a villain. She did not reward his words with a response.

After a few moments of silence, he spoke again. "But in exchange for my keeping your secret, I need your help."

"Blackmail?" she said, bringing her hands to her stomach again.

"Um, well, yes." His voice took on a pleading tone. "I need Catherine to succeed here. You can help her, take her under your wing, be her advocate. She needs nurturing."

"She needs an asylum." She pinched her lips together once the words were out. Talking to anyone was a relatively new skill for her, but talking to a man, let alone speaking so boldly, was something she had never done. Then again, she'd never been treated like this. Perhaps her defensive instincts were stronger than she'd known before she had need to use them.

He startled, his eyes going wide, and then narrowing. "She is not mad."

In for a penny, in for a pound. "Are you certain of that?"

He ran his hand through his hair before beginning to pace along the edge of the river. He cut the very figure of a distressed gentleman, with strong, broad shoulders and a perfectly crafted scowl of concern. She forced herself to not notice and looked away.

"She needs nurturing and stability," he said. "She's had blessed little of that in her life, and I am certain that if she could find her footing, she could let down her defenses and be . . . normal." He faced Lenora. "She needs to know she is safe and protected. She needs to know that she belongs. Mrs. Henry obviously respects your feelings; therefore, you could defend her if there was a need."

His explanation was so simplistic. Lenora pictured Miss Manch again, sitting in her chair, hunched and frail-looking while she grinned with satisfaction at Lenora's distress—the only one who could see her. There was more at play here than a girl needing to know she belonged. "Your gratitude for my assistance with Mrs. Henry this afternoon is to blackmail me?"

"It may take more than one more chance, and if my niece had an advocate within the school, especially a teacher whom she has already wronged, it could make all the difference. You could help soften the effect of her behavior to the other students, perhaps set a precedent for the other teachers in understanding her . . . eccentricities."

Granted, Lenora was new to teaching, but she'd already seen a variety of attitudes from the parents of the girls sent to Bath for their education and edification. Some of the parents who boarded their students in Bath for the school terms were sad to leave them; others were nonchalant. A few were obviously relieved, now free to travel to the south of France without a care thrown as crumbs to their child.

Lenora had been raised and educated at home. Her concept of family was different from that of the wealthy gentry who paid to send their children away, but she'd come to accept that way of life without judgment. Mr. Asher's attitude was different. He seemed *desperate*, which was easy enough to explain based on his niece's behavior.

"So you are blackmailing me about having been out alone after hours by insisting I be your niece's advocate in hopes that she will feel happy and loved and therefore not act out?"

He considered the summary a moment, then nodded.

"Surely you see the madness in thinking I can have any power over her," Lenora said, realizing that her nervousness had drained away. She felt offended and irritated instead, and a little surprised that she was able to converse with him so easily and honestly.

"No less mad than a respectable teacher dressing like a man and walking the streets alone at night."

She could not dismiss his point. "And what if I cannot create what you want? What if I do all I can and she still does not thrive?" Because Lenora had no idea what she *could* do. She was the wrong person for this job, but she had no choice but to attempt it.

"I truly believe Catherine will improve if there is someone to take a special interest in her." He was so hopeful, but his expression didn't last. "The headmistress at her last school felt she was only fit for a school in Germany for difficult children. From what I know it is little more than a prison; I can't send her there." The horror of the idea was clear on his face. Lenora tried to block out the sympathy that welled up inside her. "If she does not succeed here, I do not know what else I can do. I fear I have done too little too late already, which is why I must do whatever I can to remedy that now. Will you help me?"

It would be easier to remain incensed if his motives were not so pure and the look in his eyes so sincere. "It seems I have no choice."

He looked chagrined, but did not withdraw. "Thank you."

"Do not thank me for something you are forcing me to do." Yet again, her own words surprised her.

"I give you my word that I will not tell Mrs. Henry of your actions."

"Unless you end up displeased with my efforts."

He nodded at that and looked at the ground. "May I write to you for updates?"

Lenora watched him, realizing she had one more question and no reason not to ask it. "Why did you not know she plays the pianoforte?"

He kicked the dried-out husk of a walnut. "She did not tell me, nor show me, but it is not such a surprise. My family is rather musically inclined, and my mother required all of us to take lessons when we were young." He smiled as though this shared interest might chip away at her resolve to dislike him. It didn't.

She simply nodded, though she still felt it strange he didn't know his niece well enough to know of her ability. She was suddenly eager to get away. "Will that be all?" Maybe her hurry was because she wanted to ask him if he were musical, too. Yet, it made no difference, and she did not want to invite any connection between them.

"Yes, thank you." He smiled as though they were friends. A smile looked good on his face, adding light to his eyes, but Lenora did not smile back. She would go the extra measure with Miss Manch because she had to, not because she wanted to. And it would not be easy.

Chapter Six

The next day, Miss Manch arrived for the Advanced Music class wielding eyes of fury. Mrs. Henry had warned Lenora that Miss Manch had not wanted to change classes. Lenora took a deep breath and forced a smile.

"Welcome, Miss Manch," she said, then looked away, determined not to let the girl be the center of attention in this class the way she'd been in the introductory class yesterday. The other students came in and, after a quick introduction of Miss Manch, Lenora continued the instruction as planned. When Miss Manch interrupted her, Lenora interrupted her right back and introduced the day's lesson.

"As I explained yesterday, each of you are in this class because you have a level of musical proficiency. As we'll be learning and progressing together, I thought it would be helpful for each of you to be familiar with one another's abilities."

She had Miss Manch's attention. Good.

"Miss Flasch, Miss Heatherham, Miss Standone, and Miss Manch play the pianoforte. Miss Gunderson and Miss Moore are vocalists. Please take a few minutes to decide what you would like to perform for the class. I'm happy to help you find a selection if you need my assistance, and I can accompany the vocalists if they would like."

It ended up taking quarter of an hour for the girls to make their decisions. Only Miss Manch and Miss Gunderson did not ask Lenora for help. The vocalists went first, with Lenora accompanying Miss Moore; Miss Gunderson sang a cappella. Both needed help with their diction, and Miss Gunderson needed pitch work. Lenora made herself a note.

Then the pianists took their turns. Miss Manch went last but was enthusiastically supportive of the other girls, applauding and encouraging them in their performances. The other girls were drawn to her, and she acted perfectly competent and content despite being new and the youngest.

She played *Greensleeves* as she had yesterday—the only one of the four to play without sheet music—and her hands flowed over the keys like they were made for it. When she finished, she curtsied to the class, flourishing the movements and making the girls laugh.

When class ended, she walked side by side with Miss Heatherham out of the room, and Lenora wondered if she was the same girl who had arrived at class so irritated.

On Wednesday, Lenora tested each of the girls individually. She sat at one pianoforte and they sat at another. They played through several measures of the same song together, Lenora talking them through the details of the key signature, rhythms, and fingerings, then the girls played the same measures themselves at whatever pace they were comfortable, but without mistakes. Some of the girls were better than others; Miss Manch was the best if Lenora ignored her huffing breaths when given suggestions and her smug smile at the end.

For the vocal students, Lenora played notes on the piano and had them sing along as she went, pushing their range and advising them on posture and breathing to help them extend as high and low as they could.

After class, Lenora asked Miss Manch to stay. Now that she had seen Miss Manch's skill in comparison to the other girls, she wanted to discuss the possibility of moving her to level two. She hoped the girl would be flattered and that the even-more-advanced students there would further calm her behavior. Lenora often forgot that she had promised Mr. Asher to provide his niece with extra help, and she felt a wave of defiance each time she remembered. Being blackmailed made it difficult for her to sort out what was her own interest and what was self-preservation.

Miss Manch sighed loudly when Lenora asked her to stay, but settled back into her chair. Lenora thanked her, then turned around to close her lesson plan and give the other students a chance to leave the room. When she turned back, the room was empty; Miss Manch had snuck out while Lenora wasn't looking.

That night, Lenora pulled Miss Manch aside after dinner.

"I asked you to stay after class."

Miss Manch shrugged. "I forgot."

My eye, Lenora thought. "I would like you to come early to class tomorrow by ten minutes for our interview."

Miss Manch crossed her arms over her chest. "And if I don't?"

Gracious, she was cheeky. "I shall report you to Mrs. Henry and ask that you be put on a point system."

Miss Manch drew her eyebrows together and scowled. "What is a point system?"

It was something Lenora's brother, Christopher, had once told her about from his schooling. She'd brought up the idea to Mrs. Henry after Miss Manch's unexpected disappearance after class and gotten the headmistress's approval.

"You will be given one hundred points, which you lose for bad behavior, tardiness, and incomplete work. You can earn additional points through kitchen duties or copying Bible verses. Your participation in activities outside the school are dependent upon your points at the time of any given event."

Miss Manch narrowed her eyes. "Demerits," she said, as though she'd uncovered the hidden truth of Lenora's plan. Her scowl deepened.

Lenora swore there was something chilling in the girl's eyes. As though she would like to bash Lenora's head in if she had the chance. Luckily, the hallway was completely free of blunt objects.

"Not demerits—points," Lenora said, praying that her voice would remain strong. "And all within your power to manage. It is an attempt to help you better learn accountability. We would prefer to avoid the implementation if you think you can control your behavior without the system." She wanted to explain that the point system was a form of advocacy, a chance to extend her an opportunity to succeed at the school, but she didn't see that as being necessarily attractive to Miss Manch. Though she was friendly with the other girls, she did not want to be at this school. Lenora could only hope that she would want to avoid penalty enough to find her footing better than she had so far.

Miss Manch turned on her heel and returned to the dining room without another word. Were Miss Manch already on the point system, Lenora would have taken five away for rudeness.

It was a relief when Miss Manch showed up for their interview on time the next day, though she walked in laboriously, as though the effort exhausted her. Lenora almost found it funny. Almost.

"I would like you to consider moving up to the level-two class," Lenora said once they were both sitting. "Your skill is equal to the other girls there, and I think you will find greater improvement among them."

"No," Miss Manch said easily, then yawned behind her hand.

Lenora ground her teeth. "You're very talented, Miss Manch, and I would like to help you meet your potential."

"Do you get paid additional wages if I improve?"

"No."

"Then why do you care?"

Because your uncle could ruin me, she thought. "Because I

am a teacher. It is my job and my pleasure to help my students reach their goals. It is my life's work." She only squirmed a little during her explanation.

Miss Manch leaned forward so fast that Lenora pulled back without thinking. "Aren't you a teacher because you could not find a man willing to marry you?"

The sting that shot through Lenora's chest took her off guard, earning another smug look from Miss Manch. Lenora hurried to recover. "I am a teacher because I love music and—"

"*And* couldn't find a man willing to marry you."

Lenora took a breath, anger and anxiety both rising up in familiar patterns. "Would you consider level two, Miss Manch, or won't you? I will not insist upon it, but you're a bright girl, and I think you would enjoy a greater challenge."

Miss Manch leaned back in her chair. "I do not like to be challenged." She stood and put a hand to her chest. When she spoke, her voice was thick with sarcasm. "But thank you *so* much for being *so* interested in my potential, *Miss* Wilton." She smirked, and left the room.

Had Lenora a glass on hand, she would have thrown it at the door. Well, no, she wouldn't have—but she would have wanted to!

Five minutes later, Miss Manch returned with the rest of the girls for class, laughing and talking with them as though they had known each other for years, not days. For good or bad, the girl had a powerful presence.

Lenora pushed aside the emotions sparked by her interview with Miss Manch and explained to the class that she would be assessing each girl's ability to read music. Many girls had little familiarity with written music when they first came to the school and were astounded at how much opportunity was opened to them once they could read the notes on a page.

Lenora drew a staff on the blackboard at the front of the room with a stick of chalk and instructed the girls to bring out their own slates, then replicate the staff and notes as best they knew, labeling each one appropriately. It was not a test, she reminded them, just an assessment. If they were not famil-iar with written music, they should leave the slate blank. Miss Gunderson—to Lenora's surprise—pushed her slate to the front of the desk, looking embarrassed. Lenora gave her a reassuring smile and nod.

Lenora began calling out notes, and when she turned back to the girls, she saw Miss Manch quickly look away from Miss Heatherham's slate. Miss Heatherham did not seem to notice.

"Your own work," Lenora said, staring pointedly at Miss Manch, who acted as though she did not notice the attention.

Lenora finished calling out the last two notes, and then collected the slates. Miss Manch's had the same error Miss Heatherham's did and showed nothing for the last two notes. Interesting. Lenora wiped the slates clean, handed them back, and then asked the girls to fill in the notes from the first measure of *Für Elise*.

She faced the students this time in order to not give Miss Manch an opportunity to copy another girl's work. As she began collecting the slates upon completion, there was a crash from her right side. She jumped back as pieces of Miss Manch's slate skittered across the wooden floor.

"Sorry, Miss Wilton," Miss Manch said in an innocent tone. "The slate slipped out of my hands."

Lenora knew she should call Mrs. Henry—there were repercussions when school property was damaged, even by accident, which Lenora knew this was not—but she swallowed the desire. She hoped the other girls would not comment on her letting Miss Manch out of the assignment or not punishing her for the broken slate. She turned back to the board and took a deep breath, unsettled and feeling her anxiety rise.

She'd stepped over the line of loyalty to the school and was, instead, showing her loyalty to Mr. Asher and Miss Manch. It was wrong, and she hated herself for doing it, yet what choice did she have? If she didn't give Miss Manch greater margin, she risked both her own and the school's reputation. She was in an impossible situation.

Lenora continued her lecture, counting the notes and the lines of the staff. She went through her favorite exercise to help calm her anxieties: seeing three things—the blue ribbon in Miss Heatherham's hair, the lace curtain above the window, the stack of slates—touching two things—her hair and her skirt—and inhaling the scent of one thing—the smell of chalk on slate.

As her mind settled, she could focus on at least part of what was wrong with Miss Manch. Though the girl could play beautifully, she could not read music, perhaps not at all if she did not even know the basic notes on the staff. *Greensleeves* and *Rondo Alla Turca* were both popular songs. Miss Manch had likely heard them a hundred times and memorized the music. Lenora was familiar with many accomplished musicians who could play by ear. But for Miss Manch to improve further, she had to be able to read music. Perhaps it was a good thing the girl hadn't agreed to level two, where proficient reading was a requirement.

For Friday's class, Lenora pulled each girl aside to discuss their individual goals for the term. Some wanted to master a particular song or move up to a certain level of music; others wanted to improve their memorization, form, or technique. Miss Gunderson wanted to learn to read music, which Lenora was glad to hear as the girl had solid talent and would likely come to neglect it if she did not nurture it. Lenora left her interview with Miss Manch for last.

"I must ask you a direct question, Miss Manch," Lenora started, wanting to get right to the point. She kept her voice low, as she had for the other students, to ensure privacy. "Have you ever been taught to read music?"

"Of course I have," Miss Manch said defensively. "You've heard me play. You said I was better than any other girl here, though I don't believe it since they are all *so* talented." She spoke loud enough for the other girls to hear, and Lenora swallowed her embarrassment.

"Everything you've played has been memorized," Lenora pointed out, "which is impressive, but not knowing how to read music puts you at a disadvantage in regard to—"

Miss Manch cut her off with another loud commentary. "Are you trying to talk me into advancing to the level-two class again? Because I really do not want to. I enjoy the girls in *this* class. Do not make me move up and leave them behind."

A wave of pettiness spurred Lenora to also raise her voice. "Not knowing how to read music will put you at a disadvantage, Miss Manch, and disqualifies you for level two."

Miss Manch's eyes flashed, and her jaw hardened. Lenora winced internally. She should not have tried to play her game. She reminded herself to be the teacher, not a child. She took a deep breath to center herself, noting that the lace on Miss Manch's collar was not the same design as the lace on her cuffs, and then withdrew a periodical she had found a year or so earlier featuring an article that supported her desire to teach sight reading. She slid it in front of Miss Manch. "This is written by a professor of music at Oxford. I'd like you to read it, and then we can discuss his thoughts on the importance of reading notes."

Miss Manch rolled her eyes, but then stared at the page as though doing Lenora a favor. It took only a moment for Lenora to notice that her eyes were not moving from left to right. She wasn't reading.

Lenora waited her out and watched closely, feeling herself grow calmer—focusing on details always helped her. The girl's eyes moved up and down, side to side, and now and then she would scrunch her eyes as if focusing on some part, but then her gaze would move to another place on the page. After a few minutes, she sat back in her chair and crossed her arms over her chest. The action was becoming so familiar to Lenora that she did not feel intimidated by it. "So?" Miss Manch demanded.

"What do you think about what he has to say about the importance of reading music?"

"I think it is all just one stuffy old man's opinion."

"One *expert's* opinion. Did you read the part about someone being able to learn to read music in only a few months, especially if they have a natural aptitude, like you do?" The article said nothing about anticipated timelines.

Miss Manch shrugged. "I play as well as I want to, and better than most of your students." It was not a direct answer to Lenora's question, and yet it felt like an answer to a different one.

"Because of your gifts, you could excel beyond the mark of many other musicians." Lenora pointed to a sentence she'd underlined when she'd first read the article: *A proper music education is more than physical proficiency; it is the ability to communicate through the composition and musician working together.* "Read that for me and tell me what you think it means."

Miss Manch did not look at the page. She looked out the window, at the floor, at the other girls, and then at Lenora before pushing the magazine off the table. "Oops, it slipped from my hands."

Lenora made no move to retrieve the magazine and held Miss Manch's defiant gaze, wishing she could think of something clever to say. Her eyes burned, but she was the reigning champion of staring contests with her brothers and seemed to have finally learned how to keep this girl's behavior from affecting her—hallelujah. Soon enough, Miss Manch blinked. Lenora smiled even though she knew she shouldn't have.

Miss Manch did not take defeat well. She stormed out of the room, chin high and eyes blazing. Lenora did not go after her, but instead picked up the magazine and faced her class, prepared to teach the rest of her lesson. There was only slight satisfaction in having determined the root of Miss Manch's problem and why the girl kept herself in such a defensive position.

It was not that Miss Manch could not read music. She could not read at all.

Chapter Seven

Lenora toiled over her letter to Mr. Asher throughout the day on Friday. It should not have been hard to write what she needed to say: *"Your niece is amazing on the pianoforte but cannot read. How do you not know this?"*

But Lenora could not be so direct as that, so she stewed and wrote and revised in between her classes and finally, late Friday afternoon, sent the message to his house in Laura Place before removing to Aunt Gwen's for the weekend. She had never been so glad to escape the school.

Aunt Gwen greeted her effusively and said they were dining in that night, but tomorrow would be attending the Pump Room in the morning, a garden party in the afternoon, and a ball in the Assembly Rooms in the evening. Lenora would have liked to beg off—she was exhausted—but she was still her aunt's companion and did not want to disappoint her. A big part of the personal growth she had experienced in Bath could be traced to Aunt Gwen's inclusion of her in the society here. The more she interacted with others, the less she feared social situations.

They didn't reach the Pump Room until almost eleven Saturday morning, and the crowd of patrons was thin. Aunt Gwen was disappointed, but Lenora was not since she still felt on edge.

They enjoyed their promenade through Sydney Gardens on the east side of Pultney Bridge, which was not far from where Mr. Asher had taken his house. Lenora was aggravated to even think about him. There were many people she knew in Laura Place. Why couldn't one of them come to mind? She focused on the fine weather, the leaves just starting to turn golden for the season. She loved this time of year.

As she recounted her week to Aunt Gwen, she managed to make it all sound much less horrible than it really was. She left out the part about being blackmailed, of course, or going to the river . . . twice. She simply said that the girl's uncle had asked her to give the girl special consideration and she was attempting to fulfill his wishes.

"What an experience this will be for you," Aunt Gwen said. "And how well you seem to be handling it. I'm very proud of you."

Lenora let the praise fill her. "Thank you, Aunt."

"Will you discuss the girl's deficit with Mrs. Henry next week, then?"

"Yes, we have a teacher meeting Tuesday morning, and I'll bring it up then. It explains at least some measure of the girl's poor behavior—being unable to read is quite a secret to hide."

"Perhaps the relief of not needing to keep the secret any longer will invite the humility she needs to be taught. Where did this girl come from?"

"She's lived with a variety of relatives until her uncle took over her care. I do not know details aside from there being some musical heritage." She shrugged, not sure why she'd even mentioned the musical aspect. Music was not a primary skill—much as it pained Lenora to admit it. Reading, however, was essential. "This is her third school in nine months, and Mrs. Henry would not have accepted her at all save for the promise of a generous donation from the girl's uncle." She shook her head in silent reprimand of Mrs. Henry's weakness before remembering her own agreement with the man. She was in no position to judge anyone in regard to concessions made to Mr. Asher. "That is confidential, of course."

"Of course," Aunt Gwen agreed. "It seems as though Miss Manch is very lucky to have her uncle's support. I hope it pays off for both of them."

Lenora did not want to see any action on Mr. Asher's part as kindness, but it was difficult to argue. He was a young man—early thirties she would guess—and taking great pains to see that his niece was settled when he could more easily send her to that school in Germany and be free of her. It was uncharitable to think that would still be the inevitable result of his attempts, but Lenora could not help it, even if she were ashamed of the cynical thought. Granted, it would be easier to give the man credit for his devotion if he hadn't threatened her.

They stopped to converse with Mrs. Gilford—a young

married woman Lenora got on well with—before moving forward again. The promenade was as much for meeting with friends as it was for the exercise. Knowing she would not have her river walk tomorrow night left Lenora feeling restless. Perhaps she would need to resume her evening walks instead, never mind that she would be stopped for conversation or have to avoid people and carriages within the city.

When they stopped to speak with a friend of Aunt Gwen's, Lenora saw them—Mr. Asher and Miss Manch. She felt her back straighten, and she turned so she would not be facing them as they approached. Lenora tried to appear involved in Aunt Gwen's conversation but was acutely aware of the pair coming toward them. One park among so many in the city and she had to encounter *him*?

Please don't recognize me, she whispered in prayer. *Walk past without noticing so that—*

"Miss Wilton?"

She closed her eyes briefly, then summoned her politest smile as she turned. "Mr. Asher," she said, bobbing a quick curtsy. "Miss Manch."

Miss Manch narrowed her eyes. Lenora felt her heart speed up even as she tried to grab hold of the even temper she'd managed during her interactions with the girl yesterday.

Mr. Asher seemed surprised at Lenora's appearance, which embarrassed her. Dorothea had done Lenora's hair so that she had curls pinned atop her head with one perfect ringlet hanging down either side of her face. She wore a lavender day dress with matching pelisse and a gray parasol. This man had now seen her in three very different presentations, and it made her feel ridiculous.

"A pleasure to see you," she said, resisting the temptation to pat her hair or straighten her glove under Mr. Asher's attention.

"The pleasure is all mine," Mr. Asher said with a slight bow.

Aunt Gwen bid her friend farewell and turned her attention toward the newcomers. Lenora gave the introductions, counting on her aunt's manners to keep her from saying, "Oh, you are the student giving my Lenora such a hard time, and you are the girl's uncle—Lenora did not tell me of your shoulders." Of course, Aunt Gwen said nothing of the sort and merely inclined her head appropriately and made a remark about the fine weather—it had not rained today, what a blessing. Lenora fidgeted with the tassel of her handbag, and then forced herself to stop when she realized what she was doing.

The pleasantries ended, Mr. Asher turned his attention to Lenora, who struggled to hold his gaze. His intent look made her uncomfortable.

"Miss Wilton, might I have a word?"

This was not proper manners; they were in a public place, and she was being singled out in front of mixed company. She also had a good idea of what he wanted to talk about, and she did not want to address his niece's behavior here and now. It was the weekend, and she had left the school so that she might be free of it for two-days' time, not run directly into the worst portion.

"Certainly," Aunt Gwen answered before Lenora could refuse. "Miss Manch, would you attend me a bit of the way?

I should love to hear what you think of our city. You've only just arrived, have you not?" She looked from Miss Manch to Lenora, the picture of innocence. "Shall we meet you at the ruined castle in half an hour?"

Lenora opened her mouth to answer, but then closed it as she accepted her fate as inevitable.

Moments later, Aunt Gwen departed with Miss Manch on her arm. Watching them together—Lenora's favorite and least favorite people—was like watching a pony walk on its front legs: confusing and out of place. She hoped Aunt Gwen would be all right.

Mr. Asher extended his arm, and Lenora looked at it a moment before remembering the offer was nothing more than good manners. He didn't mean anything by it other than giving the appearance that he was a gentleman, which he was not. A true gentleman would never blackmail a woman.

Lenora was uncomfortable being so close to him, and she was inexperienced being alone with a man. They were in a public garden, yes, but the numerous walkways, grottos, and alcoves allowed far more privacy than she felt appropriate. Never mind that she'd been alone with this man twice now at the river, and one of those times had been at night.

She wished she could fidget with the tassel again, but with her arm in Mr. Asher's, it would be too overt. She needed something else to soothe her fractured nerves and began counting their steps—another trick she had not needed to employ for months. Not since the Mckays' garden party, where Elizabeth Bradshaw—a gentleman's daughter from Leagrave on holiday with her parents—could not stop commenting on how changed Lenora was. The more amazed Miss Bradshaw was, the more Lenora felt like a dolt. Leaving her past behind her was difficult enough without someone reminding her. Counting her steps that day had prevented Lenora from fully reverting to the girl she'd been. Counting them today would help her to maintain a professional composure despite being so close to this man.

"Did you receive my response to your letter?" Mr. Asher asked. "I sent it to the school last night and had hoped to hear back from you this morning."

"I stay with my aunt on weekends and did not receive your response," Lenora said, staring straight ahead and feeling conspicuous. Fourteen steps. Fifteen, sixteen. People would see her walking with him; they would think he was a beau. "I shall read it on Monday when I return." Twenty-two, twenty-three.

"It is a relief to know you hadn't received it. I had thought you were ignoring me."

The comment irritated her. "Because I did not immediately respond to your letter? I am not at your beck and call, Mr. Asher." Oh, she was peckish today. Thirty, thirty-one . . .

"Oh, no, I did not mean that." He sounded sincerely contrite. "Only, I had made you an offer I was eager to have answered."

Lenora stopped walking, causing him to stumble a step on the gravel path. She couldn't speak and forgot where she was in her counting. An offer? What? Evan Glenside had once made her an offer of marriage, but certainly not . . . She blinked her eyes like a fool.

"To attend you to the river," Mr. Asher continued. "I surmised that you must have a routine of some sort, since you have all the clothing necessary to serve as your disguise. Do you go every Sunday night? More evenings than that? You arrived at quarter after eleven last week—do you leave your residence at eleven, then?"

She began walking again, and he quickly fell into step beside her. She tried to angle her parasol so it would hide her flaming face from the two women who appeared from around the hedge ahead of them, coming their way. Mr. Asher inclined his head in greeting as they passed. Lenora could not manage any acknowledgment at all. At least she did not know them.

"What are you talking about?" she asked in little more than a whisper.

Mr. Asher lowered his voice and ducked his head toward her, which made her swallow. He smelled of pipe smoke and cedar—earthy and masculine. She didn't pull away from him, even though she told herself she should. "I likely ruined your evening last week and had hoped to make it right by offering to escort you when you next planned to go out. You obviously feel comfortable in the city, but it isn't safe for a woman to wander the streets at night, no matter how familiar she might feel."

It took Lenora several seconds to process what Mr. Asher had said. She couldn't accept his offer—of course not. But she had to concede being mildly grateful. "Thank you, but that would be inappropriate."

"I am only concerned for your safety, Miss Wilton, and

whatever remedy your excursion gave you. I have no intentions beyond assisting you, I assure you."

"Thank you, but no." It was embarrassing; he was the uncle of the worst student Lenora had ever had, *and* he was blackmailing her into trying to help the girl. She did not need, nor want, his help, and if she felt a tiny bit touched by his kindness and willingness to take a risk on her behalf, that was only because she had such little experience with men like him—men in general, actually.

They walked in silence for a distance and turned onto another pathway. She did not know the garden as well as Aunt Gwen, but he seemed to, and she followed his lead. His offer of escort must be to assuage his guilt regarding the blackmailing. That reason fit in perfectly with the man she knew him to be.

As they passed three younger women, Lenora heard twittering giggles behind them. Lenora glanced at Mr. Asher, who had been the object of the girls' attention, surprised to see his neck flushed. She couldn't fault the girls' notice, he did cut a striking figure, but they didn't know him the way Lenora did, and she looked ahead and stopped thinking about how comfortably her arm was wrapped around his elbow. Soon enough she recognized the path leading toward the aviary, which meant they were still some distance from the ruined castle. Had they not been walking a full hour already?

"My offer was only one part of the message I sent to the school," Mr. Asher said. "I am distressed by your report that Catherine cannot read. Are you certain?"

His niece was a topic Lenora was glad to take hold of. "If

she were more compliant I *would* be certain, but she's trying to hide it—embarrassed, I'm sure. I have not yet confirmed it. Language is not my expertise, but I will bring it up in our staff meeting on Tuesday so that we might formulate a plan to best help her."

"A plan *will* be put in place for her? She won't be dismissed from the school?"

Lenora looked up at him. "She is our student; we are her teachers. It is our job to help her improve." She left out the part about improvement being impossible if Miss Manch didn't co-operate. Nor did she ask how he could not know his niece could not read. "Have you spoken with her about it since she returned to your care last evening?"

Mr. Asher shook his head. "I did not want to put her on the defensive when she has not yet forgiven me for bringing her here. I mentioned that I'd heard she played well, I thought she might discuss that topic more easily, but she made it very clear that she did not want to talk about it." His shoulders fell. "We dance as cautious partners, Catherine and I."

Lenora considered this as they paused before the birds of the aviary. She paid them little attention, pondering over what he'd said. "She has been in your care for nine months?" She resisted asking a direct question, not wanting to appear nosy.

Mr. Asher nodded, and, as she'd hoped, filled in additional details. "I had been managing my family's interests in Jamaica since before Catherine was born. I traveled home every few years, but Catherine's father, my half-brother, was fourteen years my senior. We were not raised together, and were often at odds when it came to family matters. He was heir to his father's holdings in England, while I received my grandfather's plantation upon his death, which is why I left England in the first place. I needed to make my own fortune, since my brother would not see to my education, and my mother had no control over her own income.

"Apparently, my brother did not care for Catherine after his wife died when the baby was only a few months old. She was raised by a variety of family members since then. I'm ashamed to say I never paid much attention. I unexpectedly became her legal guardian upon the death of my brother nearly two years ago. It took some time for me to make arrangements for an extended stay in England in order to take over her care. Now that I am here, I am trying to rise to my responsibility. It is proving to be a fierce campaign. Running a sugar plantation was a far more comfortable occupation than this has proven to be."

Yet he stayed. Why? "And the family members who cared for her did not tell you she could not read?"

He was quiet, then led her further along the path. She sensed he did not want her to look at him too closely, that he was uncomfortable or perhaps ashamed? She watched the toes of her shoes peek from beneath the hem of her dress with each step and realized that she hadn't been counting for some time now.

That does not mean I am enjoying this, she said to no one but herself. But what *did* her lack of nerves mean? She'd felt this way in his company before, and suddenly something her sister Rose had told her once sprang to mind: "The right person makes up for your deficiencies. I feel more myself with him than I feel with anyone else." She'd been explaining how she'd known that her husband was the right choice. Like Lenora, Rose was shy, though not quite *like* Lenora.

If circumstances were different and Lenora were walking with Mr. Asher through the garden at night, with the lights casting a romantic glow and him wanting her to be there because of his own interest in her, she might wonder if he were the fulfillment of that explanation Lenora had never fully understood before. But he couldn't be. Not after blackmailing her. Not after causing her so much misery. Having never felt what Rose described made it impossible for Lenora to know, which meant it was *impossible* for her to feel such a thing.

Mr. Asher saved her from her maddening thoughts by continuing, regret tinging every word. "By the time I returned to England, Catherine was under the paid care of a complete stranger. My aunt and two cousins in turn had had their fill of her, and the last had cast her off nearly six months earlier. They said she was incorrigible and that they did their best before her behavior made it impossible for them to keep her. The woman in whose care she was left did not spare the rod and was not concerned with education. I *assumed* Catherine could read—she is twelve years old. The other schools she has attended since my return have said nothing of either issue." He paused thoughtfully. "If you had known her when I first collected her from that woman's house, I daresay you would be impressed by her improvement these last months despite her continued difficulties. Unfortunately, I'm running out of ideas on how to cross the remaining breach."

Lenora was contemplating what she'd learned as they crossed the bridge to the east side of the park. The sympathy for both Miss Manch and Mr. Asher was impossible to ignore, accompanied by perhaps a bit of a relief. That there were reasons for Miss Manch's difficulties was helpful to know, that her uncle was devoted enough to do so much on her behalf was impressive.

Miss Manch and Aunt Gwen came into view ahead of them. The two of them seemed rather deep in conversation, and Lenora frowned in worry. As they got closer, Lenora saw that Aunt Gwen was smiling as Miss Manch gave a detailed explanation of something. Miss Manch had many faces, and they all made Lenora nervous.

When the two couples were again face to face, they exchanged partners and shared farewells. Lenora was relieved to be free of Mr. Asher's company and let out a heavy sigh to show it. He and Miss Manch continued toward the labyrinth elsewhere in the garden, while Aunt Gwen and Lenora moved toward the bridge she'd just crossed with Mr. Asher. She hoped that meant they were heading home; if she encountered Mr. Asher during another round through the park, she might turn and run.

"I must say, Lenora, that while I do not doubt your rendition of your interactions with that young woman this week, there is a part of her that is absolutely delightful."

"Be glad you did not have a slate or need her to conform to any behavior."

Aunt Gwen laughed. "I required her to walk politely and make engaging conversation, and she did both quite well."

Lenora felt a twinge of jealously, but reminded herself that

Aunt Gwen had known the girl for only half an hour. "I'm glad she at least *knows* good manners," Lenora said out loud, feeling petulant. "I had begun to wonder."

Aunt Gwen gave Lenora's arm a squeeze. "I told her I would send an invitation for her and her uncle for dinner tomorrow night."

Lenora stopped on the walkway, and Aunt Gwen looked at her in surprise. "Dinner?" Lenora finally managed to say. "She is my student, Aunt Gwen."

"Well, yes, is that a problem? Miss McCombie and her family came to dinner last spring."

"That was different. Miss McCombie was finishing school." But that wasn't the reason she'd come to dinner. She'd come to dinner because Lenora liked her company and Aunt Gwen wanted to hear her play the violin.

"Is there some rule against students attending dinner parties with their teachers except when they are in their final year?" Aunt Gwen's expression was expectant, but she already knew the answer.

There was not a rule, and, in fact, Mrs. Henry felt it was good for the reputation of the school for teachers to have a connection outside of school with the girls and their families when possible. A significant portion of their students were sent upon referral.

Her heart pounded. Miss Manch and Mr. Asher in her sanctuary? It was that pony walking on its front legs all over again.

Aunt Gwen began walking again, which forced Lenora to follow. "They are new to Bath, and this will be a good way for them to become acquainted with other families. I will ask the

Snows and the Grovesfords, I think. The Snow girl is about Miss Manch's age, though at a country school, I believe. Still, they will know how to converse, and I would like to hear this prodigy play my pianoforte."

Lenora could think of nothing to say.

Aunt Gwen filled the silence easily enough. "I'll ask Cook to make that chocolate custard from last week; it would be just the thing, don't you think? You won't mind it two Sundays in a row, will you?"

Chapter Eight

I want your assurance that this is not another attempt at matchmaking," Lenora said as she walked from the window to the settee and back again Sunday evening. It was nearly five o'clock, but none of the dinner guests had arrived, and Aunt Gwen had commented three times now on what a handsome man Mr. Asher was, raising Lenora's anxiety with each utterance. "You promised me you would not do that again."

"And I'm not," Aunt Gwen said rather too innocently for Lenora to believe it. "As I said, they are new to the city and acquainted with you, so I thought it well-mannered of me to invite them. If I'd known it would put you in such a fit, I'd have never mentioned the idea to Miss Manch, but I could not very well rescind once I'd extended the invitation. Do sit down, my dear. Your anxiety is making my own heart skitter about my chest. I might need an early whiskey if you remain in such a state."

Lenora stopped pacing and looked hard at her aunt. "I had just finished telling you how difficult a student Miss Manch was and that Mr. Asher was heavy-handed with his demands that I pay her particular attention. I gave absolutely *no* indication whatsoever that I wanted to dine with them."

"I'm sorry," Aunt Gwen said, turning out her hands like a magician intent upon convincing his audience he had nothing to hide. "I thought you might see the side of the girl that I saw if they dined at our table." She shrugged. "I promise I did not mean to offend you, nor do I have any motive other than reaching out to a new family in the city. I will not invite them again without your approval."

Lenora resumed her pacing, irritated that she was being so uncharacteristically direct with her aunt and hating that she was looking forward a tiny bit for Mr. Asher to arrive. The man was making her crazy, and she'd only known him a week. Almost exactly a week, in fact, which was another reason she was on edge. She could not have her river walk after tonight's guests left. And she could not take an evening walk *because* of the guests. It was easy to put the blame for all of it on Mr. Asher, but as soon as she did, she felt guilty and pulled the judgment back to herself. She did not know how to *do* any of this!

Lenora stopped pacing when she saw Mr. Asher and Miss Manch coming toward the house. She backed away from the window, not wanting to look as though she were watching for them. Which she was not!

Why had none of the other guests arrived? If there were more people, she could keep from being thrust into conversation with the two people she wanted to avoid the very most. What if she were unable to speak? What if she said something foolish? What if Lenora of Leagrave took over and Mr. Asher thought her a simpleton? Why did she care so much about what he thought?

Jacobson showed the guests into the drawing room a few minutes later, and Lenora adjusted her elbow-length gloves in order to avoid Mr. Asher's gaze, which she felt lingered longer than necessary. She was wearing a royal blue evening gown with a scalloped neckline, tulip sleeves, and a split skirt to show the black silk underskirt. The gloves and sheer shawl draped at her elbows were required dress for Aunt Gwen's Sunday dinners, and Lenora had come to enjoy the opportunity to wear such fine things most nights. However, Lenora felt obtrusive tonight. He would not think she'd dressed up for him, would he?

Mr. Asher wore a traditional black coat and trousers, with silver-buckled black shoes and a deep-green waistcoat that matched the emerald pin in his cravat. His hair was combed back and formal compared to his usual haphazard style. It was irritating that he looked so handsome and comfortable while she felt so overstated and out of place.

"Good evening," he said, bowing sharply at the waist. Miss Manch, dressed in a yellow frock with her hair pinned up in such a way that she appeared older than her twelve years, gave a perfectly proper curtsy. Tonight, it seemed she was on her best behavior.

"Good evening," Aunt Gwen and Lenora said at the same time.

Aunt Gwen invited them to sit and offered Mr. Asher a drink while they waited for the other guests to arrive. When Lenora realized Mr. Asher was not going to sit unless she did, she took the seat to the right of her aunt. It put her directly across from Mr. Asher and Miss Manch, who shared the settee.

"I very much enjoyed getting to know your niece yesterday, Mr. Asher," Aunt Gwen said. "She says you have been living in Jamaica until a short time ago."

"Yes, my maternal grandfather left me a sugar plantation near Port Antonio," Mr. Asher said. "I apprenticed for three years under my grandfather and took over full management just two years before he died. I have made a few visits to London over the years, but I stayed primarily on the plantation, which has been a successful venture."

"And will you return to Jamaica?" Aunt Gwen said. Lenora was eager for the answer, too.

"I plan to make a visit next year sometime. It is two months' travel there and two months back, which will take some planning. I took on a partner after my grandfather died, and we have been managing together." He paused, as though determining what he could say. A quick glance at Catherine seemed to convince him. "I am managing my brother's estate in Cheshire, presently, and securing distribution for our sugar in Great Britain as well, so there is plenty for me to do here. I plan to make my home in England."

Lenora noticed that he said he was managing his brother's estate, not that he'd inherited, which made sense, since he'd already told her that he and his brother had different fathers.

She looked suddenly at Catherine as understanding dawned. He hadn't said it out loud, but was Catherine the heir of her father's holdings? For a daughter to inherit was uncommon, but not impossible. If any other male heir on her father's line had inherited, there would be no reason for Mr. Asher to be managing it. Interesting.

Lenora noticed that he fiddled with the edge of his coat; his own anxiety coming forth?

"You'll remain in England long-term, then?" Aunt Gwen asked.

He nodded as though it was slightly painful for him to admit it. Sacrificial, perhaps. It seemed he would have preferred to stay in Jamaica. Perhaps he regretted his decision now that he was in the middle of it. "I've enjoyed getting to know Catherine and look forward to making a mostly-traditional English gentleman's life here."

Miss Manch glanced at her uncle, a look of sincere appreciation on her face. It was perhaps the first glimpse Lenora had seen of an ordinary girl. Mr. Asher smiled back at his niece but also looked a bit relieved. Perhaps she was not so kind when they were alone? Mr. Asher *had* said she did not want to be in Bath.

The other guests finally arrived, diluting the attention so pointedly fixed on Mr. Asher. Lenora was actually disappointed. She'd liked learning more about his life—well, anyone's life, she told herself. There was nothing special about his life in particular. But he'd lived on a tropical island in the Caribbean. Lenora had read about Port Antonio, so different from England. Did he prefer that climate to this one? How large was his plantation? Did he manufacture both sugar and treacle there, or did he sell off the renders to someone else to make the treacle?

Lenora sat next to the elderly Mr. Grovesford at dinner and allowed him to go on at length about his upcoming travels to Sussex to spend the winter with his wife's sister. Lenora had never been to Sussex—she'd never been anywhere but Leagrave and Bath—and so she asked him to tell her all about it, and by the end of the meal she felt like an expert on the county.

The women withdrew to the drawing room, Lenora bringing up the rear. Miss Manch sat beside Aunt Gwen. Mrs. Snow sat on Aunt Gwen's other side, and Lenora stood near the fire next to Mrs. Grovesford. The woman was always cold, it seemed. The men joined them some quarter of an hour later. Mr. Asher did not seek out Lenora, though she was irritatingly aware of his placement in the room.

Aunt Gwen invited Miss Manch to play the piano, and the guests were all impressed by her proficiency as she played what seemed to be her favorite piece, *Greensleeves*. Lenora enjoyed watching the girl play, noticing the way the music brightened her face. Lenora never felt more herself than when she was playing the pianoforte. The guests applauded, and Miss Manch smiled beneath their praise.

Lenora looked at Mr. Asher, who fairly glowed with pride. He caught her glance, and she looked away, feeling her cheeks turn pink. She was trying very hard not to pay attention to him, but it was proving difficult.

After Catherine's performance, Aunt Gwen asked Lenora to

entertain them, and she took her place on the pianoforte with relief, choosing from her memory a sonatina that could remain in the background and allow people to continue visiting. As she played, she kept looking at the clock as she typically did on a Sunday evening. Each time she noted the time, she mourned that she would not be going out tonight—or ever again. Oh, how she would miss her private time in the quiet city. She focused on her music.

Aunt Gwen allowed Lenora to play until the guests began to leave, something Lenora's family had often done in Leagrave to protect her from anxiety-producing social events. Aunt Gwen was not usually so accommodating, allowing Lenora to play for only half an hour before inviting her back into conversation. Lenora took her aunt's forbearance tonight as an apology for putting her in an awkward position.

Lenora left the haven of the pianoforte to share in the farewells. The Grovesfords and Snows left, and Lenora returned to the drawing room to find Aunt Gwen and Miss Manch on the far side where Aunt Gwen was explaining the portrait of her father that hung on the wall. Lenora's grandfather had been a land owner of some renown in Nottinghamshire. Her uncle now ran the estate, but she had never had the chance to visit. Not only was it some distance from Leagrave, but her father's duties as vicar and patriarch of eight children also made it difficult for the family to travel.

Mr. Asher stood near the doorway of the drawing room, as though he were waiting for her. To walk past him would be rude, so she stood next to him and hoped Aunt Gwen would run out of things to say soon.

"When do you go out?" he whispered.

She looked at him in surprise, felt her cheeks flame, and faced forward again. She should have been rude and passed him by after all. She was astounded that he would bring it up. It was the type of topic people were expected to sweep beneath the rug and forget existed. She said nothing, wishing she had a fan to hide behind.

"Please let me escort you," he said under his breath. "You have been watching the clock all night, and I cannot bear knowing you'll go out alone."

"I am not going," she said, lifting her chin, though it did not make her feel more confident.

"I don't believe you." He took a sip of his brandy.

"Well, you should." She forced a smile and crossed to Aunt Gwen in time to hear her explain how she had been her father's caretaker after her mother died and what a dear time it had been. Lenora glanced at the clock again out of habit. It was nine o'clock. If last week hadn't happened, she'd be on the streets in two hours' time, leaving the frayed edges of her anxiety behind her with every step. But last week *had* happened, and she would be in her bedchamber in two hours' time, missing the river, missing the night. Mr. Asher's offer opened the door she'd closed just a sliver.

Impossible, she told herself. Last week had been horrifying— crouching in alleys and slinking behind shops. *Never again,* she reprimanded, *but . . .*

Mr. Asher must have followed her across the room, as she became aware of him behind her a moment before he spoke. "Catherine, it is time we made our good-byes."

The girl turned sharply toward her uncle, her eyes flashing in a way that brought Lenora and Mr. Asher up short. "It is only nine!"

"Catherine," Mr. Asher said in a chiding tone that Lenora found rather brave considering the menace of his niece's glare.

The girl let out a heavy sigh, but did not argue. "All right." She turned to Aunt Gwen and embraced her. Aunt Gwen hugged her back, just as she would Lenora or one of her other nieces, which sparked an unwanted bit of jealousy in Lenora. Miss Manch did not deserve the same consideration as family. "Thank you so much for having us, Mrs. Simmons. It was quite truly the most enjoyable evening I have had in months."

"Having you was a delight," Aunt Gwen said, placing her hand on the girl's cheek.

Catherine ducked slightly, as though she were embarrassed by the praise. Was she playing Aunt Gwen as proficiently as she played the pianoforte? But why?

Lenora forced her smile to stay in place as they walked the guests to the door.

"Shall you call a carriage?" Aunt Gwen asked as Jacobson opened the front door. There was a breeze tonight, but also a quarter moon. It would reflect so beautifully on the river, as though fairies were skittering across the surface.

"Not tonight," Mr. Asher said as he buttoned his overcoat. "The night is mild, and I rather fancy long walks at night."

Lenora made the mistake of catching his eye. He raised an eyebrow as though issuing his invitation again. She looked away but felt the renewed tug. The reason she had decided not to go out was because he'd caught her, but if he *escorted* her, she would not have to fear him, or anyone else. He was already using her walks against her. How could he take further advantage if she accepted his offer?

"Well, then you are very brave," Aunt Gwen said, shivering dramatically. "I hate to be out after dark, and I'm afraid the weather is already turning. At least there is no rain yet."

"Yes, at least that," Mr. Asher said. "Though I don't mind the rain."

Lenora didn't mind the rain either. She'd come home a dozen times from her night walks soaked to the skin. She would simply lay her clothes before the fire and let them dry overnight, packing them away before Dorothea came to wake her. But not tonight. Not ever again. To lose the freedom she credited with developing her courage was painful, and she sensed Mr. Asher knew it.

"I hope to see you again soon," Aunt Gwen said as Mr. Asher and Miss Manch stepped over the threshold. "And best of luck in school this week, Catherine. The first week is always the hardest, but now that you know your teachers and classmates and what is expected, I have no doubt this week will be far more comfortable."

Catherine smiled sweetly, then scowled at Lenora when Aunt Gwen turned her attention to Mr. Asher's good-bye.

Lenora clenched her hands at her side. She needed her river.

She needed fortification to deal with this girl tomorrow and the four days that would follow. Lenora looked at Mr. Asher one last time and amazed herself by giving one crisp nod. He hid his surprise quickly but nodded back, just once, before stepping toward the street. The door closed behind them, and Lenora followed Aunt Gwen back to the parlor so they might discuss the evening and Aunt Gwen could enjoy her whiskey.

Lenora's chest tingled. She'd agreed to let Mr. Asher escort her to the river. Why had she done that? She knew, though. She was eager to get out of the house, to sort her thoughts, to enjoy her river. But she wouldn't be alone. Would the experience be damaged by the lack of solitude? In that moment, as she sat next to her aunt and commented on how pleasant the night was, she realized she didn't care. She had regained something precious she thought had been lost. She would enjoy it for every moment she could, come what may.

Chapter Nine

When the door to Mrs. Simmons's terrace house closed behind them, Aiden looked at his niece with grateful relief. She'd been lovely tonight—well-mannered, poised—and he'd been so proud of her performance on the pianoforte. It was the first time he'd heard her play, and she was exceptional.

He felt as though they had finally overcome the animosity that had been between them since he'd announced she would be enrolled in Mrs. Henry's school in Bath. He'd told her the day before they left the estate in Cheshire—*her* estate in Cheshire, though he had not yet disclosed that fact to her—and she'd been livid, convinced in her own mind that, after she'd been turned out of two schools between February and May, he had given up. He hadn't; he'd only used his time in following up on the only school Miss Keighly thought would give Catherine a chance.

All that angst seemed behind them now, and it was such a relief to be back to an easier, if not easy, relationship. He put out his arm and bowed to her somewhat dramatically. "Might I escort you home, m'lady?" he said in exaggerated tones.

She looked at him as he straightened, then rolled her eyes and walked ahead. Sheepish, Aiden put down his arm and caught up with her, hoping no one had seen him be spurned by a child. Perhaps they had not overcome the difficulties as well as he'd hoped. He decided to act as though nothing had happened. "I enjoyed spending the evening with you, Catherine," he said, trying to soften her a bit.

"I think you mean that you enjoyed spending the evening with Miss Wilton." She smiled with self-satisfaction as he startled.

"I beg your pardon," he said, truly stunned by the accusation.

"You watch her," Catherine said in a knowing voice.

Aiden forced a laugh. "I do not watch her."

"Yes, you do," she said. "You looked her direction sixteen times during the time between our arrival and going in to dinner. Then you looked her way two dozen times when she was playing the pianoforte."

"I don't think that's true," Aiden said, still trying to chuckle, though it was hollow even to him. Had he watched her? Well, he'd noticed she glanced at the clock quite often. He was uncomfortable about Miss Wilton going out alone tonight, that was the reason. If indeed he glanced at her more often than was proper, he couldn't tell Catherine that. And he hated that she'd noticed.

"It is true," Catherine said, assured of her certainty. She

looked at him, her eyes dancing with mischief. "And she watches you, too. When you aren't looking. Nervous, though—like you are the cat and she is the bird."

Aiden swallowed but managed to keep his smile in place. He rolled his eyes and shook his head, but he wanted to groan and ask what she meant. He certainly hadn't noticed Miss Wilton watching him, but then he hadn't noticed himself watching her either.

"You are making up stories," he finally said with a sigh. "If indeed she was watching me, it was surely to figure out how such a nice man could have a niece that caused so much trouble for her this week." He ruffled her hair, and she pulled away and scowled at him. He felt that she was a tiny bit embarrassed about her behavior at school. Good.

"And you looking at her?" Catherine said after a few minutes. She watched her shoes as she walked, her hands inside her pockets.

"I do not think I did that."

She snapped her head up. "You did!" she said with accusation, and he realized that he'd inadvertently called her a liar.

"All right," he said, thinking of an explanation fast. "I might have noticed how different she looked tonight as compared to how she looked at the school when I first met her." It had been surprising to see her in such different costumes, as though the woman underneath changed with each set of clothing. Though she didn't, not really. The schoolteacher he'd spoken to on the riverbank Monday was the same woman he'd walked with yesterday—one who spoke her mind and did not simper beneath his dominance the way the woman in Mrs. Henry's office had. She was a puzzle, this Miss Wilton, but he was not trying to solve her. Only ensure Catherine's success. Any way he could.

A wide smile split Catherine's face, giving Aiden a niggling suspicion that he should have thought longer and harder before he answered. Sometimes talking to Catherine felt like handing over arrows she would store in her quiver for later.

Aiden cleared his throat, determined to change the subject and wishing he'd done so earlier. "You seem to like Mrs. Simmons."

Catherine shrugged. Aiden clenched his teeth. "And we quite enjoyed hearing you play. You are quite talented. I was very proud of you."

She looked up at him, doubtful, then away without a word. What had earned him that look? That he was proud of her?

"Did you enjoy performing?"

She didn't answer, running her fingers along the fence posts of a small park they passed on their way toward the bridge. "Yes," she finally said.

Aha, progress! "Is that your favorite piece—*Greensleeves*?"

She shrugged.

Heaven help me! He nearly commented on Miss Wilton's playing—she was *very* good—but remembered that he did not want to bring her up. At all. In fact, he felt this entire conversation had run its course. He was not going to pander to Catherine for the duration of the walk.

He put his hands in his pockets and began whistling under his breath, realizing after a minute that he was whistling one of the tunes Miss Wilton had played. Beethoven, he thought, but wasn't sure. Though he could play the pianoforte, he didn't. A decade in Jamaica without an instrument or reason to keep his skills sharp meant he had almost forgotten he had ever known how to play. He would like to try again, if he had the chance. Perhaps the ability would come back to him if he practiced.

"How do you do that?"

The softness of the question took him off guard, but he tried not to show his surprise as he looked down at Catherine, who was walking slower and looking up at him.

"Do what?"

"Whistle."

Was that sheepishness in her tone? He worked hard to keep from smiling too much.

"Oh, well, the skill is a bit different for each person, but you, um—" He had to practice the right position with his tongue before he could explain it. "You put your tongue against your bottom teeth, then narrow your lips so only a small amount of air comes out." He had to whistle a note to come up with the next instruction. "Then sort of lift your tongue a bit, but keep it against your teeth." He whistled again.

With an expression of deep concentration, she pursed her lips and blew, but did little more than blow spittle. She harrumphed, her fists clenched at her sides. She seemed to take any failing as a personal fault of character. He hurried to encourage her.

"Good, you've got the position of your lips right," he said, though he had no idea, really. "Hold them tighter together, try to flatten out the back of your tongue, and lift the center."

"That makes no sense at all!" she said and stormed forward. He caught up with her.

"Giving up is what makes no sense, Catherine." He was nervous as he spoke the words; it didn't take much to make her turn on him. "Just keep practicing between here and home. No one can see you, and the only way to learn to whistle is to keep trying. I tried for years before I mastered the ability."

Actually, he'd learned from watching his brother— Catherine's father. For the first ten years of his life, he'd wanted nothing more than to be like his older brother, but Edmund wanted nothing to do with a shadow, which left Aiden to observe and imitate as best he could. And he was a quick study. He'd learned to whistle like Edmund, dismount like Edmund, and even laugh like Edmund. Aiden's admiration of his older brother had been endless, until he was ten years old.

They had gone fishing—Aiden ecstatic to have an outing with his brother—only to have Edmund break Aiden's pole and push him into the river. Aiden had thought it an accident, but Edmund had watched his brother with a strange smile, then walked away while Aiden sputtered and tried to call for help even as the water quickly swept him downstream. A fisherman nearly a mile downriver had pulled Aiden from the water, barely conscious and with his lungs filled with water. Edmund had claimed Aiden ran off, and Aiden did not dare tell his mother the truth.

Aiden avoided his brother after that, and there had been no

love lost on Edmund's part, which made it all the more surprising when Aiden had received notice from the family solicitors that he had been granted guardianship of Catherine as well as named the custodian of the estate left to her until she married or reached the age of twenty-nine.

At first Aiden had been angry that Edmund would take such liberties with Aiden's future. He knew Aiden had meant to stay in Jamaica and make a life for himself there. But after some time to come to terms with things, Aiden had accepted this change of circumstance. The truth was that he missed his homeland, missed the connection of family. Catherine was nearly all he had left, and he had felt driven to rise to his responsibility. How often since then had he wondered if Edmund's decision had been rooted in his desire to torture his younger half-brother, even after death.

Catherine pursed her lips together again, slowed her walk, and kept trying. Within a few yards, she made a single wisp of a whistle.

"There," Aiden said. "Now try to find that same position."

Catherine nodded quickly, her face bright and focused, and made another attempt but without the same success. For the rest of the walk home, Aiden encouraged her and prodded her forward. They had just reached the first house on their block when she made a clear whistle that lasted nearly a full second. Aiden applauded. Catherine grinned and whistled the rest of the way home. All in all, it had been a pleasant evening.

They entered the house, met by Hyrum, the man-of-all-work Aiden had hired with the house. He helped them with their coats, and Aiden said good night to Catherine. He turned toward the parlor, where he planned to enjoy a glass of brandy before going out to meet Miss Wilton. The reminder sent a rush of heat through him as though he already had the drink in hand.

He was simply doing the right thing, he told himself, and yet that did not explain the rush of pleasure he'd felt when she'd accepted his offer of escort. Nor the sensation he'd experienced just now. Surely all his awareness was due to his having forced her into helping him secure Catherine's place at the school. They were a team, of sorts, both working toward the girl's success. And it was such a relief to have another person involved in her care.

He had lifted the decanter to pour when he thought of Miss Keighly. Wasn't Miss Keighly involved in Catherine's care? She was the one who had found Mrs. Henry's school, after all, and sent the first letter of request for special consideration. Aiden hadn't been particularly pleased that she had sent the letter without informing him, but it was easy to forgive when Mrs. Henry had responded with a willingness to explore the idea. He shook his head, not wanting to think on that. Tonight had been a success on many fronts—Catherine had showed how well-behaved she could be, Aiden had met other people here in Bath, which helped him feel more settled, and he felt that he and Miss Wilton had smoothed over some of the tension between them.

A sound behind him made him turn so quickly that he sloshed brandy on the sleeve of his coat. He muttered a curse, then realized the interruption was Catherine. She smiled at having caught him using foul language. "You were supposed to go up to bed," he said.

"I'm not tired."

"You go back to the school in the morning, and it is nearly ten." He glanced at the clock for confirmation. He would be meeting Miss Wilton in an hour. He looked back at his niece. "Tired or not, it is time to go to bed. Where is Paulette?"

Catherine shrugged. Aiden let out a breath and replaced the decanter.

"Come with me," he said, heading toward the servants' quarters, where the silly maid was surely flirting with Hyrum instead of tending to her responsibilities. Catherine needed to be in bed and asleep before he left. She was entirely too observant for her own good, and he did not relish her asking him any questions if she knew he'd gone out again.

Chapter Ten

At five minutes till eleven, Lenora, dressed in her men's clothing, slipped through her window, made her way to the street, and looked around. They had not discussed a time, but Mr. Asher had referenced eleven o'clock during their promenade Saturday morning, and she assumed he would comply with that.

But maybe she was wrong and he wouldn't be here. That might be the best of everything. She would have her walk alone and, should he call her out for it, she could explain that it was a misunderstanding regarding what time to meet. Yet she already felt more anxious knowing she was not as invisible as she'd believed she was before last week. She glanced around again, wondering if a dozen sets of eyes were following her. The idea made her shiver, but she lifted her chin and began walking toward the river.

Within a few yards, Mr. Asher melted out of the shadows ahead of her but stayed close to the building where he'd been waiting. Lenora swallowed before moving toward him, her palms sweating. She was embarrassed to have him see her dressed this way, and also for allowing his escort. She felt as though she were admitting a weakness, and she was worn out from all the weakness she'd endured for so many years of her life. Being independent here in Bath had made her feel strong, and yet she'd agreed to let this man—this blackmailer—escort her as though she were a frightened little child.

"Good evening," she whispered when she reached him.

He put a finger to his lips, then pointed in the direction of the river.

She paused another moment, but then began walking, expecting him to fall in step beside her. Instead, he let her move several feet ahead before he followed. It seemed Mr. Asher was honoring her need for solitude, which was thoughtful of him.

When she reached the wall behind the shops, she looked back at her silent escort, feeling as though she should say something but not knowing what. There was an odd kind of intimacy between them, and yet he hadn't said a word or gotten within ten feet of her for the duration of their walk.

Mr. Asher lifted his pipe in salute and waved her toward the stairs. He took one of the crates from a pile that hid the gate from the alley and turned it over for a seat.

The briefest skiff of disappointment washed over her, knowing he would not be coming to the river, but she quickly quashed the regret. He *shouldn't* come with her to the river. This was *her* time, *her* meditation, and if he were there, she would not get the full effect.

She gave him a grateful nod—without a smile so as not to seem *too* grateful—then climbed ungracefully over the wall and moved down the stairs. At the riverbank, she brushed off the stone wall with the sleeve of her coat and took up her usual position of knees to chest and chin on knees. She stared at the water that glittered with the quarter moon as she'd known it would.

She tried to review the last week and make a plan for how she would deal with Miss Manch in the coming one, but the man at the top of the stairs kept invading her thoughts. If she thought about him enough, would she understand why he cared so much about a niece who was so difficult? And was he becoming more handsome each time she saw him, or was that simply a trick of her imagination?

Chapter Eleven

Lenora divulged Miss Manch's illiteracy at the teacher meeting Tuesday morning. The writing teacher admitted to having suspected the same thing, but she'd been unable to test it as Catherine had manipulated her way out of both assignments the week before.

"The girl is smart," Madame Hargreaves, the French teacher, said. "Her memorization skills are sound. And, truly, she has not been difficult for me." She shrugged, but could not hide how pleased she was to have good behavior from the girl every other teacher struggled with. Since memorization was the focus of beginning French, rather than writing or reading the language, it wasn't surprising to Lenora that Miss Manch had done well in that class. She *was* smart. Too smart in some ways.

"Yes, her memorization is excellent," Lenora said, wishing she wasn't so nervous about leading this discussion. She was usually on the listening end of these meetings. "She's a gifted musician despite being unable to read a single note."

"She's been a terror for me," Miss Carlyle said, her eyes magnified by her thick glasses. "She stabbed me with a needle yesterday." She held up a finger as though they could see the pinprick. "She does not like needlework and is very agitated by the time our hour is up."

"Which explains why she's always in such a state when she arrives in my classroom." Miss Bowman taught etiquette. "She's been difficult but not impossible. She's been taught manners, which makes her far above some of my other students who don't know their salad fork from a curtsy. I think it helps that we are always moving and practicing things. Some students are better with action than with lecture or recitation."

Miss Carlyle shifted in her chair, apparently displeased with the remark since needlepoint could be considered an active class.

Mrs. Henry listened to everyone's comments, then turned toward the writing teacher. "Miss Grimes, would you be willing to implement the skill-building methods you used for Miss Jonavin a few years ago?"

Miss Jonavin was before Lenora's time, but she'd heard of the girl. She was slow-witted, but her older sisters had attended Mrs. Henry's institute, and their parents had begged Mrs. Henry to allow their youngest daughter to attend as a day student. By the time Miss Jonavin finished her fourth year, she was improved beyond what anyone had expected and now served as a companion to her grandmother in London. She was an example of what effort and dedication could bring about. However, all accounts indicated that Miss Jonavin was sweet and eager to please both her teachers and her parents.

"I *could* help Miss Manch build her skills," Miss Grimes said with reluctance. "But I would need one-on-one time to implement the exercises. I only taught three hours when Miss Jonavin was a student here, and now I teach five. Beyond that, I feel Miss Manch rather undeserving of special attention. We are not a school that caters to misbehavior."

"Illiteracy is not misbehavior," Mrs. Henry said.

"Being incorrigible and disruptive certainly is. Why are we so determined to give this girl additional attention? We've dismissed other students for far less serious offenses than what she has already shown in barely a week."

Mrs. Henry and Lenora exchanged a glance. Miss Grimes had a point. That Mrs. Henry had trusted Lenora with the truth tugged at Lenora's loyalty. Mrs. Henry had her reasons to make exceptions for Miss Manch, and Lenora had her own.

"I could help with your first-year course, Miss Grimes," Lenora offered, knowing the class consisted mostly of basic poetry and composition. "I do not have students during that hour. If I taught for you a few times a week, would that free you enough for the extra time with Miss Manch?"

She considered bringing up the point system she and Mrs. Henry had already discussed, but felt that was a topic for the headmistress to explain.

"She can study during my class whenever she needs to," Miss Carlyle said, frowning at her injured finger. "Perhaps it will both spare me additional bloodshed and allow me to be more attentive to the other girls." Needlepoint was a required class, but no one argued it was less important than the girl learning to read.

They discussed a few other options and finally agreed on the course of action, some teachers more reluctantly than others. Lenora would teach first-level poetry on Mondays and Fridays, a study hour would be held in Mrs. Henry's office during needle-point class, and oral assignments and exams would be offered for all of Miss Manch's classes until she was able to do written work.

"I hope all of this effort is worthwhile," Miss Grimes said, shaking her head. "For a pleasant girl, this is reasonable, but for a difficult one . . . it is unprecedented."

Mrs. Henry cleared her throat, and she spoke with a tone of finality. "We will all need to, well, lower our expectations of Miss Manch for a time, I believe. Her uncle brought her here so she might benefit from routine and stability. Let's make that—and her skill training with Miss Grimes—the emphasis for the next few weeks and then reevaluate in one month's time. I would like each of you to designate one student in each class who will fetch me if Miss Manch's behavior is disruptive. Let *me* extend the reprimands. Perhaps that will free the rest of you from her poor graces."

On the first day of the "Miss Manch Plan," the student des-ignated by Lenora to report to Mrs. Henry went for the head-mistress after only ten minutes, when Miss Manch would not stop talking to her neighbor. Mrs. Henry came to collect Miss

Manch, and after fifteen minutes, the girl returned to the classroom and acted appropriately throughout the remaining hour, though she scowled at Lenora each time they made eye contact.

For the rest of the week, Lenora included Miss Manch in performance work and adjusted some of her lessons to incorporate more basic elements of music, such as beat and dynamics. She hoped the other students would not be frustrated by the backtracking, but they did not seem to notice. She did not want to delay the entire class for the sake of Miss Manch, and yet when she finally seemed to understand tempo and could keep the beat, Lenora let out a celebratory cheer in her mind. That Miss Manch was obviously pleased as well made her feel better at having given this girl the extra attention she seemed to need.

Saturday morning was too wet and rainy for an outdoor promenade, and when Lenora returned from the Pump Room with Aunt Gwen, she found a note from Mr. Asher waiting for her. Aunt Gwen lifted her eyebrows, but Lenora ignored the look and took the letter to the second-level, parlor where she could read it in private.

> *Dear Miss Wilton,*
> *I would like to extend my escort to you tomorrow night, if you are of a mind for a walk. Please send regrets only. If I hear nothing, I shall assume your agreement and proceed as last week.*
> *A. Asher*

Lenora bit her lip, looking around as though she had anyone to hide this from as she refolded the note. She did not consider sending her regrets for even a moment.

The weekend unfolded as it had the week before, and she merely nodded her notice of him when he stepped out from the shadows Sunday night.

Again, he kept his distance and remained at the top of the stairs.

She struggled to keep her thoughts away from him as she looked over the river, a light rain pocking the surface of the water. They'd exchanged two other notes during the week. In each one, he'd thanked her for her efforts with his niece, and she'd been unable to resist allowing herself to feel the pride of it.

She was making a difference with Miss Manch, and although she was uncomfortable with her original motives, her feelings were changing. She was beginning to care about Miss Manch for her own sake, and beginning to better appreciate the girl's uncle. He'd sacrificed two Sunday nights for her benefit now.

She rested her chin on her knees and thought about Evan Glenside, the only other man she'd ever spent private time with. They'd first met with a hedge between them, and since she had never had much of a conversation with any man, she'd taken it far too seriously. After Cassie had drawn him in with the letters where she'd pretended to be Lenora, Lenora had gone on two drives with Mr. Glenside. She'd felt awkward and nervous the whole time. He'd escorted her to a dance, and she'd barely spoken to him. She could sense his discomfort when they were together but had no idea how to remedy it.

When he proposed, she'd been relieved. She would be married. She would become a wife. Mr. Glenside himself was of little factor. She'd never felt comfort with anyone outside of her family and so did not consider it a hindrance that they were so uncomfortable in one another's company. She'd never kissed him. Never felt any kind of connection.

When he broke the engagement after learning of her and Cassie's deceit, she'd felt stupid and humiliated. It was why she'd begged to come to Bath in the first place. But she had realized rather quickly that she wasn't heartbroken. In fact, some part of her had felt as relieved at the jilting as she'd felt at the proposal, but in a different way. Surely she and Evan could have made a marriage work, but not in the same way he and Cassie were thriving.

It had been easy for Lenora to give up on future prospects after that, and no man had captured her thoughts and her senses since then. Until now. It was ridiculous to give so much notice to Mr. Asher. He was her student's guardian. He was handsome and, she could finally admit, kind—despite the blackmailing. He was only attentive to her out of guilt or gratitude, or perhaps some of both, and yet she thought of him more and more with time. She smiled more easily when she saw him.

She stared at the river while exploring memories of their interactions. Tonight, sitting alone in the rain while he smoked his pipe some distance above her, she could admit that she'd come tonight because of him, not because of the river. The thought both embarrassed and thrilled her. Fantasy, she concluded after listing all the reasons her thoughts were folly. But, perhaps, at the age of twenty-six, she could indulge in fantasy. Just a little.

The rain increased until she finally left the river. She nearly fell when trying to step over the wall. He hurried to catch her, and did he hold her elbow a bit longer than necessary? And did he step back too quickly once he realized the same thing? She thanked him, smiling sheepishly, and he simply nodded, before waving her forward.

Some heckling from a group of men on the way home caused Mr. Asher to close the distance between them. By the time they reached Gay Street, he was close enough for her to smell the pipe-smoke on his coat. She thanked him with a nod when they arrived at Aunt Gwen's house. He returned the gesture without a word.

She went through the back garden and up to her room. At the window, she peeked through the blinds, just able to make out his form in the shadows. That he'd watched to make sure she arrived safely touched her. She pulled open the drape a bit more so he could see her wave. He waved back and finally turned to leave, disappearing around the corner within a few steps.

As she laid her clothing out to dry, she smiled and admitted that she enjoyed her silent walks with him more than the walks she'd taken on her own. Because he assured her safety, she told herself, but she didn't quite believe it. Just fantasy, she told herself.

She was already looking forward to next Sunday.

120

The second week of the "Miss Manch Plan" did not go as well as the first. Miss Manch was belligerent during her individual sessions with Miss Grimes, and then tore the sleeve on another girl's dress when the girl teased her during tea about needing extra help. Lenora intervened in the argument and suggested a walk to help Miss Manch calm down. Mrs. Henry agreed.

Lenora and Miss Manch walked for nearly two hours through the city, and then through a section of wood, most of it in silence, because Lenora had no idea what to say. Miss Manch's temper faded the longer they were among the trees and grasses, until Lenora suggested they return. Catherine had been told she must apologize to both Miss Grimes and the girl before she would be allowed any supper. She apologized easily enough, but the next day, one of the class reporters came to Mrs. Henry in tears, saying that Miss Manch had called her a tattletale and threatened to stab her with a pen nib if she reported on her again. Neither Lenora nor Mrs. Henry doubted Catherine would do it.

Lenora was discouraged. If Miss Manch lost her connection with the other girls, things would only get worse. Lenora wrote to Mr. Asher, explaining her concerns. Her heart was more and more engaged with Miss Manch's success, but she was increasingly worried that she did not know how to properly help the girl. Mr. Asher responded that he would speak with her that weekend when his niece returned home.

Sunday afternoon, the weather turned. Lenora watched the windows closely in hopes the rain would lighten, but it did not, and she was forced to send a note to Mr. Asher saying she would not be taking her walk. She regretted missing it for more reasons than one, and then felt peckish when she returned to the school the next morning. She would not have gone out in such a downpour on her own, but it was missing Mr. Asher that set her mood on edge, and she hated that. It would not serve her to let her fantasy interfere with regular life.

The third week showed little improvement in Miss Manch's behavior. Lenora had started thinking of her as Catherine due to Mr. Asher referring to her as such in the notes they passed back and forth almost daily.

Catherine's relationships with other girls were continuing to break down. On Thursday, she made good on her threat and poked the reporter with the nib of her pen. She was sent to her uncle's house for the night, and Mrs. Henry called a special meeting for all the teachers after dinner. She announced that the point system would be implemented, though the majority of teachers wanted Catherine dismissed and could not understand why Mrs. Henry was so determined to avoid it.

Lenora stood by Mrs. Henry, though it made her stomach tight to argue with Miss Grimes. When Miss Grimes suggested Lenora be the one to inform Catherine of the plan, Lenora felt she had no choice but to agree.

After a particularly difficult class on Friday, Lenora asked Catherine to stay and told her the point system would be implemented Monday morning.

"I did not stab her," Catherine insisted, arms crossed tight over her chest as she glared at Lenora. "She walked too close to my desk, that is all."

"You did stab her," Lenora said. "And there is no point arguing otherwise. This is truly your last chance; do you not understand that?" But then what, Lenora wondered. Would Mrs. Henry dismiss Catherine if the point system did not work? Where would that leave Mr. Asher's bargain with Lenora? She didn't think he would expose her; after all, he knew how hard Lenora had worked, but Catherine would be out of options.

"I do not want another chance," Catherine said, leaning forward. "I hate it here. I hate the students. I hate the teachers, and I especially hate *you*."

Lenora flinched and felt an unfamiliar desire to take Catherine by the shoulders and shake her. "I am trying harder than anyone to help you, Catherine. Do you want to go to a school for troubled girls in Germany?"

"I want to get away from *you*," she snapped.

Lenora knew Catherine said it to hurt her, that she likely did not feel any more animosity toward Lenora than she felt toward any other teacher, but she couldn't avoid feeling hurt by it all the same.

"Well, you can't. We have not given up on you just yet."

"Then I shall fail at the point system, and you shall have to dismiss me."

Lenora let out a breath. "I hope you reconsider. The point system has bought you one more week, but it will be up to you. I should personally hate for you to be sent off to Germany, and I know your uncle would hate to see you go as well."

Catherine stared at her thoughtfully, far too long than could be considered polite. "I think it is my uncle you want to keep on. That is why you won't dismiss me, because you are in love with Uncle Aiden."

Lenora could not stop her cheeks from flushing hot, nor could she resist the excitement of knowing Mr. Asher's Christian name—Aiden. But she was finished with this meeting, and her heart was racing at having validated Catherine's accusation. Or at least, as far as Catherine knew. Lenora was not in love with Mr. Asher. Whatever it was she did feel, it was the fantasy of an avowed spinster, nothing more.

Besides that, this was all his fault. If he hadn't threatened Lenora, she would never have worked so hard to keep Catherine at the school this long. The last three weeks of her life would have been far simpler.

"I assure you, Miss Manch, that I will shed no tears when you or your uncle leave this city but shall be appeased with knowing that I gave my very best effort to give you the opportunity to succeed. Your failure will be due to your own actions, not mine."

She did not stay to read the expression on Miss Manch's face, but as she left the room—*her* classroom—she could feel the girl's glare burning into her back. She walked out of the building and down the block until she found a park where she could sit and drop her face into her hands. She struggled to hold back tears of frustration, embarrassment, and flat-out exhaustion. She had never worked so hard to help a student, and it was coming to nothing. Catherine *would* fail. She *would* leave Bath. And Mr. Asher—Mr. *Aiden* Asher—would go with her.

Good riddance, she told herself. But she didn't quite believe it.

Chapter Twelve

Dear Miss Wilton,

Please let me apologize—again—for Catherine's outrageous behavior this week. I have spoken to her at length and restricted some of her privileges in hopes that she will better understand the severity of this situation. I do not know why she is so intent on failing, when so many people are working so diligently to help her find success. I cannot properly express my gratitude for the sacrifices you have made on our behalf. While I know that I forced your hand, you have proven to be a woman of determination and grace.

I also want to apologize for having blackmailed you when we first met. I was desperately hopeful that this school would change Catherine's pattern, but I used you quite badly in the process. I would never dream of exposing you after all you have done and, come what may this next week, I will ever be glad to *have known you and had your assistance with this task. It troubles me beyond words that Catherine has not taken advantage of this opportunity.*

Sincerely,

A. Asher

Mr. Asher's letter did little to relieve the tightness in Lenora's chest. In some ways she was ready to be done with Catherine—the girl was an ungrateful terror. And yet Lenora had seen moments of pride in her accomplishments, focus, and ordinariness. Recalling those moments reminded Lenora that Catherine was still just a little girl. Was there something they had all missed that might break through her exterior? She had no answers. Mrs. Henry had given one more week to see if she might rise to the opportunities provided for her. Lenora did not dare to hope.

Lenora accompanied Aunt Gwen to the Assembly Rooms on Saturday night, glad for the distraction, and visited with Miss Randall. They were friends, but not close enough to make special appointments to see one another. When they were at a shared event, they enjoyed each other's company, which was all Lenora really wanted, actually. She did not long for bosom friendships the way some women did, though she enjoyed having more acquaintances here than she had ever had before.

As always, the large crowd triggered her anxiety, so she began counting candles, and then feathers in women's headdresses. So many women were dressed in pale green tonight. Interesting. Perhaps that was a new fashion. As Lenora had never followed the fashion plates, she had worn her purple silk gown with the silver beading along the stomacher. She felt pretty, and determined to enjoy herself. She did not want the weekend wasted on worries about Monday that she had no power to control.

Lenora had been able to set aside her counting after the first half hour, surprised to see Mr. Asher arrive with a few other gentlemen. He scanned the room until his eyes found her, then he smiled and began moving her way.

Her stomach flipped, and it was all she could do not to smooth the skirt of her dress or straighten her neckline.

Mr. Asher's party arrived, and introductions were made before the men began to mingle with the other guests. Lenora did not expect to see Mr. Asher again, but, after a break between sets, he made his way toward her. He easily joined in the conversation, but did not show her particular attention. Lenora remained on the edges of the group, trying to quiet the butterflies that had been awakened by his appearance.

"Would you care to dance, Miss Wilton?" Mr. Asher asked when there was a break in conversation. The women around them went quiet, and Lenora felt her cheeks heat up at being the center of attention. She was rarely asked to dance. In fact, she had only danced a handful of times since coming to Bath, and her partners were always sons and nephews of Aunt Gwen's friends.

"No, thank you, Mr. Asher," she said, embarrassed for what felt like an offer made out of sympathy. "I had not planned to dance tonight." She had certainly never planned to dance with *him* and did not feel up to such closeness. Until now their relationship had been professional, excepting the river walks. Still, something told her dancing with him would not be wise.

"Oh, do," Aunt Gwen said, tapping Lenora on the arm with her fan. "It's been ages since you've danced, and you will forget the steps entirely if you do not keep up your skills."

Lenora felt her face flush even deeper, but Mr. Asher seemed to take Aunt Gwen's encouragement as an answer and put out his arm. She felt she had no choice but to allow him to lead her from the woman who had thrown her to the wolves—though at least it was a handsome wolf. No amount of deep breaths and counted steps could calm her nerves now.

"I did not mean to put you out," Mr. Asher said as they stopped at the edge of the dance floor to wait for the set to finish.

"I did not mean to seem petulant. I am . . . I am not very . . . I do not usually dance."

"Why is that?"

She opened her mouth to give a polite answer, and then wondered why she should be anything but honest. The thought was surprisingly calming. He already knew the worst of her and would likely be leaving Bath within a fortnight once Catherine failed her final chance at school. She watched the dancers as she spoke so she would not have to see his reaction. Honest or not, she did not want to see pity or judgment in his expression.

"I am twenty-six years old, Mr. Asher, a teacher, and an independent woman. Ballrooms, even in Bath, are filled with more women than men, younger and lighter on their feet than I." She sounded so pathetic, but it was a relief to tell the truth. Standing so near him made her thoughts swirl like the mist from the river in winter.

"Would you prefer *not* to dance with me?"

Lenora's cheeks flushed yet again. "That is not what I meant. I would like to dance with you. I mean—" She paused for breath and focus. "I would not *not* prefer to dance with you, which, as that is a double negative, means I—" Another breath. More focus. "The invitation simply took me by surprise, and I am not very good with surprises."

"Well," he said in a lighter tone, "I find that interesting since you seem to be full of them."

The music began, and he led her to the floor. It was a few seconds before she recognized the song as a waltz. She paused, and he interpreted it as her wanting to start where they stood rather than further toward the center of the floor. He put his hand at her waist, and she put her hand on his shoulder. He took her other hand and held it up. She could feel the fire in her neck at the prospect of having to admit yet another failing.

"I have never waltzed, Mr. Asher. At least, not with a man." She spoke softly but still glanced about, as though someone might overhear and burst into laughter.

He raised his eyebrows. "With a goat, perhaps?"

She smiled despite herself and looked at her feet as he led her into the first steps. "With my sisters. My understanding was that such a scandalous dance as a waltz was not allowed in Bath."

"Perhaps someone was feeling wicked and bribed the orchestra quite generously." He winked, and she pulled her eyebrows together. Did he mean him? He bribed the orchestra to play a waltz so he could dance with her? No, that couldn't be it. Could it?

When she didn't answer, he continued. "No doubt there will

be letters of complaint published in tomorrow's paper. We shall keep it slow, and you may pretend I am your sister if you would like. Right foot back, left foot back and left, right foot back—one, two, three, one . . ."

She kept glancing at her feet, but her thoughts were tangled in what he'd said. When she'd danced with her sisters, they would tie up their skirts so they could see the steps.

He let go of her waist long enough to tip her chin up, sending a shiver down her spine. "Watch my eyes, do not think too much about the steps, move with me."

The flush in her cheeks spread quickly through the rest of her, but she did as he said and held his eyes. Within a few more steps, she felt as though they were one person moving across the floor. If she held his eyes, she could follow the steps without thinking about them. When she thought about the steps, on the other hand, she stumbled. He resumed counting each time she missed a step in order to get her back in rhythm, and after another minute, she was moving in perfect time with him.

Looking into his face and being so close to him was thrilling. And frightening. She felt so many things she had not felt before. This closeness made the fantasy of it all too real. Had he truly arranged for this dance?

She reminded herself that he was blackmailing her—except he'd apologized for that in his last letter and said he would keep her secret without any expectations from her any longer. But then his niece was a nightmare, and she was all but certain that Catherine and Mr. Asher would be leaving Bath soon. But then she was distracted by small specks of gold in his eyes. When he smiled, the lines beside his eyes lengthened like the petals of a daisy. He wore his hair longer than was fashionable, and when it fell over his forehead, she wanted to brush it away.

Where on earth are these thoughts coming from? She was a vicar's daughter, for heaven's sake, nearly a spinster, and an inexperienced woman to boot. *That* was why his proximity was so overwhelming; she had such little experience to draw from. She'd danced with other men—even her former fiancé—and only felt anxiety. But she'd never waltzed with a man, certainly not a man who had arranged one specifically for her. It was no wonder that Bath did not often include a waltz at these events. It was a wicked dance. She feared she would never recover.

"You look lovely, Miss Wilton. The color favors you a great deal. Your eyes seem brighter, and your hair reflects more light."

Lenora's cheeks were in a perpetual state of flush. "Thank you." Had a man ever given her such a direct and sincere compliment? She wished his words were something tangible that she could fold in half and store in her pocket. For an instant, she imagined asking him to write them down. The thought made her smile, or perhaps it was his compliment, but she felt some of the tension ease from her shoulders. He would leave Bath soon, and she would never see him again. She could put a bit more effort into enjoying *this* moment. A moment he had created.

"I enjoy seeing you outside of the school," he said, then hurried to add, "Not that I don't like seeing you *in* school, but you are different when you are not there."

He was one of the few people who knew how very different she could be. He spread the fingers of his hand at her waist and pulled her an inch closer, sending a shiver up her spine and back again. The way he looked at her made her feel as though he could see every part of her, and approved of what he saw.

"Will you be going out tomorrow night?" His voice had dropped to a whisper.

"I would like to," Lenora whispered back.

He said nothing, but when he winked conspiratorially, she winked back.

She winked! At a man. At *Mr. Asher!*

Too soon, the waltz ended, and Lenora felt almost drunk— not that she'd ever actually been drunk. She imagined it felt like this, though—unaware of the details of her surroundings, unable to think about the past or the future. Mr. Asher led her back to her aunt and kissed her hand before vanishing into the crowd. Had his lips *lingered* on her hand?

When she came back to herself and stopped staring at the square of floor where he'd been standing, she turned to find Aunt Gwen watching her.

"Did you enjoy your dance, dear?" Aunt Gwen asked, her eyebrows raised. "A waltz, no less."

Lenora sat on the bench and tried to avoid her aunt's eye, afraid of what Aunt Gwen might discover if Lenora let her look too close. She could not stop smiling, nor could she say anything but the truth, even though a lie would have served her purposes infinitely better. "Yes, Aunt. I enjoyed it very much."

Chapter Thirteen

Aiden moved his knight and glanced at the clock—9:47. Thirteen minutes and he'd insist Catherine go to bed. He should have insisted an hour ago, but she had suggested chess and, with things being so difficult, he couldn't refuse an opportunity to spend time with her any more than he could forget the connection he'd felt with Miss Wilton when they'd waltzed last night. The click of two chess pieces making contact drew his gaze back to the board, where he quickly assessed what had happened during his musings.

"You moved your pawn two spaces," he said, looking at his knight that now lay on its side. He'd noticed that Miss Wilton could give equal attention to numerous conversations and activities going on around her. Apparently, Aiden did not have that ability.

"No, I didn't," Catherine said innocently—too innocently.

"It was right there." She pointed to an empty square between where her pawn had actually been and where she'd moved it.

He held her eyes. "I will not play with you if you are going to cheat."

Catherine rolled her eyes, let out a heavy sigh, and reset the pieces. "I was trying to determine if you were paying attention to the game."

Well, he couldn't offer much argument. He wasn't paying attention. His thoughts were already on the river, and although he told himself the tension he felt about tonight's escort was due to the drizzly weather and Catherine's desire to stay up late, he suspected it was more about his anticipation to see Lenora Wilton. It seemed every time he was with her, he saw some new facet of her personality, some hidden aspect of her nature that intrigued him in a way no other woman had.

Catherine moved her piece correctly, and Aiden quickly captured it with his rook. She grunted and propped her head up on her hand as she surveyed the board. She moved another pawn one space to the left. Aiden could have captured it, but decided to be merciful. She was still learning the game.

"How are you feeling about school tomorrow?" Aiden asked, hoping the topic would keep his mind focused on his niece and the game. He glanced at the clock. Eleven minutes.

"I hate school," Catherine said flatly. "And I especially hate Miss Wilton."

Aiden felt his defenses rise up, but he forced himself to take a breath. He moved his knight again. "Miss Wilton has been very fair with you, Catherine."

"She hates me."

"I assure you she does not." At least, he didn't think she did. Certainly, she didn't praise Catherine, but then Catherine hadn't given much effort worthy of praise. "She has tried harder than anyone to help you be successful at Mrs. Henry's school."

Catherine huffed. "She's put me on the point system. I am certain it was her idea."

"*You* are the reason you are on the point system," Aiden reminded her. "You could have easily been dismissed instead, but you have been given another chance."

Her fingers pinched the head of the pawn she was in the process of moving. "I do not want another chance. I hate it there." She moved the piece, taking out Aiden's rook. He hadn't noticed that his mercy toward her pawn had left him vulnerable.

Instead of taking his next move, Aiden folded his arms on the edge of the table and leaned forward. "You would rather go to the school in Germany? It is little more than a sanatorium."

She didn't meet his eye and began lining up her "fallen" pieces along the edge of the board. "I would rather not go to school at all," she said, too casually to actually be a casual comment. "Why can I not simply go to the estate in Cheshire?"

"You need an education."

"In needlepoint and etiquette?" She rolled her eyes.

"In literature and French, in music and poise. In a few years' time, you will make your debut, and the match you make will determine your future. You must be able to make a good presentation." Yet she could not even read. Was it folly for any of them to expect she could learn so much now when she hadn't thus far? She was fighting them every way she could.

She narrowed her eyes. "What if I don't want to make a match? What if I simply want to be a homely music teacher at an all-girl's school?"

Aiden clenched his teeth, ignoring the barb at Miss Wilton. "You still need an education."

"Which I could get in Cheshire with a private tutor. I do not like living in the city. It is too crowded."

"You need to learn how to socialize." She'd been isolated most of her life, interacting with adults who did not treat her well. She needed to learn how to exist in the polite world— that was how Miss Keighly had explained it. *Miss Keighly.* He groaned in his mind, thinking of Miss Wilton and how he felt when he was with her. He did not feel the same with Miss Keighly. He had not expected to feel it with any other woman. He would need to resolve that situation.

"I can learn to socialize in Cheshire so long as you do not lock me in the linen closet."

His head ached. Catherine needed to learn how to behave. Could he even find a tutor who could not only control her but also teach her to read and everything else she needed to learn without beating her as the others had eventually done? And yet, schools were not working either.

He had circled such thoughts a hundred times the last few days and found no solution. He straightened, looked at the board, and then pushed it away. "It is time for bed."

"But we aren't finished with the game!"

Aiden stood. "It is time for bed," he repeated. "Tomorrow is an important day, and one I hope you will appreciate." He rang the bellpull, and then moved to the sideboard where he poured himself a brandy. He raised the glass, but then looked at his niece, glowering by the table. "I do not understand you, Catherine. You are surrounded by people who are doing their best to help you, yet you refuse to take advantage of it."

"I am surrounded by people determined to make me miserable, is what you mean."

He put down his glass sharply, nearly breaking the glass, as the temper he had tried to keep in check leaped up hotter than he could control. "You think I am trying to make you miserable? I have turned my entire life on its ear for you, Catherine. Miss Wilton has made great sacrifices to give you the best opportunity to improve, and you continue to be completely rotten. I am running out of ideas, and if you had any sense in your head, you would be trying your very best to make this school work!"

Her expression did not change. She did not show remorse, or hurt, or irritation. In fact, if anything she looked pleased at him having lost his temper.

Paulette appeared in the doorway, eyes wide. Aiden turned his back to her and to Catherine, finally lifting the brandy and taking a long swallow.

A crash behind him caused him to spin around. The chessboard and all the pieces lay scattered across the floor. Catherine smiled smugly at him, then stood up from her chair and walked toward the maid, not even trying to avoid the pieces but stepping on them instead. They were pewter, and unikely to be damaged, but she had made her point.

His hand tightened around his snifter.

Catherine passed Paulette in the doorway, who, after some hesitation, turned to follow her charge.

Aiden held back a curse, finished his brandy, and then set about righting the board. Exhaustion overcame him. What else could he possibly do? Perhaps nothing. Perhaps this was the end of his options and Germany was all that was left. The idea made him sick to his stomach. He wanted success for Catherine. He wanted to make up for the cruelty she'd experienced and find the girl he knew lived behind all her defenses. But if she would not meet him halfway, all his efforts would be for nothing.

It wasn't until he'd placed the final piece in position that he glanced at the clock again and remembered the river. A flash of energy coursed through him, anticipation and relief making up for the heaviness of the last several minutes. He hurried toward the front door and retrieved his coat and hat himself rather than ring for Martin to assist him. Tomorrow would come, but tonight, he would escort Miss Wilton to the river and find some peace.

Chapter Fourteen

M r. Asher was waiting for Lenora as he had the previous Sunday evenings, as though last night's dance had not happened. It was cold and drizzly, but Lenora needed the river, and she wanted to see him before having to face his niece again on Monday. Every time her dread of the coming week rose up, she thought of Mr. Asher and the river until the dread went away. She would have to face Catherine one way or another, but why spoil the day with anticipation of misery?

Lenora wondered if he would walk with her now that they had shared their waltz, but he waved her ahead of him as usual without a word. As on the other nights, he followed her from a distance and stayed near the shop when she reached the stairs. As she went down the stone steps alone, she wondered if perhaps he hadn't felt the same connection. Perhaps he'd orchestrated the dance, but found it not nearly as enjoyable as he'd expected. But it wasn't her imagination that there had been *something* between them. Was the something enough? Was that something what love grew from? Was this the something her sister Rose had tried to explain? That Cassie had found with Evan?

Her thoughts embarrassed her, and so she watched her feet, placing them carefully on the steps slippery with rain. She chose a spot on the stone wall that was further from the river but protected by the leaning trunk of the walnut tree.

She wrapped her arms around her knees, rested her chin, and thought about how she'd felt the warmth of his hand at her waist through the fabric of her dress. The way he'd looked at her as though he wanted them to be alone. Wanted to draw her closer to him. The way her whole body shivered and tingled, and how her anxiety had fallen silent—like the way snow muffled the air on a winter morning. Lenora had never felt such things before and wanted desperately to know if Mr. Asher had felt them too, but she could never ask him. She was being ridiculous.

What a relief that Lenora had supported Cassie and Evan being together despite not fully understanding their connection until now. What if she'd denied them because of her own embarrassment and pride? What if they'd never been able to have one another because of her?

What if she could not have Mr. Asher even though she felt this way?

She pushed aside the memories of how astoundingly aware of him she'd been and forced herself to consider the fullness of the situation. She was his niece's teacher, and Catherine was volatile and dishonest, sneaky and disruptive. *And* Mr. Asher's ward, which meant any woman who chose to spend her life with him would have a life sentence with Catherine, too.

The argument was moot. Lenora had accepted a solitary life, but she would walk away from that in an instant if Mr. Asher's arms were an alternative. Admitting it to herself was freeing, and foolish. Catherine would not last the week at Mrs. Henry's school. Everyone knew it.

The fact that her thoughts were racing from reasons to be with him to reasons to keep him at a distance was confusing. She liked order in her life, and Mr. Asher had thrown her life into chaos in more ways than one. But those gold flecks in his eyes. His hand at her waist. The way he'd focused so intently on her throughout their waltz.

A sound to her left startled her, and she turned to see Mr. Asher at the base of the stairs. They held one another's eyes across the darkness, and Lenora thought how very alone they were here.

"I thought you might need my coat," he said as he began undoing the buttons. "It seems the weather is turning faster than I expected."

"I cannot take your coat, Mr. Asher." Lenora moved so she was sitting on the edge of the wall, facing him in her men's trousers and knit cap. How she wished she were in a gown—blue—with her hair pinned up and a string of pearls at her throat.

He continued unbuttoning his coat as he walked toward her. She stood and waited for him to come under the meager protection of the walnut tree.

He stopped a few feet in front of her, his breath clouding

around his mouth. "It's getting colder," he said. "The rain is coming harder. We cannot stay much longer, I'm afraid."

She hadn't noticed the change of temperature or cadence of the rain.

He swung the coat off his shoulders and around hers, and as he brought the collar together at her neck, she stepped toward him, bold as brass and yet calm as a summer's morn. His hands stilled at her throat, the edges of the coat still in his hands.

They stared at one another with only inches between them. The feelings and sensations of last evening's waltz came back to her, testifying that what she'd felt had nothing to do with the dancing and everything to do with the two of them and what happened when the space between them disappeared.

She lifted her chin as though by instinct, knowing somehow that it would serve as a request and feeling certain he would answer. She felt a sense of not being in her body, of watching this scene play out as though on stage.

He will be leaving Bath soon, she told herself. *All the more reason.*

She stared at him, the first flicker of fear that he would put her off beginning to grow when he took a step forward, his face relaxing as he let go of the coat. He reached up and took off her cap, then ran his hand along the side of her face. An expression of tenderness came over him, but he looked torn.

"Lenora," he whispered, and she was undone.

She rose onto her toes and put her hand behind his neck as though she had guided a dozen men to kiss her before this very first wanton act of her life.

She could smell the pipe smoke on his breath as his face lowered to hers. And then she could taste it.

Chapter Fifteen

As Lenora reviewed her lesson before class the next morning, she could not suppress a smile. The memory of the night before was like a warm blanket, wrapping itself around her every time she reached for it. When would she see Mr. Asher again?

After the kiss—the amazing, overwhelming kiss—he'd held her against him, and she'd slid her arms around his back. She'd listened to his heartbeat. He'd kissed her hair, and after too long and not nearly long enough, the sky had opened, and the cold could no longer be ignored. He'd held her hand up the stairs, then hung back to follow her home. It would not do to see two people in men's clothing holding hands in the streets late at night. When she'd reached the gate to Aunt Gwen's garden, they'd shared a look across the sidewalk, before she'd turned and gone through the back garden as though she were a princess being returned to her castle.

Every moment since then had been woven with thoughts

of him. His arms around her back. His lips against hers. The rain dripping off his hair and running down her neck. Part of her wished they could have verbally confirmed what had passed between them at the river. Another part felt that the moments were perfect just as they were, that words would have ruined the splendor. She considered sending him a note and asking him to meet her at the river again that night, and then shook her head in surprise at herself. Who would have ever guessed that Lenora Wilton would have such a secret as this? Who would have thought that such improper behavior could feel so deliciously good?

When *would* she see him again? Certainly, she wouldn't have to wait until next Sunday.

"Miss Wilton."

Lenora looked up at Mrs. Henry and remembered that she was a music teacher today. Her first class would start in half an hour. She needed to focus.

"Good morning, Mrs. Henry," Lenora said to the headmistress, smiling. "What can I help you with?" She suddenly remembered that Mrs. Henry had been planning to meet with Catherine that morning to implement the point system. "How did things go with Catherine?"

"Are you having personal relations with Mr. Asher?"

Lenora felt the blood drain from her face as she stared at the older woman, only now noting the hard set of her face, the concern in her eyes. *How did she know?*

"I—uh." Lenora looked at the hardwood floor between

where she sat and where Mrs. Henry stood, waiting for the answer Lenora never imagined having to give.

"Have you been sneaking out at nights to see him? Have you been dressing as a *man* on the streets of Bath in order to meet with him undetected?"

Bursts of shock and fear and humiliation filled Lenora's head and chest. Mrs. Henry knew that much? How? Who could have told her? Mr. Asher? But he wouldn't reveal her. Would he? He *had* blackmailed her. But that kiss, that connection . . .

"Well, have you?"

Lenora swallowed again. "How do you know this?"

Mrs. Henry's gray eyebrows shot up. "So it is true?" The displeasure in her voice made Lenora curl in upon herself and feel as though a hundred fingers were pointed her direction.

"It is not true, or, rather, it is . . . but I do not sneak out at nights to see him."

"Were you with him last night? Alone on the riverbank, kissing him wantonly with no regard for your reputation or mine. I encourage you to think very hard before you answer. You were seen."

Seen? How? By whom?

Lenora put her elbows on the desk and covered her eyes like a child who believed she was hidden if she could not see anyone else. All her mother's lectures about respectability and living above reproach assailed her and closed her throat so she could not speak. Her heart raced. She felt dizzy and sick.

"I cannot believe this," Mrs. Henry said with a tone of disgust.

Lenora kept her face in her hands and focused on her breathing, the feel of the hard floor beneath her feet, the temperature in the room. If she did not ground herself in this moment, she felt as though she might burst open, pieces of her flying in every direction.

"My school is a paragon of respectability, Miss Wilton. Families send their daughters here from all over the country with the comfort of knowing that their girls will be protected from scandalous natures and nefarious persons. I made the expectations of your position here very clear. I chose to overlook your failed engagement and lack of experience due to both your excellent musical skills, which I thought would be nothing but a credit to my establishment, and the fact that your father is a man of the church. Now you have brought into question the character and virtue of the other teachers and our students. To say I am completely ashamed is to show the limitations of the English language. You will have your things moved from this premises immediately, and your name shall be struck from our establishment by the end of the day."

Lenora dropped her hands from her face and quickly focused on the window to her right, the desk before her, and the pianofortes on the side of the room—*see three*. She rested her hand first on the desk and then on the side of her chair—*touch two*. She inhaled the lingering scent of cinnamon buns from breakfast—*smell one*. Centered and grounded, she found her voice. "I am being dismissed?"

"Your contract states that you will do nothing to embarrass

the school, nor will you have relations with family members of our students. You have broken both creeds with your behavior."

Her contract said that? She didn't remember, but would it have changed her actions if she had? Remembering the power of that kiss was answer enough. *Nothing* could have kept her from Mr. Asher's arms last night. What passed between them was bigger than anything she'd ever felt in her life. Every other element of her existence had bowed to it, and she would not take back that moment for the world. Admitting so much, and actually choosing it over the life that until yesterday had seemed her only future, gave her strength.

She took a deep breath. "Mrs. Henry, please let me explain." And so she did. She told Mrs. Henry about her walks early in her stay in Bath and how they evolved into her wearing men's clothing and walking at later hours to find the solitude she craved. She talked about Mr. Asher having discovered her at the river, quite by accident, and then offering to escort her. She did not mention he'd blackmailed her into giving Catherine special treatment—that would reflect poorly on both of them.

"I did not go out last night with any expectation of misbehavior, Mrs. Henry, but, yes, I kissed him when he brought me his coat." Her cheeks burned. Speaking such private things out loud gave them a tinny sound, like something cheap and disposable. "I did not remember the part of my teaching agreement about not having relations, but I understand that I violated your trust all the same. I am shocked that someone saw us, and I am humiliated to have been reported on. But I am not a wanton woman, and I am very, *very* sorry for any ill reflection I have made on you or your school."

"I gave you a chance." Mrs. Henry's voice was sad.

Tears filled Lenora's eyes to know she'd disappointed this woman who had been so good to her. "I am so sorry. Perhaps I can speak to whoever saw us and explain."

"The letter I received was anonymous. The sender feared repercussions if I knew his or her identity."

Repercussions from Mrs. Henry? Then it must be a teacher or student. She felt some relief that it had not been a town gossip who might spread the word far and wide, thus damaging Lenora's reputation publicly. But someone had wanted to damage her nonetheless. Should she fight to keep her position? She thought of the kiss and all that it meant to her. Would she regret leaving her position to be with Mr. Asher? A modicum of peace settled within her. She was still upset and embarrassed, but maybe, just maybe, this was an impetus to something better. Lenora took a steadying breath and rose to her feet, determined to be calm.

"Might I step down from my position rather than be dismissed?" She faced Mrs. Henry across her desk. "I can leave immediately if you wish, or I could stay on until a new teacher is found to take my place."

"I cannot employ a teacher embroiled in scandal, Miss Wilton."

"Falling in love is a scandal?" Lenora said, boldness loosening her tongue. She had kissed Mr. Asher with all the passion of her soul, so surely she could speak plainly to Mrs. Henry. Her future had changed, everything had changed, and the knowledge was unbelievably invigorating.

"Publicly kissing an engaged man most certainly is."

The world stopped. Lenora did not breathe as she fell back into her chair. Only one word bubbled up in her throat. "Engaged?"

Chapter Sixteen

A iden sat in Mrs. Henry's office with his hands in his hair as the headmistress explained the letter she'd received and her dismissal of Miss Wilton that morning. Mrs. Henry was horrified but willing to overlook *his* part in it so they could make one final attempt at Catherine's education. The point system would still be implemented and move forward as planned, only without Miss Wilton's participation.

Aiden felt like the very worst of men.

"Must Miss Wilton be turned out?" he asked. "I am more the guilty party in this." How had he let this happen?

"I cannot overlook her participation. She violated her contract and the morality of this school." She shook her head. "But I am entertaining the idea of allowing her to resign rather than be dismissed so as to protect our reputation. I told her I will send my decision to her aunt's house in the morning."

"She has already removed from the school, then?" Aiden asked. He wanted to talk to her, *needed* to talk to her.

Mrs. Henry did not answer, but then she did not need to. Miss Wilton was gone. Because of him. "You must promise me that you will have no other relations with any other teachers," Mrs. Henry said. Did she think him a libertine who regularly preyed on innocent schoolteachers? He felt sick. "And, I would strongly suggest that you take your engagement to Miss"—she looked at the paper in front of her—"Keighly to the next level and make an honest man of yourself."

He lifted his head, a chill running through him.

He'd told Mrs. Henry he was engaged when he'd first corresponded with her regarding Catherine's possible enrollment. He had wanted to demonstrate that he was doing his best to give Catherine a solid foundation. But Aiden hadn't used Miss Keighly's name in any of his letters or conversations with Mrs. Henry. There was only one person in the entire city of Bath who knew it.

"I would like to speak to Catherine," he said.

Mrs. Henry frowned. "She is in class, Mr. Asher. Seeing as how we have just implemented the point system, I feel it essential that we keep her to a schedule."

He sat up straighter and held the headmistress's eyes. If she wasn't going to dismiss him or Catherine after such a scandalous situation, she wouldn't do so for his wanting to talk to his niece. "I would like to speak to Catherine—*now*."

Ten minutes later, Mrs. Henry showed Catherine into her office, where Aiden waited with barely restrained fury. Mrs. Henry said nothing as she left uncle and niece alone.

"You followed me," he said firmly, arms crossed as he stared at her. "You followed me and then reported to Mrs. Henry so that Miss Wilton would be turned out. Who helped you write the note?"

Catherine blinked up at him with innocent, wide eyes. "Miss Wilton was turned out?" she asked, her expression shocked. "Whatever for?"

It was her clasping her hands to her chest with exaggerated drama that completely gave her away.

"I should whip you for this," Aiden said through his teeth, unsure if he had ever felt so violently angry in his life. Catherine had done this with a full understanding of the consequences and she didn't care. He'd never imagined she would do something so malicious, even at her worst.

Catherine dropped her hands to her sides and leaned forward, every degree of softness gone from her face. "Then whip me," she said. "Everyone else has."

Her response shocked him, drained away some of his anger, but not enough that he could turn his attention away from her admission the way he suspected she wanted him too. He held her eyes, thinking back to what Lenora had once said about something being very wrong with his niece. "Why would you do this to her? She's done nothing but try to help you."

Catherine relaxed, shrugged her shoulders, and walked

around Mrs. Henry's desk, where she flopped into the chair, looking completely at ease.

Aiden sat in his chair and stared at her, wanting so badly to understand her motivation. Was it because of the point system? Because she believed that if she ruined this chance, she could be tutored in Cheshire?

And yet the particulars were impossible to pin down. How could she have followed them without being noticed? Why was it last night of all nights that both he and Miss Wilton let down their defenses?

Catherine propped her elbow on the desk and rested her chin on her hand as though terribly bored. With her other hand, she traced the wood grain with her finger. He watched her for a few seconds, overwhelmed by defeat.

He wanted to lean over her, and tell her that if she wished to be whipped, he'd do it—but he couldn't. Something—the same something that had prompted him to come to England and propose marriage to Hazel Keighly and buy Catherine's way into this school and blackmail Miss Wilton for help—held him back.

Catherine had been beaten by the woman responsible for her care, had been locked in closets as a form of punishment. No one had wanted her after his mother died. Had the rejection broken something inside of her, much as war broke too many soldiers? Would Catherine not allow herself to trust anyone for fear they would hurt her eventually?

"Do you truly not care about what you've done? You have been cruel to people, Catherine," he said in an even tone he knew she did not expect. "You have hurt someone very special to me." There, he'd said it, and the truth reverberated in his chest.

She looked up, her eyes still hard. "More special than your fiancée?"

"I will not discuss that," he said, sick to his stomach at the reminder. An engaged man did not *forget* his fiancée. He did not kiss a woman when he'd promised himself to another woman.

"I like Miss Keighly," Catherine announced. She'd only met Miss Keighly twice, but she had responded well to Miss Keighly's confident manner, turning meek instead of antagonistic. "I think what you have done to her is perfectly shameful. She is a far better match for you than stodgy Miss Wilton." She made a face as though she'd eaten rancid cheese.

Was that her motivation? She preferred Miss Keighly to Miss Wilton and wanted to thwart a growing attraction? To ask would extend the topic, and Aiden was quite finished with it for the present. She was attempting to control adult situations, and he would not play into it.

"There will be no ices this week or next." It was a weak declaration, but she loved their Saturday ices. Her eyes flashed, and he was glad to have at least come up with something—though unequal to what she'd done—that would be a punishment.

"Then I will not go out with you on Saturday at all!"

"That is your choice," he said. "The dresses we ordered last week will be put on hold until you apologize to Miss Wilton."

She rolled her eyes. "All right, then, I am sorry."

"A written apology in your own hand."

She narrowed her eyes.

"Who wrote the letter delivered to Mrs. Henry?" Whoever it was knew the secret too, a secret that could destroy Miss Wilton.

Catherine shrugged.

"I will have a name." As soon as he spoke, however, he knew who it had to be. "Paulette?"

Catherine shrugged, but he knew he'd guessed correctly. At least it hadn't been another student.

Aiden could likely buy Paulette's silence. He would deal with that later. "Who else have you told?"

She sighed dramatically. "No one," she said as though he should have assumed as much. Then she smiled and added, "Yet."

"You will not tell anyone," Aiden said, hoping she was telling the truth about not having gossiped about what she'd seen and done. "And you will write a letter of apology to Miss Wilton or you will have no dresses."

She leaned toward him. "I would rather you thrash me. I know you want to."

The words cooled his temper, as she surely knew they would. Anytime she reminded him of her past abuse, he pulled back. But he would not be manipulated by the reminder. He had treated her with nothing but decency, and it was wrong of her to insinuate that he was like every other caregiver. "I do not want to *thrash* you, Catherine. I want you to learn. I want you to behave in a way that will open doors, not close them."

She flopped back into the chair and stared at the ceiling.

"I love you, Catherine."

"No, you don't." She closed her eyes. "No one loves me."

His immediate answer was to say that was not true, but he paused instead. Had anyone besides his mother ever truly loved this child? Did he? If he did not, then why was he going through all this misery? That, in and of itself, was proof that he did love her.

"I have changed everything in my life to care for you and to see you well, and I am not going to send you to Germany unless it becomes the only option. You can do better than this, and I am determined to do anything possible to ensure it."

She cracked open an eye and cocked her head. "By seducing my teachers? Perhaps you should try Miss Bowman next. She's fat as a cow and ugly as a post. She would likely respond very well to your advances."

Chapter Seventeen

Mrs. Gwenyth Simmons came into the parlor where Aiden waited, but she remained in the doorway, and her expression was polite, rather than warm as it had been on prior occasions. "Lenora is not seeing anyone, Mr. Asher."

He looked at the floor and sat back down even though Mrs. Simmons remained standing. "She is here, though?" That meant her aunt had not turned her out; that was a relief. He pushed his hands through his hair and wished the certitude he'd felt when this idea had first come to him was as strong now as it had been when he'd thought it.

He had wanted to talk to Miss Wilton—Lenora—before making this proposal to Mrs. Simmons, but perhaps a letter of explanation would be better. She could read a letter in private and consider his position without feeling pressed to respond in the moment she faced him. He needed to fix this, all of it, as soon as possible.

He heard Mrs. Simmons's skirts rustle as she crossed the room and sat on the settee across from him. He looked into her expectant face. He didn't know how much Lenora had told her, but it was apparent she knew enough to be quite displeased.

"I would never turn her out, Mr. Asher. She is my niece, and I care for her a great deal. But she is distraught."

Of course, she was. He took a breath and let it out slowly. At least he could explain himself to someone, and then perhaps her aunt could help Lenora understand.

"Hazel Keighly is a family friend," Aiden began. "We grew up together in Cheshire, and when I returned to England to become Catherine's guardian, our paths crossed once more. She is twenty-nine years old, practical, orderly, and the type of woman I felt would make a good mother figure for Catherine, who needs stability above all else. Miss Keighly fully understands the reasons for my proposal, and we agreed to wait until Catherine was settled before we married. It is more of an arrangement between us than an official engagement, based on necessity and individual needs on both our parts to secure our futures."

"An engagement is an engagement, Mr. Asher, and I presume you fully intended to go through with the marriage up until last night."

Aiden paused, but then nodded. He still thought of Miss Keighly as a friend more than a fiancée. They had finalized nothing and had not even corresponded since his coming to Bath. It was easy to forget about their future plans when the present had demanded so much of his attention.

"And now?"

He looked through the doorway toward the rest of the house, where Lenora was hiding somewhere. Was she angry? Heartbroken? Both? He ached to see her face, desperate to explain himself. "I would like to talk to Lenora."

"You are engaged to be married to someone else."

Aiden turned back to Mrs. Simmons. "I need to explain," he said. "I need to assure her of my feelings so she does not think I am some cad who took advantage of her. My engagement to Miss Keighly is of no consequence, truly, and will be an easy enough matter to remedy." Surely she was no more committed to the marriage than he was, seeing as how she had not written to him or pressed for a date. In fact, she had treated their arrangement as more of a favor to him than anything else. He would offer her a settlement, she would take it, and that would be that.

Mrs. Simmons's expression hardened. "Did you know that Lenora was jilted by a man who went on to marry her sister? That is why she originally came to Bath, to be free of the humiliation and to live an independent life. Have you any idea what it felt like for her to realize you had showed her such attention when you were committed elsewhere?"

Aiden blinked, his heart in his throat. "I knew nothing of a broken engagement."

"And if you had?"

"It would mean nothing to me other than I am sorry for the pain it may have caused her. I have no prejudice against her for her past." Was Lenora still in love with this man?

"So, you plan to break your engagement to Miss Keighly and court Lenora with such a scandal fresh on your heels?"

"It was an agreement, not a love match, and Miss Keighly is as mild in regard to the promise as I am. I shall write to her today and dissolve things between us. It will not be a scandal such as you fear."

Mrs. Simmons looked doubtful.

"Within the week, Miss Keighly will agree to break the engagement, and no one will be the wiser. The only people who knew of it were Mrs. Henry and Catherine."

"Not your families?"

"I am not in good company with my remaining family right now due to their treatment of Catherine during my absence, and Miss Keighly said we should not go public until we had set a date, which we have not done. I only told Mrs. Henry to assure her that I was building a stable foundation for Catherine."

Mrs. Simmons considered his words, then stood and moved to the bellpull. A footman arrived, and she asked for whiskey instead of the tea Aiden had expected. "Two glasses," she said before retaking her seat and looking at Aiden.

"You seem quite certain," Mrs. Simmons said.

Aiden sensed she was letting down her guard and willing to at least consider that what he was saying was true.

"I am certain," Aiden said with a nod, though there was a small niggling of making such a promise. He and Miss Keighly had never discussed the possibility that one of them might change their mind, but—no, he pushed away any doubt. She would understand, and she was of such a practical nature that she would very likely encourage him to pursue his heart. If one *could* marry for love, one should do so.

"How soon do you expect Miss Keighly will agree to your terms?"

"Upon receipt of my letter," Aiden said eagerly. "She will understand my wanting to follow my heart." As it was, his heart was lifting with every word he spoke. This would work; it would follow the course he described, and the pain Lenora felt now would be short-lived. "I will ask her for a quick response." If his head hadn't been so much in the clouds last night, he'd have written Miss Keighly as soon as he returned from the river. How he wished that was what he'd done. "I can write Lenora a letter as well—explain myself."

Mrs. Simmons nodded. "I think a letter would be helpful for Lenora. She does not trust easily and will remain in retreat until she is convinced, both of your intentions and of the state of your engagement. Even then, it may take time for her to fully trust you and heal her embarrassment. She feels foolish and used."

He nodded sadly. "I shall write an explanation, leave nothing out, and when I receive Miss Keighly's letter, I will forward it to her to prove the way of things."

The footman returned with a tray holding a decanter of the liquor and two glasses. He proceeded to fill both glasses halfway before leaving the room. Mrs. Simmons picked up her glass. "I'm sure it goes without saying that I never drink so early in the day, but I am making an exception."

Aiden reached for his glass. "As am I."

They both threw back the drinks in one swallow. Aiden took the liberty to pour them both another, though he did not drink his right away, as he turned his thoughts to the other reason he had come. He'd have liked a more natural transition from the topic of Lenora to that of Catherine but could not think how to manage it. Seeing as how they were drinking whiskey at one o'clock in the afternoon, perhaps he did not need to stand on such ceremony.

He lifted his glass and met Mrs. Simmons's eye over the brim. "I also came to talk to *you* about Catherine."

Mrs. Simmons furrowed her brow. "What about Catherine?"

"She enlisted a maid to write the anonymous letter to Mrs. Henry that exposed us. She must have followed me last night. That is how Mrs. Henry learned of our . . . meeting."

Mrs. Simmons frowned and shook her head in disappointment—exactly the reaction he had hoped for.

He set down his glass, stood, and began pacing. "I do not know what to do with her, Mrs. Simmons. I have tried every tactic I can think of, and the school has gone to such lengths, yet she has ruined everything. Mrs. Henry is allowing her to stay at the school for now, but I worry what Catherine might do next. She and I had formed an accord until we came to Bath; since then, things have been difficult. This morning, she was downright horrid when I confronted her. She claims not to care if she is sent to Germany, but I sense an odd sort of preservation about her actions. As though she is trying to push away everyone who cares for her, who gives her special interest or attention. I am afraid that in the process of pushing us away, she is squandering every last opportunity for a normal life."

"It is heartbreaking." Mrs. Simmons's sorrow was sincere. "I wish I had more experience with children so that I might know how to advise you."

"I did think of one possible solution." He stopped pacing and sat on the edge of his chair. "Of everyone I have seen her interact with, she behaves the very best for you."

Mrs. Simmons pulled her eyebrows together. "What do you mean by that?"

"She seems to like you, Mrs. Simmons. Trust you."

"Well, I like her too, but—"

"You are the only person who does. Well, the only adult who does. Everyone else thinks she is a menace, and rightly so, since she acts as such. But she is on her best behavior with you."

Mrs. Simmons shifted in her chair, as though both uncomfortable and pleased. "I am flattered," she said, but she also seemed confused.

"I wonder if she might spend more time with you." He had to speak fast before he lost his confidence. He felt just as he had when he'd blackmailed Lenora that day on the riverbank. He was asking for something that polite people did not ask for. It felt awkward and inappropriate, yet just as he'd felt with Lenora that day, it seemed necessary. "As punishment for what she's done, I've canceled a dress order as well as our Saturday outings for the next two weeks—it is not enough, but they are the only things she seems to value—and I wondered if she might spend those days with you instead."

"Spend the day with me?" Mrs. Simmons said with a slight sputter. "And do what? I spend Saturdays at the Pump Room and along the promenade with Lenora. I do nothing that would be of interest to a child."

"Could she please attend you to the Pump Room on Saturday? I shall make up some job she must do for you—straighten your yarns or read aloud or something to explain it—but mostly I just want to see how she does in your company. I want to see if she will end up in a fit as she does in most situations or, as I suspect, if there is something about the relationship you two share that evens her moods and might be the grounds for some success on her part. Something to build on."

Mrs. Simmons did not look entirely convinced; in fact, she looked nervous. "I am just who I am, Mr. Asher, and I do not like the contrived feel of this at all. And what if she does throw a fit—what am I to do about that?"

"I will be on hand," he said, thinking fast. "Have your footman fetch me for the slightest reason. I know it is a great imposition, and I will owe you dearly for your assistance, but of everyone I have seen Catherine interact with all these months, you are the only person who seems to bring out the best of her every time you meet."

Mrs. Simmons smoothed her skirts and adjusted the lace cuff of her morning gown. She let out a breath. "Very well, I shall do as you ask. I doubt Lenora will want to go out in public that soon anyway. Bring Catherine around at nine thirty on Saturday; I like to be to the Pump Room by ten o'clock. The waters are more potent in the morning, you know. Maybe they will do her some good as well."

Chapter Eighteen

Lenora lowered Mr. Asher's letter to her lap Monday night and leaned her head against the window of her room at Aunt Gwen's house—her only room now that she'd been turned out from Mrs. Henry's school. She stared at the rain-washed city and wished her mother were there, holding her and telling her everything would be all right as she'd done after Evan broke their engagement. Even though Lenora had known her mother could not guarantee that everything *would* be all right when she'd said it, Lenora had liked hearing it, liked her mother's arms around her, liked the reminder that she mattered and that someone loved her enough to hurt with her.

She felt completely alone now. She had Aunt Gwen's sympathy, but that was not quite the same. According to the letter, she also had Aiden's regret, but that was not enough either. She could not forget the moment she learned he was engaged to someone else. She would not allow herself to forget it.

A tear slid down her cheek. If her mother were here now, would she give comfort, or would she let out a frustrated sigh and wonder how on earth Lenora had landed herself in the middle of a scandal yet again? How could Lenora make a mess of what other women made look so simple? What had she been thinking, kissing a man she already knew to be untrustworthy?

What she had been thinking was that it was all so romantic, like a fairy tale, destiny catching up to her and rewarding her for doing the right thing for Cassie and Evan. It was all the fantastical notions of a ten-year-old girl who had expected a storybook ending. Foolish girl. Simple-minded child. There was a reason she had felt invisible for most of her life.

Lenora glanced at the letter again, imagining Mr. Asher toiling over every word as he tried his best to explain. His engagement was a matter of agreement for Catherine's sake, he'd written. He said he cared deeply for Lenora. He said he was sorry he had not told her of the engagement but there had not seemed to be a time or reason. He wanted to see her and explain everything in person, but barring that, he would send round the letter from Miss Keighly as soon as he received it. She closed her eyes.

He cares deeply for me, she told herself. He did not say he loved her.

In the letter, he explained that Catherine had followed them last night—though how she'd managed it was still a mystery—and that she had a maid help her write the letter, which she then slid under Mrs. Henry's door, knowing full well that the consequences would be severe. She had wanted Lenora to suffer.

Last night's kiss may have distracted from that truth, but

Catherine was intent against her. Even if the situation with Mr. Asher could be repaired—which she did not foresee—she would encounter this same venom from Catherine over and over and over. Lenora was not built for such conflict, so perhaps this heartache was a blessing in disguise. Perhaps it was what she needed to prevent her heart from running away from her and resulting in a lifetime of misery. And yet, even if this turn of events was meant to prevent greater pain in the future, it was still painful now.

People would talk. Wonder. Speculate. Lenora imagined walking through the promenade knowing that people were sharing gossip about her. She imagined encountering their questioning eyes and accusing smiles. It would be Leagrave all over again. She could not stand the thought of going through the censure and pity again, and yet she was out of places to run.

More tears leaked from her eyes. Mr. Asher had awakened feelings within her she had never known existed, yet he was engaged to another. He had held her in his arms knowing full well he was promised to Miss Keighly, knowing even as he awakened her heart that he would break it. She had thought she could trust him. She had allowed herself to be vulnerable with him. She had let herself love him and risked the careful, respectable life she'd built to make up for the marriage she'd given up wishing for. For a few hours, she had believed he loved her too, that her future was new again, and her wishes to belong somewhere were fulfilled.

What a foolish girl she was. Again.

There were other girls' schools she could apply to, but it

was the middle of the term, and Mrs. Henry had agreed to allow Lenora to resign but would certainly not give her a letter of recommendation.

Beyond that, there was no Aunt Gwen to go to in another city. Lenora had lost, literally, every good thing in her life because she had trusted Mr. Asher. She had believed what was not true—that he loved her and wanted her and had come into her life to fulfill the joyous wishes she'd given up on.

Lenora wished she could go to the river, but that had been taken from her too—again. Only this time, she would not go back, not ever.

Where else can I turn for peace?

After another minute, without insight or answers revealing themselves, she accepted that she would find no peace. She pushed the letter to the floor, pulled the edges of the blanket tighter around her shoulders, and began to sob.

Chapter Nineteen

A iden arrived at Mrs. Simmons's house at 3:30 on Saturday afternoon, his palms sweaty and his neck hot with anxiety. He held two bouquets of flowers in one hand and took a deep breath as he heard footsteps come to the door. Mrs. Simmons's man answered the door and led him into the drawing room, where Mrs. Simmons and Catherine looked up from the hoop in Catherine's hands. Both of them smiled quite naturally. Mrs. Simmons ushered Aiden toward a chair.

"Shall I take your flowers, sir?" the footman said.

"Oh, yes, thank you," Aiden said, turning back toward the servant. "Two vases, please—one for Mrs. Simmons and the other for Miss Wilton."

The servant looked to Mrs. Simmons, but kept his professional smile in place as he took the bouquets and quit the room. Aiden wished he could ask about the shared look, but this portion of the visit was for Catherine's sake.

Lenora had never replied to his letter, sent five days ago now, but he'd sent another yesterday afternoon asking for a private visit today when he collected Catherine. By the looks of things, the day had gone well for Catherine and Mrs. Simmons. He had not been summoned to intercede.

Unfortunately, it had not been a complete success as he still had not received Miss Keighly's letter of agreement to terminate their engagement. He'd asked her to respond immediately so he might proceed with the choice of his heart. But he could not wait another day to talk to Lenora. He felt as though each day created more distance between them.

"The flowers were very thoughtful of you," Mrs. Simmons said, though there was something sad in her smile that made his heart skip a beat. She turned to Catherine and brushed the girl's hair, worn loose today, behind her shoulder. "Catherine was a great deal of help. I'm so glad she was able to come."

Mrs. Simmons did not strike him as a woman who said what she did not mean. She looked back at Aiden. "We organized all my threads, which had become quite a jumble in my workbasket, and then I offered to help her begin a cushion."

Hadn't Mrs. Henry said that Catherine was specifically opposed to needlepoint? What kind of magic did Mrs. Simmons employ?

"It sounds like a wonderful day," Aiden said. He turned his attention to Catherine for the first time since his arrival. "Did you enjoy yourself, Catherine?"

"Very much," Catherine said, though her eyes remained intent on the needle, thread, and screen in her hand.

"Why don't you go to the second-floor sitting room, Catherine, and continue working," Mrs. Simmons said. "Remember to keep your stitches small, yes, just like that. I'd like to speak with your uncle for a few minutes."

Catherine looked at Aiden, instantly suspicious, and then at Mrs. Simmons. "Are you going to tell on me, Aunt Gwen?"

Aiden tensed. She *had* misbehaved after all?

"Have I something to tell about?" Mrs. Simmons asked, raising her eyebrows.

Catherine seemed to consider that, then nodded and took her screen with her as she left the room. Mrs. Simmons waited until they heard the girl's feet on the stairs before indicating that Aiden should close the door, which he did, both eager and anxious about the amount of ceremony put into this conversation.

"I hope you do not mind that I gave her leave to call me Aunt Gwen, as my niece does. It feels so much more comfortable, but I fear I was presumptuous to make the offer without speaking with you about it."

"Not at all," Aiden said, shaking his head. "Did she behave herself?"

Mrs. Simmons nodded. "She is delightful, Mr. Asher."

He blinked. "Really?"

Mrs. Simmons nodded. "We went to the Pump Room, and although she was fidgety as I talked to my acquaintances, she did not spout off or cause a disruption. We walked about the promenade, and when she saw a group of children playing tag she asked if she could join them. She played with them for nearly half an hour until the game ended, at which point she returned to my company and took another round before we came back home. She was meticulous in separating out my colors, and though she told me straightaway that she did not like needlepoint, I offered to sit with her through every stitch, and she agreed. She seemed to enjoy it." She paused, then shook her head. "She is not skilled at it. Girls of her age should know their stitches and basic design, and she does not have a good grasp on either."

"Mrs. Henry said she is very poorly behaved in her needlepoint classes."

Mrs. Simmons shrugged. "Who enjoys doing what they are not good at?"

Excellent point. "I do not know how to thank you," Aiden said. "This is better than I had hoped for."

Mrs. Simmons nodded. "I'm glad. Now, please tell me about your mother, Mr. Asher."

Aiden was taken off guard both by the request and the wave of nostalgia that came with it. "My mother was all that was good and kind," he said. "She passed nearly seven years ago, I believe. I was in Jamaica and did not hear of her passing for some months. It was a terrible loss."

"She helped to care for Catherine, did she not?"

"My mother took over her care when Catherine was about a year old."

"Catherine's memories of her grandmother are very clear, considering having been only five or six years old when your mother passed. She said they took long walks during the day, picked flowers, and talked about fairies and princesses and haunted woods."

Aiden smiled. "Yes, that sounds like my mother. She was a nurturing soul. I think it was very distressing to her that neither of Catherine's parents cared for her the way my mother cared for me and my half brother—Catherine's father."

"When she died, Catherine went into the care of her father, though it does not sound as though she knew him very well before that time. He hired a nurse who cared for her?"

"That is my understanding. He left her at the Cheshire estate with a series of governesses—I understand he himself very rarely came to visit. When he died, the estate was closed up until I could come to England and set the affairs in order. Catherine was passed along a string of family members who tried to manage her but, I'm afraid, did not do well at it."

"I tried to ask about the other people who cared for her, and she became closed off to it. She only wanted to speak of your mother. I wondered if perhaps she had put the woman on a pedestal after her passing."

"My mother *earned* the pedestal," Aiden said with a soft smile. "What I would not give for her to be with us still."

"I am very sorry."

He nodded, though his throat was thick. There'd been little time to mourn his mother, and he missed her every time he thought about her.

"I am near the same age as your mother when she'd have had the care of Catherine, am I not?"

"I'm sure I don't know how old you are, Mrs. Simmons."

Mrs. Simmons gave him an indulgent, if not an approving,

smile. "Let us assume that I am your mother's age. Do I remind you of her?"

Aiden looked at her closely, noting some similarities in their bearing and slender build. There was something more regal about Mrs. Simmons, however, where his mother had been relaxed and playful. He remembered being seven or eight years old and hiding behind a hedge with her, taking off their shoes so they could run to the meadow barefoot. She'd made him promise not to tell anyone, not even his father, and the forbidden aspect made it even more enjoyable.

"My mother was gentle, but strong and nurturing without being . . . I'm not sure how to say it, but without coddling, if that makes sense." He struggled to sum her up in mere words.

"I shall take all of that as a compliment," Mrs. Simmons said. "I think the fact that I remind Catherine of her grandmother is what accounts for how well we get on. That, and the fact that I require very little from her. I'm an old woman; I like to sit and visit, not zip from one thing to another or make other people account for their time. I imagine I am very different from her teachers, and, perhaps, very different from her caretakers, who I gather were rather put out by the extra child thrust into their hands. She obviously did not have access to proper education, or perhaps there is some difficulty in her learning ability, but she is very bright, and, when she is enthusiastic about a task, she can be very attentive."

Aiden was encouraged by Mrs. Simmons's assessment, but unsure what his next step should be. "I'm grateful for you spending the day with her. It eases my mind to know that she has the ability to control her behavior. I just need to figure how to direct her enthusiasm, and hope I can do so before Mrs. Henry has had her fill."

"I have a suggestion."

He looked up, hungry and eager to hear her ideas.

"For it to be successful, however, would take a great deal of work and cooperation from Mrs. Henry and . . ." Her voice trailed off.

"Yes?" He leaned forward in his chair.

"Lenora."

Chapter Twenty

N o," Lenora said flatly. She'd paced the length of the parlor more times than she could count. Back and forth, over and over, in an attempt to calm her anxieties, which felt fit to bursting. She looked at the curtains, the rug, the porcelain vase on the table beside the windows. She felt her feet within her shoes, the scratchy lace at the throat of her morning gown, and smelled the flowers—flowers sent by Mr. Asher. She refused to look at them.

"It would allow you to stay in Bath," Aunt Gwen said.

"I do not want to stay in Bath," Lenora said, shaking her head in an attempt to convince both of them. "I've made my arrangements, Aunt Gwen. Mary is expecting me, and . . . I hate that girl." Lenora had never hated anyone in her life, not Evan when he broke her engagement, not Cassie for falling in love with Evan herself. No one in her life had hurt her as much as Catherine had. Except perhaps Mr. Asher. But she did not hate him either. She did not know what she felt toward him anymore. It was too confusing to sort out.

Aunt Gwen held her eyes. "I do not believe you mean that."

"I do," Lenora said, but she wasn't entirely sure about that either. Having never hated anyone, could she know what it felt like? If it was not hatred, it was the greatest dislike she had ever experienced. And extremely complex. It wasn't just Catherine, it was everything she was connected to—termination, embarrassment, failure, Mr. Asher. Lenora stopped pacing and faced her aunt. Her chin quivered. "I cannot tell you how it hurts me to even have you ask this of me."

Aunt Gwen stood quickly from her chair and crossed the room. Lenora hung her head, the tears—a familiar companion this week—rising fast. Aunt Gwen took hold of Lenora's hand with both of her own. "Do you believe I would ask you to do something that would hurt you? I am not asking for Catherine's benefit alone; I believe this might heal you, too."

Lenora could not speak around the lump in her throat but shook her head. To expect healing to come from spending more time with Catherine Manch was idiotic, and she was tired of being an idiot, though she had proved herself rather adept at the role.

"Please sit down and let me explain."

Aunt Gwen led Lenora to the settee, where they sat side by side. Aunt Gwen patted her hand, and Lenora wondered if it was the physical touch that made her compliant enough to listen to the whole of this foolhardy plan.

Aunt Gwen talked about her day spent with Catherine,

the insight she'd gained regarding Catherine's relationship with people who failed to care for her, and her opinion that Catherine would never thrive in a school environment without the basic skills of reading and writing. What she needed were positive connections to a few people who could help her overcome her weaknesses while maximizing her strengths.

The plan was to have her move into the terrace house with Aunt Gwen and Lenora during the week, much like she lived at the school now. Aunt Gwen would serve as a mother figure, and Lenora would serve as the girl's private teacher. Catherine's abilities were so delayed for her age that Lenora's home education would be sufficient expertise for quite some time. Lenora could help her excel in music as well as more academic topics. Mr. Asher would pay Lenora's salary and cover all of Catherine's expenses. She would stay connected to the school for activities and group projects so as to enjoy structured social opportunities, and she would continue to stay with her uncle on weekends. As her abilities improved, she would attend school for specific topics until she was able to transition back to being a boarded student.

Aunt Gwen had obviously put a great deal of thought into this plan, which seemed reasonable for a girl who needed help. But Catherine was not simply an ordinary girl who was behind in her learning—she was mean and divisive and the catalyst to Lenora's broken heart. But Lenora listened to the entire presentation while she stared at the floor and struggled to understand Aunt Gwen's willingness to support a plan that would absolutely turn her life on its ear.

And Mr. Asher's part? That was the hardest to bear. After

all that had happened between them, he expected her to teach his niece as though Lenora were any other teacher. He expected her to sacrifice for Catherine and himself, give up what was left of her pride, and use her ruined career for their benefit. It made her feel as insignificant as she'd ever felt in her life.

She imagined him coming to Aunt Gwen and saying, "Shame about what happened, but I think I have a way to use it all to my advantage." He was the type of man to blackmail a woman, convince her to trust him, and eventually persuade her to fall in love with him. It was not beyond reason that his manipulations extended further, and for a moment it felt as though the entire situation had been contrived from the very beginning. He'd needed someone vulnerable but skilled, meek but hungry to be loved. Lenora had been the perfect target.

"I truly think this is Catherine's best chance," Aunt Gwen concluded. "And I think the three of us—you, me, and Mr. Asher—can make it happen."

"I want no part of it," Lenora said, though she felt bad when Aunt Gwen's face fell. "Mary is expecting me, and I need to leave Bath and the memories here." She couldn't expect Aunt Gwen to understand. Her aunt made friends easily and . . . fit. Lenora did not have such close friends to buoy her up, and she did not have past success to give her confidence in her ability to rise above this. She needed to run; it was the only escape that had ever worked.

"Mrs. Henry accepted your resignation without giving cause. We shall simply explain that you did so in order to be a private tutor for Catherine."

"Which is a lie." Lenora shook her head. "That's not right." Her piety, which she had allowed to grow soft, had been pricked quite sharply in light of her lapse of moral behavior. If she had adhered closer to what was proper and right, she'd have never been in this mess.

Aunt Gwen tightened her grip on Lenora's hand until Lenora met her eyes. "You have been wronged, Lenora. No one—not me, not Mr. Asher—denies that, but I truly believe that helping her will help you."

"She is the cause of this," Lenora said. "She knew full well what would happen, and she did it with malice and, likely, a thrill of victory. To expect *that* girl to then heal what she has done is beyond even your optimism."

"I am not expecting Catherine to heal you. I am expecting you to heal yourself through teaching and showing mercy and reaching out to someone who does not deserve your help but who could benefit greatly from it." She paused. "And I don't want you to leave. Having you here has been wonderful. It has extended to me love and a sense of family I have not felt since I was a child. To have you leave, and like this, breaks my heart."

Lenora closed her eyes, feeling manipulated again and yet touched as well. Aunt Gwen made her feel important, she always had, but the idea of dealing with Catherine day in and day out . . . She took a breath. Was that harder than leaving? Harder than stepping into Mary's already brimming household and having to find a new fresh start?

But the gossip. And the memories. Having to see Mr. Asher.

"Could you please give it a chance?" Aunt Gwen said when

Lenora did not answer, her tone pleading and sincere. "Perhaps for one month, structured however you like. You can choose the boundaries of acceptable behavior, you can end each day at any time you like, you can employ any method and timetable you wish—however you feel would be best." She took a breath and delivered her final attempt. "She has treated you badly, Lenora, but I also know that you *do* care for her. You were the first to see through the mask she has worked so hard to keep in place. I do not suggest this simply because you can do it—any number of teachers could do it—but because I know that you will put your heart into it, and the forgiveness that will be required will only do you good."

Lenora was left without argument. She had felt the balm of forgiveness before—both giving and receiving—and her soul longed for that comfort to soothe the raw and bitter feelings throbbing in her chest. And she *had* come to care about Catherine, even to see similarities in the fact that both of them had found ways to keep the world at a distance. It was that caring that made the betrayal sting so sharply. To agree to be her private tutor would be to risk greater pain—Aunt Gwen could not convince her otherwise—but she could also see the potential of strength to come. Much like coming to Bath had allowed her to become better and more secure within herself, accepting this challenge could keep her from reverting to the frightened girl she'd been for so long. Even if the arrangement did not work out in the long-term, attempting to do her best could help her be better for it rather than be broken by it.

"I will accept the arrangement for two weeks," Lenora said.

"Then I will decide if I can continue longer. I will need you to let me stay away from society during that time."

"Two weeks then, and you shall have all say." Aunt Gwen wrapped her arms around Lenora's shoulders. She was Lenora's mother's sister, and when Lenora closed her eyes, she could pretend she was in her mother's arms. Aunt Gwen held her tight, kissed her temple, and said, "Everything is going to be all right."

Chapter Twenty-One

Aiden stayed in the shadows Sunday night, hoping against hope that Lenora would go to the river so he could explain himself in person. It had been a full week since his escort had ended with her in his arms. It had happened so fast, and yet, if he were honest, it had been a slow and delicious simmer. Starting during their first few interactions, then the greater comfort they achieved when they were together, and then the night they waltzed in the upper rooms. It had all led to the moment when his head bent to hers, the cold rain only emphasizing the heat growing between them. Even thinking of that kiss now seemed to raise the temperature of the October night, which could no longer be described as crisp. It was cold.

His toes were tingling, and he had not felt his nose for a quarter of an hour. The light was on in Lenora's bedroom, and he waited for her to blow out the candle as she always did before leaving the house. The light stayed on. Another quarter hour passed. Then another quarter. The candle went out, but the night remained silent. At midnight, he concluded she was not coming.

His letter of explanation, his agreement of Mrs. Simmons's plan, and his hoping for forgiveness was not enough. He let out a discouraged breath, the air clouding in front of him, and turned toward his house, where Catherine slept. He'd made sure she was asleep before he left and charged a footman to keep watch so the girl could not go out at night again. Tomorrow he would take her to Mrs. Simmons's house, and her lessons would begin.

Before reaching the bridge, however, he changed his mind and continued down the street to the gap in the shops that led to the secret steps he had discovered his first night in Bath. The morning of his first day, his shoes had been oddly scuffed, as though someone had scraped them across stone. His pipe, left on the mantel of the Cheshire estate, was filled with tea, and his favorite walking stick, the thin black lacquered one with the ivory swan's head handle, was broken into three pieces and left in the entryway. He'd ignored all of Catherine's "subtle" protests and physically placed her in the carriage for their journey to Bath while counting the hours until he could take her to school Monday morning. When they reached their rooms that afternoon, he'd met with the proprietor to finalize the arrangements and returned to the study to find the book he'd been reading disemboweled. He'd charged the staff to watch his niece and took to the streets rather than shake the girl into submission.

He had already been at the river when someone came down

the steps, prompting him to pull into the shadows to avoid discovery—perhaps he wasn't supposed to be in this place he thought he had to himself. He hadn't known for certain that the visitor was a woman until she'd bolted up the stairs with her plait falling down her back, leaving him to hold his foot he'd feared was broken.

Tonight, the city was lit by a half moon, and he could easily see the stone steps and the water pooling in the uneven portions from this afternoon's rain. How he wished he could see Lenora again; how he wished she would let him explain in person about his agreement with Miss Keighly.

After talking to Mrs. Simmons the first time, he'd returned to his study and written a letter that said, in effect: *Dear Hazel, against my expectations, my heart has been captured by a woman whom I don't believe I can live without.* He expected her reply any day. Perhaps she wasn't at her family home in Cheshire, and the letter was chasing her to London or her grandmother's house in Yorkshire—that could take a week or more. Yet here he was, alone on the banks of the river where he'd first met Lenora Wilton. He had not seen her since their kiss, yet she'd agreed to make one more attempt to tutor Catherine and help the girl reach her potential.

Catherine.

He sat down on a dry section of what he thought of as Lenora's wall and lit his pipe, puffing to catch the tobacco and then inhaling deeply. He smoked and watched the river and thought of the women in his life, and the one woman he wanted in it but wasn't. Maybe Lenora hadn't felt what he'd felt. But if that were the case, why would her reaction be so strong?

He let out a heavy breath, knowing he should have told her he was engaged when they'd waltzed that night. Or he should have walked beside her as they went to the river instead of playing escort as though the waltz had never happened. He should *not* have given in to his baser desires and taken her his coat, knowing full well he'd wanted an excuse to be close to her. To smell her perfume, to gaze into those dark blue eyes in the moonlight.

If he'd written Miss Keighly *before* he'd held Lenora in his arms, or even immediately upon returning home from the river that night, things might be different. Lenora would still be with Mrs. Henry's school. That delicious sizzle would still be building between them.

Yet how did he explain that he'd forgotten proposing marriage to a woman he'd known all his life—the safe and easy and practical choice upon which to build a future for Catherine? He'd never felt anything more than physical attraction for any woman until meeting Lenora, and now that he understood how deeply a man could feel, he could not unfeel it or settle for less.

He puffed on his pipe and then tapped out the ashes. It was late and fiercely cold, and a new week would start in the morning. Lenora had agreed to teach Catherine for two weeks. Perhaps she would see another side of the girl and take pity on both of them. If she could forgive Catherine, perhaps she could also forgive him.

When he received Miss Keighly's response, he would show

the letter to Lenora. Once she knew the engagement was broken, she would be able to forgive him, right? And if he could kiss her again, then *surely* she would.

In his mind, everything lined up like soldiers in formation. In his mind, it was all so clear. Like leaving his plantation to care for his niece. Like proposing engagement to a respectable woman he could make a life with in hopes of giving Catherine the family she deserved after how poorly she'd been treated in his absence. Like falling in love with a woman he did not expect and therefore being able to change his mind and build a new future. Why was reality so very different than his expectations?

Chapter Twenty-Two

Catherine moved into the terrace house Monday morning. Lenora watched through an upstairs window until she saw Mr. Asher walking away. When he looked up, she pulled back, hoping he had not seen her. She'd told Aunt Gwen that she did not want to interact with him, and Aunt Gwen had agreed to ensure as much.

Whatever her relationship with Mr. Asher had been before, Lenora would keep it purely professional this time. She needed time to prepare for even that level of relationship, however.

A few minutes later, Catherine and Aunt Gwen came into the upstairs parlor. It was small but nicely appointed in shades of yellow and lavender. Compared to the spacious parlor on the main level, complete with a large bay window, this room saw little company but would be just right for the schoolroom.

Lenora swallowed her rising anxiety and lifted her chin. She had her hair pulled up and wore one of her teaching dresses, wanting to set the right tone. The desk from Aunt Gwen's bed-chamber had been brought in to serve as a workspace. Lenora felt as tight as a sail and twice as battered; she had not been sleeping well and hadn't gone to the river last night—the first Sunday she'd missed in months.

"I shall leave you two to your studies," Aunt Gwen said. "I'm going to the Pump Room with Mrs. Grovesford."

"Can I go with you?" Catherine asked, a pout in her voice.

"You have school, dear," Aunt Gwen said sweetly while Lenora arranged the primer, slate, and letter board Aunt Gwen had procured. "But I shall see you for tea this afternoon." She kissed the girl's forehead, and Lenora pushed down an unex-pected wave of jealousy.

"Please take your seat," Lenora said, once Aunt Gwen left the room.

Catherine let out a huff, but took dragging steps across the floor.

Lenora did not smile as Catherine sat in the chair across from her. "Good morning, Catherine."

Catherine mumbled something.

"I said, 'Good morning, Catherine,'" Lenora said, her hands clasped on the top of the desk. "You are to say 'Good morning, Miss Wilton' back to me."

"Good morning, Miss Wilton, back to me."

Lenora held her eyes, glad that Catherine couldn't hear her racing heart. "I will not abide rudeness. This is your first warn-ing. You will have two warnings every day, but on your third offense, I will leave the room and you will explain it to Aunt Gwen."

Catherine rolled her eyes.

"This is your second warning."

Catherine looked at the desktop, her jaw clenched.

Lenora took a breath and began the day's lesson. "You have proved to be very good at memorization, which will greatly help this process, but we need to work on actual writing and, therefore, words. In order for us to know where to start, I need to assess your current level." She was careful to keep her tone slightly animated and positive, so Catherine would know she was not holding the warnings against her.

"Miss Grimes already did that."

"Yes, well, since you and I will be working together from now on, I need to do my own assessment."

Catherine shrugged, and Lenora considered whether or not to count it as a third offense.

"Sorry," Catherine mumbled before Lenora could decide, and, relieved, Lenora nodded. "We will need to start below your ability, so I'll need your patience as we move forward." Lenora turned the letter board to face Catherine. "Do you know your letters?"

"Of course."

Lenora stared at her and again debated the idea of ending their lesson. They had been together for less than five minutes. But this girl was twelve years old and having to start at the very beginning. Lenora would give her some margin. But only some.

"Good, then this shall be easy. What is this letter?" She lifted the board and pointed to a letter.

"N."

"And this one?"

"Q."

"And this?"

"H."

"Excellent. What sounds do they make?"

They went through every letter, and Catherine gave the correct sounds for each one, only missing a few of the secondary sounds for letters *J*, *G*, and *Y*. They moved on to the primer, which had lists of two-letter words Lenora expected to go through it quite easily, but Catherine read "no" as "on" and "if" as "fi." Three-letter words revealed similar mistakes of getting the order of the letters wrong, though Catherine seemed bored and unaware of her errors.

"I know all of this," she said as they finished reviewing the first-level primer.

Lenora said nothing as she placed the second-level primer on the desk between them. It was what a seven- or eight-year-old would typically study. That was when things began to turn poorly. Catherine read "hour" as "or" and "left" as "felt." She had to sound out the word "away" and did not correctly pronounce the different *A* sounds in the word. Even though Lenora did not comment, Catherine seemed to know she was making mistakes, and the tension in the room began to rise. When she said "jump" as "goomp," she suddenly pushed the primer toward Lenora, who caught it before it fell in her lap.

"I do not like this and want to do something else." She crossed her arms over her chest and glared at Lenora.

"What would you like to do, then?"

She pulled her eyebrows together. "What?"

"I said, what would you like to do? Maybe I can make a lesson out of it."

"What does that mean?" she asked warily.

"Every *thing* is represented by a word," Lenora said, thinking off the cuff. "And you know those words, so you choose something to do and we can make labels for the items involved or write out the words on the slate."

Catherine considered this. "Anything?"

"Within reason," Lenora said, then made herself smile in hopes of cutting through the tension between them. "Shooting pistols, for instance, would be an unreasonable request."

"What about taking a walk?"

Lenora's smile softened, remembering the walk they'd taken during the last week at the school. "Excellent suggestion," she said, pushing back from the desk. "I'll bring the slate, and we'll practice the names of things we see along the way."

"I did not say that was what I wanted, I just asked if a walk was a possibility."

Lenora laced her fingers on the desktop and raised her eyebrows while unclenching her teeth. Could nothing about this girl be simple?

Catherine's expression turned smug, which should have been a warning. "I want to see my uncle."

Lenora's heart skipped a beat. "Choose something else."

"But that's what I want. I want to see my uncle. You can label the door as we leave, the streets as we pass them, the door of his house in Laura Place, then paste a label on his fine eyes, and his thick hair, and—"

Lenora stood and left the room. She did not speak, she did not look back, and she did not feel bad about it either. Catherine could run out into the street for all she cared. She was not the girl's babysitter. If Aunt Gwen wanted to be the mother figure, then she could deal with her daughter figure and sort it out.

Lenora took the stairs to her room, shut and locked the door, and then stood in the middle of the room with clenched fists at her sides. *She is a monster,* she said in her mind. And yet, Lenora had worked with Catherine up close today. The girl knew her alphabet and the sounds of the letters. She could string *some* words together but not other words, even simpler ones. Catherine seemed most familiar with nouns—door, rock, bird. Why?

Lenora wished she could consult with Miss Grimes, but the idea of talking to anyone from the school made her insides shrivel like last year's potatoes. She was a second-class teacher now, dismissed from her first and only position because of the very girl she was now trying to help. Her interest in having decoded some of Catherine's deficiency was easily eclipsed by the girl goading her about Mr. Asher.

Lenora closed her eyes and felt fresh fire wash over her face and neck and chest. She tried not to think of Mr. Asher's fine eyes and thick hair, but of course, trying not to think about them meant they were the *only* things that would come to mind.

I should have gone to Mary's, she thought, looking at the days ahead with absolute dread. Why had she believed she was up to this? She had agreed to this plan in hopes that Aunt Gwen was right and it might somehow help her, but she could not—*would not*—continue if Catherine made a game of taunting her. Her battered heart could not take that kind of abuse.

Chapter Twenty-Three

Lenora skipped tea because she was unable to think of a single reason to put herself in Catherine's company. Instead, she began transcribing some sheet music she'd inadvertently brought home from the school for her personal collection. She desperately wanted to lose herself in playing the pianoforte or walking by the river. Taking comfort with the pianoforte would require going to the main parlor and likely crossing paths with Catherine. Going to the river required leaving the sanctuary of the terrace house, and she wasn't ready for that either. Perhaps she should take up the flute; she could play in her room and maybe find some peace.

Aunt Gwen knocked with three short raps and then opened the door. "Could we talk in the schoolroom?" Already the second-floor parlor had taken on a new identity. Lenora wondered how long it would remain as such. Based on today's attempt, she did not see this arrangement succeeding.

Lenora searched her aunt's tone and expression for censure but found none. She nodded and followed her aunt to the schoolroom. Once seated in the chairs next to the desk, Aunt Gwen asked for Lenora's version of events.

"I imagine Catherine gave a different account," Lenora said when she finished, keeping her tone even.

"Slightly, yes. She claims that you dislike her and were irritated. And of course, she made no mention of having brought her uncle into the discussion."

Exactly what Lenora had expected Catherine would have said. "I *was* irritated." She was willing to concede her part, though she did not say out loud that she disliked the girl. She honestly had no idea how she felt toward Catherine. "But I did my best to hide my feelings and act professionally, Aunt Gwen."

"I have no doubt of that, my dear." Aunt Gwen patted Lenora's arm. "Not being able to read words seems to have made Catherine rather good at reading people, and she seems to know how we feel even when we are trying very hard to hide it." Aunt Gwen smiled at her little joke.

Lenora did not smile in response. For the first time, she felt as though she and her aunt were on opposite sides of an issue. Lenora did not like the isolation of it, and yet she had to hold her ground or risk stepping into quicksand that would swallow her up.

"So," Aunt Gwen said, but didn't continue, as though waiting for Lenora to fill in the blanks.

"So," Lenora repeated.

"Have you had enough, then?"

That Aunt Gwen would let her quit after the first day spurred an odd stubbornness in Lenora, bringing back all the lessons she'd been taught about being a woman of her word and following through on her promises, no matter how difficult or miserable. Catherine Manch, of all people, would not be the reason for Lenora's lack of character, though the offer was tempting.

"I said I would do two weeks and I will do it. I explained to Catherine that she would get two warnings for bad behavior each day, and then I would leave. That is what I did, and I am prepared to do it again every day for two weeks. I gave my word, and I will keep it."

"She did not mention the implementation of a warning system either. She said you were peckish and harsh and then walked out on her because she wasn't doing well in her reading."

Lenora said nothing. She didn't need to. Aunt Gwen was not defending Catherine; she seemed to have an objective view of the situation, which helped lower Lenora's defenses.

"I will speak with her and enforce your stipulations."

"And tell her to make no mention of her uncle."

Aunt Gwen sighed. "Lenora, dear."

Lenora braced herself for a lecture she did not want nor feel she deserved.

"Do you think that perhaps you are being a bit hasty in your determination to avoid Mr. Asher completely, and without letting him explain himself? He does not share affection for this woman and has—"

"You mean his fiancée?" Lenora kept her chin high, her

stubbornness strengthening her resolve again. She would not bend on this either. Mr. Asher had fooled her, and she would not condone his actions nor make herself vulnerable to further embarrassment and heartache.

"It was an arrangement based on the sole purpose of providing stability for Catherine. He has written to the woman and expects her response and agreement to break the engagement any day."

"He did not tell me he was engaged, Aunt Gwen. He took advantage of my not knowing and entertained himself at my expense. He is not someone I can or will ever trust again."

"You have been sneaking out of my house for months and did not tell me. Should I not trust *you*?"

Lenora looked at her hands in her lap. "Did learning of what I'd done break your heart, Aunt?" She looked up. "Did it cause you to plan out your future in one direction only to be left empty and abandoned when you learned of the deception? Not that my night walks were right—they were not—and I am very sorry for having deceived you."

"It did not break my heart, but it did make me feel rather foolish, and sad that you couldn't confide in me."

Lenora was not sure what to say about that. Her river walks had been lost in all the mayhem that followed Catherine's letter to Mrs. Henry. But she *had* been going behind her aunt's back, which she knew was wrong of her. Still, her poor behavior did not reach the level of Mr. Asher's deception. To say nothing of the fact that she'd lost her river and her position and her reputation. Mr. Asher had lost nothing and gained a feather in his cap and private tutoring for his niece.

"If something had happened to you on those walks to the river, have you any idea how I would have felt?"

"If I had told you, you would have forbidden it."

"Yes, and if Mr. Asher had told you he was engaged as a matter of course? What would you have done? Not allowed him to escort you to the river?"

Lenora had no answer. "I would not have felt foolish when I learned of his engagement from Mrs. Henry. I would not have felt that he had kept the information from me and taken advantage of my . . . hopes."

"Yes, I suppose that is difficult to argue," Aunt Gwen said. "You do not trust easily, and you did trust him. I was not there that night—no one was but the two of you—and I have little experience with . . . midnight trysts. If he kissed you with full thought and intention, then yes, he should have divulged his situation beforehand."

What she didn't say was obvious—if Lenora was the one who kissed *him*, then he'd not have had the chance. He'd said her name; the word had sounded breathless and full of the same desire she'd been feeling. Had his tone also held regret? Had he been about to tell her when she'd silenced his words? She gave herself a mental shake, afraid that acknowledging the possibility might unravel her further. She needed to be strong, impenetrable, and self-preserving.

"I need Catherine to not mention her uncle. She uses him to distract from her frustrations and turn the tables. Any mention of her uncle in any context will be counted as a warning for the day's lesson."

"I think that is a reasonable request," Aunt Gwen said, standing. "And thank you for not giving up." She let out a heavy breath and raised a hand to her forehead. "How on earth did I get in the middle of a situation like this?"

For the first time, Lenora smiled. "I believe it was your idea."

Aunt Gwen laughed. "Touché."

Lenora started Tuesday where they'd ended on Monday, and when Catherine's irritation began to rise, Lenora suggested they do some French recitations. Pure memorization would help build Catherine's confidence since she was skilled at that type of learning. They conjugated verbs for nearly an hour. When they returned to reading and Catherine became tense again, Lenora suggested an early tea, wishing Aunt Gwen was there to displace some of the ever-present awkwardness. Unfortunately, Aunt Gwen was visiting a friend that afternoon and unable to join them.

Once the tray arrived, the silence only increased the discomfort, forcing Lenora to find a solution other than critiquing the girl's etiquette, which was not on the list of duties she'd agreed to fulfill. Two afternoons a week, Catherine attended Mrs. Henry's school for needlepoint and etiquette, relieving Lenora of those topics.

After a few minutes of strained silence, Lenora attempted

ordinary, polite conversation as she would with any other student. "When did you start to play the pianoforte, Catherine, do you remember?"

Catherine gave Lenora a cautious glance as she blew on her tea, as though Lenora's question was not to be trusted.

Lenora counted a full minute before she took another uncomfortable step in the conversation. What she wanted to do was simply maintain the silence—she was very good at that—but she believed this "relationship" would not last the month, so she had nothing to lose in making attempts. Perhaps she would look at it as practice for the new life she would need to make after she had fulfilled what she felt she owed her aunt. And maybe, just maybe, she could do Catherine some good.

She wished she did not feel so nervous and took a moment to look at the teacups, the silver tray, and Catherine's shoes, then felt the warmth of the cup in her hand and the cushion of the chair before inhaling the earthy scent of the tea. Centered, she made another attempt.

"I started to play when I was four years old," Lenora said as though *that* had been the question she'd asked. "My mother plays—Aunt Gwen does, too, did you know?—and Mother was teaching my older sister. I remember I was playing with something—dolls, maybe—in the corner of our parlor during my sister's lesson but was distracted when I realized the sounds of the keys were different from one another. When they left the room, I went to the piano and started hitting the keys, trying to make the same sounds they had made. Without realizing it, I played the same melody my mother had been teaching my sister—a simple version of 'Come, Thou Almighty King.' My mother came back into the room and helped me finish the melody line with my right hand. I played it back almost perfectly my third time through."

Catherine was watching her, but didn't speak. She took a sip of her tea.

Lenora had never relayed her story quite like this. She gave the basics to her students every year, that she'd started at four and grown up playing hymns by ear, but never these details. Saying it out loud replaced some of her discomfort with pride. She had a gift, she'd always known it, and she had pursued it relentlessly. That was something to take righteous pride in.

"My mother instructed me until I was eight years old, at which point I surpassed her ability and began taking lessons— both organ and pianoforte—from Mrs. Bombshaw. She was the church's organist and did not read music either. Everything she played was memorized." She looked up to see if Catherine was paying attention. She was, and so Lenora continued.

"My mother had taught me the staff, but most of what I learned was by ear—the way you play. By the time I was eleven, I played two dozen of the more popular hymns well enough that I became Mrs. Bombshaw's relief when she was unable to play. By the time I was fourteen, I played the organ every other Sunday and knew every song in the hymnal by heart. I had also realized how much easier it was for me to be with an instrument than it was for me to be with people."

As soon as she'd said it, she regretted sharing something so personal and hurried to think of something to put on top of the information in hopes Catherine would not hone in on the vulnerability.

"Mr. Thompson moved to our village about that time. He was a professional musician—I think he played twelve different instruments—but he had been taught music note by note. He was intrigued by my ability and asked my parents if he could teach me to read music, impressing upon both of them how essential it was for me to progress beyond the hymns."

Lenora smiled, thinking back. "How I hated his lessons. He made me start with simple notes and childish songs I'd mastered years ago. He made me read the music I played, which meant I made mistakes."

She thought back to those years, remembering how frustrated she had been, but she avoided contention at all costs and hated displeasing anyone so much that she studied the music sheets Mr. Thompson gave her the way other people studied books. She would go over the sheets until her eyes crossed or the candle burned out at night.

"I had to transcribe every piece of music, then read the notes aloud like a book before he would let me play it. If I didn't get every detail right, he would rap my knuckles with a ruler, then tear up the sheets and order me to start again. I would spend weeks playing the same notes until they echoed in my head every minute of every day. I could easily memorize a piece, but he would not let me play from memory. He forced me to look at every note—*read* every note—until the piece was perfect, then he would take the music away, and I could finally *enjoy* playing. For a long time, reading music felt like a punishment."

Lenora suddenly wondered how different things would have been if she'd had a temperament similar to Catherine's. Would she have rebelled against the lessons, insisted she would not do them, stomp on Mr. Thompson's foot, and run from the room? If she had, she'd have never learned what she knew.

"And then, Aunt Gwen sent me my very own sheet music— *The Wanderer Fantasy* by Schubert, a new composer my teacher did not know nor want to learn about. He wanted to expand my classical repertoire and had no use for modern composers who, he felt, polluted the music with unusual timings and harmonies. I was so upset that he would not let me practice the gift from my aunt, but then realized I could *read* it and therefore figure it out myself. I spent months, literally, learning that piece without Mr. Thompson's knowledge. I practiced two hours for his lessons, and at least two more on my own."

"Every day?" Catherine asked with heavy skepticism.

"Every day except Sundays. My father is a vicar, and the Sabbath was a day of rest, though I still played the organ for church. I played and played until the piece was perfect, and then I mustered all my courage and played it for Mr. Thompson. When I finished, he sat back in his chair, and we both knew that I was done with my lessons. I had exceeded him, the master, and could not be content with only what he wanted to teach me any longer."

Lenora smiled at the memory, at how proud she'd felt, how proud she felt now to remember it. Learning that piece and playing it for him had been the bravest thing she'd ever done to that point. She looked at Catherine and wondered why she would give the first telling of such a story to her, of all people. Lenora picked up another shortbread from the tray.

Catherine took one as well. "Did you not feel completely pathetic that you had nothing else to do in your life but play the pianoforte for *four hours* every day?"

Lenora leveled her gaze on the girl and shut off all the warm feelings she'd allowed to bubble up. It was her own fault; she knew that Catherine would use anything she could to feel powerful. Interestingly enough, though, Lenora's feelings were not so very hurt. Perhaps upon later reflection, Catherine would better understand what Lenora had been trying to teach her.

Lenora would not be as proficient as she was if not for a natural ability similar to Catherine's, but she would also not have reached the level she had without learning to read music; it had opened up a whole new world. If Catherine chose to take advantage of the opportunity Lenora was offering, she might very well become the best student Lenora had ever taught.

"This is your first warning. We'll resume lessons in ten minutes."

Chapter Twenty-Four

Catherine lit up whenever Aunt Gwen was present, sparking jealousy in Lenora, though she wasn't sure who she was more jealous of—Catherine for being so happy to see Aunt Gwen, or Aunt Gwen for getting such a warm welcome from Catherine.

Lenora watched how her aunt interacted with the girl, but when she attempted the same type of techniques, Catherine would become obstinate and argumentative. Lenora stopped trying to imitate anyone and walked out of their lessons after only forty-five minutes on Wednesday when Catherine brought up her uncle again and refused to read aloud.

Lenora skipped reading on Thursday and instead opened a history book about the early Spanish campaigns. As it turned out, Catherine loved history. They made it through the entire five hours that day with only one warning. Lenora was lifted by the success and could sense that Catherine was pleased as well, though she would not say as much, only commenting how glad she was when their lessons were over.

On Friday, Lenora began teaching Catherine how to read the music staff, curious to know if the same difficulty the girl had with letters would translate into music notes; it did not seem to. Catherine found it frustrating to read notes on a page, but Lenora had anticipated that and did not spend too much time on that first lesson, content to teach the bass and treble clef and where on the staff each note was located with its accompanying key on the pianoforte.

Then Lenora taught Catherine a duet she had been taught by her mother years ago. It was simple, but because it had a split melody, it took some effort on Catherine's part to master her portion, especially when Lenora was playing her part. Because Catherine's skill was essentially mimicking, she had to concentrate on what she remembered rather than what Lenora was playing.

By the second hour, Catherine had learned her part well enough that she and Lenora performed it for Aunt Gwen after tea. Aunt Gwen applauded, and Lenora received her first thank you from her student. She had not anticipated how validating it would feel to receive any amount of gratitude.

"You are very welcome, Catherine," Lenora said as she stood from the chair she had pulled alongside the piano stool. "You have an amazing gift."

That evening, Catherine went to the theater with some girls from the school. She would return to her uncle's apartments for the weekend after the event. Lenora and Aunt Gwen enjoyed the fire in the parlor without Catherine's usual prattle, which was always directed at Aunt Gwen, of course. The silence was welcome and reminded Lenora of how things used to be when it was just her and her aunt in the evenings. She wished she felt as light as she did then, however, and that thoughts of Mr. Asher did not continually fill her. She missed being a part of the school, missed the sense of purpose, belonging, and independence she'd found through her position. Now, she felt trapped in her aunt's house, struggling to teach a difficult student. It had been nearly two weeks since she'd seen Mr. Asher. Two long and mournful weeks.

"Will you attend the Roman Baths with me in the morning?" Aunt Gwen asked once she'd finished reading the day's newspaper. She always read it at night before bed.

Lenora was working on one of her transcriptions. "No, thank you, Aunt." She might still live in Bath, but she did not feel like one of them anymore. She'd lost her place here as assuredly as she'd lost her place at Leagrave the last time she was embroiled in an engagement-centered scandal.

"I missed your company last week, and people will ask after you if you miss a second week."

"I cannot abide the gossip, Aunt. Please understand."

"That is what I am attempting to say, Lenora—no one *is* talking. I think Mrs. Henry's agreement to accept your leaving so that you might teach private lessons prevented the gossip you feared."

"I appreciate your kindness, but the truth rarely stems such juicy gossip and you know it." Lenora set down her music sheets. The transcriptions had been a good distraction these past weeks. She only had a few more pieces left to copy before she could send the music back to the school.

Aunt Gwen smiled. "I always befriend the most atrocious gossips so that I am always in the know. If there was talk, I would have heard it by now. I *have* been asked about your resignation from the school so early in the term, but I explained that you had been retained as a private tutor by Mr. Asher, and that was that."

Hearing his name sent a shiver through her. "Then it is only a matter of time."

"I believe the potential scandal was avoided, Lenora."

Lenora was quiet. Hadn't Catherine told the other students? If they knew, word would have spread. But it *had* been two weeks. Was she relieved to know she was not being whispered about behind hands? Did that really matter when her heart felt floppy in her chest? It did not change that she *had* been terminated, nor that it had *not* been her choice to leave. It did not change that Mr. Asher had not been honest with her, nor that she'd been reminded, again, that she was never a man's first choice. The kiss on the river was little more than fantasy now, complete with curling edges and muted color. It felt like a step out of time that she hoped would fade from her mind completely one day.

"Believe me, dear," Aunt Gwen continued. "If there were a story about the music teacher at Mrs. Henry's school passionately kissing the handsome uncle of one of her students, I'd have heard about it a dozen times over."

Lenora blushed at her aunt's words. Who was Lenora Wilton to think she could passionately kiss a man and not be punished for it?

"Please come with me to the Roman Baths tomorrow," Aunt Gwen said. "I miss your companionship after so many months of being able to take it for granted."

"Perhaps Catherine could attend you." Catherine had accompanied Aunt Gwen last week, and even though nothing could have convinced Lenora to attend so soon after being turned out, it had been hurtful to be replaced so easily.

"She will be with her uncle." Aunt Gwen touched Lenora's arm, then waited until Lenora met her gaze. "And I want to be with *you*, Lenora. Please come. See for yourself that no one is whispering about you. This is not Leagrave."

No, it is not Leagrave, she thought. *It is far worse than that.* She had not loved the man who jilted her in Leagrave. Her pride and expectations had been wounded, but not her heart. This time, every part of her suffered.

In the end, Lenora did go to the Roman Baths, though she found them uncomfortable. She did not put herself forward, content to stay to the sides in her brown bathing costume. She'd worn an unadorned bonnet so as to avoid the obvious conversation a more elaborate one would attract. Aunt Gwen, however, wore one of her most elegant bonnets specifically to receive compliments. A number of acquaintances came to them—looking like disembodied bonneted-heads bobbing across the water—to trade compliments and gossip.

By the time they returned home, Lenora was nearly convinced that Aunt Gwen was right. The scandal had not spread. Several people had expressed surprise at her leaving her position, but she sensed no suspicion that there could be more to the story. Lenora still *wanted* to hide, but she did not feel like she *had* to.

Lenora listened to Aunt Gwen talk about Sunday's upcoming dinner party as they entered the front door of the terrace house. The Davisons had returned to Bath after nearly a year, and Mrs. Davison was one of Aunt Gwen's dearest friends.

Lenora pulled the ribbon of the bow beneath her chin that held her rose-sprig bonnet in place, and then stopped dead in her tracks. Standing at the base of the stairs, hat in hand, was Mr. Asher.

She was not ready.

Chapter Twenty-Five

A iden took a breath as Lenora stepped back from him, treading on her aunt's foot in the process, the ribbons of her
bonnet tangled in her fingers. One would think he was holding
an axe above his head.

"My dear!" Mrs. Simmons exclaimed, pushing against
Lenora's back, which caused her to stumble. Aiden reached out
to catch Lenora's arm, then kept hold of her elbow once she was
righted. She stared at him, confused and shocked, but, dare he
say it, perhaps glad to see him?

The look only lasted a moment before she stepped to the
side, necessitating that he release her arm. She turned away completely, fiddling with the bonnet in her hand and brushing at
the tendrils of hair around her flushed face while looking into
the small looking glass placed above the umbrella basket at the
entryway.

"Good afternoon, Mr. Asher," Mrs. Simmons said, polite

but obviously surprised at his arrival. She smiled at him, but glanced at Lenora, concerned. "We were not expecting you."

"Catherine wanted to show me her room. I hope it is all right that we came."

"Certainly."

"I took a liberty, and I am sorry. I should have sent a note, or waited until I returned Catherine on Monday."

"It is fine," Mrs. Simmons said, but she glanced at Miss Wilton again just as Catherine traipsed down the stairs.

"Aunt Gwen!" Catherine said, running into Mrs. Simmons's arms, forcing the older woman back a step, and hugging her tightly. "Can we stay for tea?"

"It is impolite to invite yourself, Catherine," Aiden said, but he glanced at Lenora and wondered if things might soften between them if he were to stay for tea.

Lenora was watching him in the glass but flicked her gaze away as soon as she realized he'd noticed. She had to be hurting as much as he was, so shouldn't they put an end to it? He had not yet received Miss Keighly's response, but surely one private conversation would help them both feel better.

"I'm going to Mrs. Grovesford's for tea today, Catherine, and your uncle is right. It is poor manners to invite yourself."

Catherine let go of Mrs. Simmons and took a few steps away, a pout on her face.

"And it is impolite to pout," Mrs. Simmons added, lifting her eyebrows.

"Very well," Catherine said. She clasped her hands behind

her back and stood up straight. "I beg your forgiveness for my poor manners, Aunt Gwen."

Mrs. Simmons smiled. "You are forgiven." She inclined her head, and Catherine's expression softened. She did not like to displease Mrs. Simmons, though displeasing anyone else did not seem to affect her much.

Lenora did not say anything and moved toward the stairs that would lead to the first level. Aiden watched her ascend, then looked at Aunt Gwen, who waved him forward encouragingly. He was not one to disobey his elders.

"Miss Wilton," he said, turning on his heel and taking a few steps after her. She paused on the stairs, but only looked over her shoulder. "Might I have a word?" he asked.

She said nothing, but looked pained and let out a breath of resignation. She nodded once before continuing up the stairs. He looked at Mrs. Simmons, who gave him a smile.

"Perhaps Catherine and I shall walk to the corner and back," Mrs. Simmons said as she put a hand on Catherine's shoulder and turned her toward the door.

Aiden entered the parlor and saw Lenora by the window with her bonnet in her hands and still wearing her pelisse. She turned to face him, the light from the window making her look as though she were outlined in charcoal, as if she were a work of art. She held his gaze a moment before turning her attention to her bonnet.

He wanted to go to her but couldn't ignore the signals she was giving that he keep a distance. It was difficult not to let his mind go back to their exchange on the riverbank—the last opportunity he'd had to be this close to her. Thinking of the moment filled him with the same sensations now that had overcome him then. This woman intrigued him—a surface of poise and propriety, but underneath, a curiosity about the world. He wanted to uncover the deep thoughts he knew hid behind her eyes. He wanted to be someone she trusted. He wanted to explore the passion she'd shown him a shadow of already when she had put her hand behind his neck and invited him in for a kiss. *She'd* done that. He wanted her to do it again.

"I wrote to Miss Keighly," he said. "I explained the situation and asked for her understanding."

Lenora turned away, staring at the street below and not speaking.

He moved forward until he stood a few feet behind her. His awareness of her prickled, and he had to clench his hand into a fist to keep from brushing the backs of his fingers across the smooth skin of her neck. Did she feel the pull between them as he did?

She barely turned her head toward him before facing forward again. "You should have told me," she whispered, her hurt and distrust louder than her words.

"Yes, I should have." He still did not know when he would have had the chance—until they had waltzed, he had not fully realized the energy between them—but he should not have kissed her when she was unaware of his status. He should have broken his engagement with Miss Keighly as soon as he realized how strong his feelings for Lenora had become. "I underestimated the situation, Lenora. Both the engagement to Miss

Keighly and my feelings for you. I thought I had more self-control." He'd meant the last comment to lighten the mood, and perhaps compliment her by explaining how his feelings for her had blinded his senses. Whatever she'd heard, however, was different than his intention. He watched her head go down and her shoulders fall forward.

"Lenora?" He'd only ever called her by her Christian name one time before today—the moment before she'd put her hand on his neck and pulled him to her.

"I suppose you have likely encountered that often, then. The inability to control your actions regardless of your commitments."

Aiden was shocked by the vehemence of her words, though she'd little more than whispered them. Did she mean . . . ? He reviewed what he had said, unsure if he was properly understanding her. "I am not a rake, if that is what you are implying."

"I beg to differ."

She'd been bold with him before, but not like this. Not with cruelty. *She is protecting herself,* he said in his mind. He decided to respond with equal boldness. "I have never felt anything toward a woman like what I feel for you."

She faced him, but he sensed that it took all the strength she had left to do so. She wanted to hide from him; she was afraid of being alone with him—as though she were a glass he could shatter with the merest flick of his wrist. His heart ached.

"I have been Miss Keighly," she said. "I have been counted as so little by a man I thought cared for me."

"I explained to you in my letter that my arrangement with Miss Keighly was not a love match."

"But you made a *promise* to her, Mr. Asher—a legally binding one that assured her of security and devotion. You pledged to spend your life with this woman, but you are willing to bring it to an end with such little consideration of the impact it shall make on her." She took a shaky breath. He could see tears in her eyes, but determination in the set of her face. "I cannot reconcile the displays of your character with the type of man I could allow into my heart. If you can break your commitment to her so easily, what might happen five years down the road? Or ten, or twenty? A woman needs to trust and respect a man above all things. I have been taught as much all my life, and I am humiliated to have forgotten it in a moment of weakness."

A slap would have left less of a sting. "You are questioning my honor and character because I have fallen in love with you?"

She flinched at him proclaiming himself, and yet the words felt as natural for him to say as anything he had said before. He *did* love her, and he'd truly believed she loved him too. Had he been wrong?

Her mask of impenetrability was quickly recovered. "You blackmailed me into giving your niece considerations she did not deserve. You omitted telling me of your engagement. And you kissed me despite being promised to Miss Keighly. All of those things together have made me realize that you are not the man I thought you were. I will continue to teach Catherine and do my best by her, but I ask that you forget what has passed between us and keep your engagement in place. I will wish you happy and forget everything else. It is the right thing to do."

Heat crept up his neck—anger and embarrassment. He was *not* a cad, nor a man who took his obligations lightly, as she accused, but arguing would only prove her point. Despite all that had passed between them, she had chosen how she would see him. Any attempt he made to talk her out of her feelings would only reinforce that choice.

"That is all you have to say? That I should marry a woman I do not love to please *you*?"

She turned away from him, and though he sensed she was faltering, he suddenly wondered if he *wanted* to prove himself.

He straightened, drew his feet together, and bowed at the waist. "You have made yourself quite clear, Miss Wilton. I will take no more of your time. Good day." He turned sharply, almost militantly, and quit the room without looking to see if she turned to watch him go.

Mrs. Simmons and Catherine were coming up the walk when he burst through the front door, causing them both to startle. Mrs. Simmons smiled hopefully at him, but he only shook his head and pressed his hat onto his head. "Come along, Catherine," he said, his tone sharp enough that she did not argue.

Catherine almost had to jog to keep up with him, but he did not slow his pace and wished he could run in an attempt to burn through the emotions. Had he ever felt so . . . reduced? So small and insignificant and absolutely humiliated? His chest ached, wanting to convince Lenora that he was not the man she was determined to see. But what made sense in his mind did not seem to translate to reality. For the first time since stepping off the ship that had brought him home, Aiden truly wished he'd never come back to England.

He reached the rented house and pushed through the door, startled to see his man standing in the foyer as though waiting for him.

"Mr. Asher?" Martin asked.

Aiden gritted his teeth but stopped instead of taking the stairs that led to his study on the third level. He was only mildly aware of Catherine stopping behind him, apparently unnerved enough by his behavior not to press him. That was a good thing because he did not feel that he could deal fairly with her right now.

"Yes?"

"A woman is here to see you, sir. She said she would wait in the drawing room until precisely two o'clock, at which time she would leave an address for you to call upon. As it is only a quarter to the hour, she is still waiting. We have already provided a tea tray at her request."

Aiden felt his stomach drop. He moved slowly up the stairs toward the drawing room, trying to convince himself that there could be another woman in England who prized punctuality and schedule as much as the one he feared waited for him. He felt Catherine slip her hand into his and looked at her worried and yet irritatingly curious face. He stopped on the stairs and turned toward Martin, who remained in the foyer.

"Could you ask Paulette to accompany Catherine to her

room and stay with her until I come for her?" A good scolding regarding her part in writing Catherine's letter had resulted in Paulette's sincere apology and promise to keep Catherine in hand, which she had done a remarkable job at since.

"Yes, sir," Martin said with a slight bow, disappearing toward the kitchen, where Paulette was likely helping Cook with supper.

"I do not want to go to—" Catherine broke off at the look Aiden gave her. Paulette came running to the bottom of the stairs, then slowed her steps and gave a quick curtsy before taking Catherine by the hand. Catherine tried to resist, but Aiden glared at her, and she dropped her head.

Aiden waited until the two of them disappeared at the end of the hall, then he turned to the drawing room door and steeled himself for what awaited him on the other side.

A woman in a navy dress with white adornments looked up from a small notebook. She set down her pen and closed the book. Miss Keighly's looks were more classic than beautiful, but she exuded confidence and practicality, traits which had been attractive to him eight months ago when he was desperate to create a stable family for Catherine.

She stood and put out her gloved hand for him to cross the room and kiss, which he did. Another woman, older and plainer, sat in the corner of the room—Miss Keighly's maid, he felt sure. She would need such a companion for when she traveled a hundred and sixty miles to confront her fiancé instead of sending the letter he'd been expecting a fortnight ago. Once again, his plan had gone awry, and he was at the mercy of whatever fate seemed determined to wring out of him like a dishrag.

"Mr. Asher," she said with a smile as he stood from his bow. "I made plans to come as soon as I received your letter. I would like to discuss such a hasty change and see if we might be able to address the situation directly. Where would you prefer we discuss the particulars? There is a lovely tearoom just down the road that I visited when I was in town last fall for my cousin's wedding, and there is a particularly cozy table in the corner that might be the very place for us to work this out in private. What do you think of that?"

Chapter Twenty-Six

M iss Keighly listened attentively as Aiden explained his feelings for Lenora. He did not mince words. There was no reason to be less than perfectly and humiliatingly honest. Saying them out loud further convinced him of how real his feelings were. Not that it was *easy* to tell the woman to whom he was engaged that he loved someone else—it was terribly uncomfortable—but it was his only option. He had to convince her to end their agreement, one made in haste and desperation on his part before he understood what he was choosing *against*. He did not explain that Lenora had turned him out that very afternoon and felt him a man of low character, nor did he recount the kiss on the banks of the River Avon that played through his mind continually. As that detail had not gone public, he did not wish to cause either of them further embarrassment.

"Hmm," Miss Keighly said, tapping the pointer finger of

one white-gloved hand on the table. "Miss Wilton is Catherine's teacher, you say?"

"Yes. She was the music teacher at the school, but has since agreed to a private position now that we are beginning to understand the depth of Catherine's difficulties." At the time he'd made an offer of marriage to Miss Keighly, they had both believed Catherine needed nothing more than structure. Perhaps now that they realized how much she truly needed, Miss Keighly would be discouraged by the commitment.

"And the arrangement is working well?"

"Yes."

"How long do you feel Miss Wilton will serve in this capacity?"

Aiden scrubbed a hand over his face. He felt restless now that he'd revealed himself and eager to move past Hazel's desire to understand the particulars. He wanted to simply say, "I don't want to be engaged to you anymore. Might we please part as friends and continue on our way?" He might never earn back Lenora's respect, but once the engagement was off, he could at least try.

He had kissed the woman sitting across from him exactly once, a proper peck on the lips that had been more a seal of their agreement than an exchange of affection. The idea of taking her in his arms the way he had Lenora felt impossible. She would never mold to him as Lenora had, her lips would not be so soft or eager. He adjusted his position in the chair, pushing away the sensations brought on by the memories. Miss Keighly was watching him, waiting for his answer, which required him to remember the question.

Oh, yes, how long Lenora would be Catherine's teacher. "Until Catherine is prepared to return to a formal school, I suppose, which will require both her academics and behavior to be much improved."

"What is your best guess? Will Miss Wilton be her teacher through the Christmas holidays, or do you expect her service will continue throughout the next year? Two years, perhaps?"

"I really have no idea." He thought of the arrangements he'd made—at great expense—to ensure Catherine's acceptance to Mrs. Henry's school. That had been set on its ear like every other plan he'd put into play, including his plan to marry Miss Keighly and provide a stable family unit for Catherine. He hadn't rescinded his donation to the school; Catherine was still involved there as much as was possible. "If I could make a guess on when Catherine will return to the school, I would make it." He paused, realizing that Miss Keighly seemed oddly interested in the timeline. "Why does it matter?"

"Well, your affection for this woman is obvious in the way you speak of her, but once Miss Wilton is no longer engaged as Catherine's teacher, I am not opposed to another appointment—discreetly, of course. Such a relationship would be inappropriate as long as she is working with Catherine, however."

Aiden blinked. Hazel could not be saying what it sounded like she was saying. Yet she looked at him expectantly and did not try to restate or clarify her point. Aiden took a deep breath that did blessed little to clear his mind. "You are implying that I would take Miss Wilton as . . . a mistress?"

Hazel smiled a bit indulgently. "I am a woman of the world, Mr. Asher, and understand the ways of men. Discretion would be paramount, of course, and any children would not be publicly acknowledged but—"

"Stop," Aiden said, covering his face with both hands. He could not bear to hear more.

"She could do worse for herself, I daresay," Hazel continued. "And if you feel affection for her, then—"

He slapped his hands against the table and stared at her. "I beg of you, stop this line of discussion."

She shrugged, but did as he said, lifting her teacup to her lips and taking a genteel sip. She made a face, scanned the room for an attendant, and waved the young man over. When he arrived, she pushed the teapot to the edge of the table. "A fresh pot, please. Hot."

The attendant took the pot. Hazel picked up one of the raspberry biscuits from the platter in the center of their table and took a small bite, chewed thoughtfully as though determining its quality, and then took a larger bite. When she finished, she dabbed at her lips with her napkin. "I'm sorry if my talk has shocked you, Mr. Asher. I am only attempting to find a remedy for our situation that can satisfy all parties."

"I believe I was rather clear in my letter, Miss Keighly, regarding the remedy. I am very sorry for how things have transpired, but I would like to end our engagement in whatever way will create the least difficulty for you. I hope that our mutual respect and years of accord might allow this to proceed smoothly."

"I feel you made the decision rather rashly, Mr. Asher. You also seem to believe that I would *want* to discontinue our agreement, which I do not."

He had to repeat her words in his mind twice before he could answer. "You would prefer to continue our agreement even though I would not?"

The attendant returned with the hot tea. Hazel put up a hand to keep the attendant from leaving while she took a sip. Apparently satisfied at the tea's temperature, she smiled and nodded her acceptance. The boy bowed awkwardly and left them to their privacy again.

Miss Keighly lifted her cup. "I believe that love will grow between us in time, and we both have great potential to find happiness together through this arrangement. I am sympathetic for this . . . infatuation you feel, but I do not think the emotional charge you have experienced is sufficient reason to make permanent changes. The truth, Mr. Asher, is that in the months since our agreement, I have become rather accustomed to the idea of marriage. I have enjoyed the warmth and congratulations of my friends and family and have become quite taken with the idea of being Mrs. Aiden Asher."

Unbelievable. Lenora did not believe the depth of his feelings for her and had been worried about his hurting Miss Keighly. Miss Keighly, on the other hand, *believed* his feelings for Lenora—did not even discourage them—but did not see them worthy of dissolving an engagement.

He could officially break the engagement himself and accept the damage it would create to their reputations, the doors that would be closed to both of them. People would judge him harshly, while Miss Keighly would be regarded with pity, just as Lenora had been after her suitor broke off their engagement.

On the other hand, if Hazel were the one to beg off, they would both be the recipients of sympathy because he would be seen as the rejected party and her reasons would be accepted since a woman was expected to *only* cry off if she were convinced that the man would not make her happy. But Hazel didn't want to beg off, which meant Aiden would either have to do it or keep the agreement intact.

His desire to break the engagement stemmed from his wish to court Lenora, who did not want to be pursued by a man of his poor character. Would he be a fool to publicly reject a woman who was willing to take on his difficult niece? Or was he a fool to think he could ever find happiness with a woman who could treat their marriage as nothing more than a contract? That she had no expectation of fidelity seemed a reflection of how little she would value him overall.

And yet, she was here, and Lenora not only had dismissed him quite boldly, but she did not want him to break his engagement. And Catherine was still in need of the stability a marriage would create. Miss Keighly came from a family whose connections would only improve Catherine's situation and eventual interactions with society.

Aiden didn't know what to say, but finally nodded, surrendering to this course as exhaustion overtook him, much like malaria had once claimed him in Jamaica. He'd spent a full week in a fog where he'd wished simply to have it over with, even if his misery ended in the grave. Now, the woman he loved had told him to keep his engagement in place. The woman he did not love wanted the same thing.

"Very good," Miss Keighly said. "I think this is a good time for us to formalize our agreements. My father's man of business is working up a contract that he shall send to your solicitor once it is complete, at which time you can suggest any changes. Would you like to add in the mistress clause, then?"

"No, thank you," he said, his face flushed and a headache coming on. He picked up a scone, hoping for distraction, and took a bite, dropping crumbs onto the table. Miss Keighly reached across and brushed the crumbs to the side for him, then gave him a disapproving look. Would this be his life?

A ward who had aged him ten years in nine months, a wife who would live according to contract, and another woman who had his heart but would not have *him*.

What a brilliant life he'd created for himself. In this moment, he wondered what had ever made him think he could charge back to England and right all the wrongs.

Chapter Twenty-Seven

Aiden returned home and explained to Catherine that Miss Keighly would be staying in town for a few days.

"She came from Cheshire?" Catherine said, unable to hide a delightful look in her eye that did nothing to help Aiden's growing headache. "What a lovely surprise."

He restrained himself from blaming her. "We are having tea with Miss Keighly at the White Hart in two hours. I would like to lie down until it is time for us to leave." Miss Keighly had taken rooms there for the next fortnight while they finalized their plans.

"I am invited?" Catherine asked hopefully.

"Miss Keighly's companion, Mrs. Hobart, will return here with you if you are not on your best behavior."

"Oh, I will be on my *best* behavior." It was spoken as though Aiden had invited her to the circus. The girl had an unhealthy desire for drama. He almost hoped Catherine wouldn't behave herself at the tea so that Hazel would see what she was getting herself into, then regretted the thought. He needed to move forward with the agreement he had made, which meant helping form a positive relationship between Catherine and Miss Keighly.

He laid on the bed with one arm thrown over his eyes for two hours, until it was time for their appointment at the White Hart. Over tea in the well-furnished sitting room reserved for hotel guests, Miss Keighly engaged Catherine in polite conversation, which Catherine was perfectly responsive to. Miss Keighly complimented Catherine's frock, and Catherine fairly glowed. Apparently, she had decided she would be on Miss Keighly's side of things. What luck.

After tea, they returned Catherine to Laura Place—even her protests were muted in Miss Keighly's company—and then he escorted Miss Keighly back to Milsom Street so she could see the shops. Glimpses of the river appeared here and there between the buildings, and at one point she stopped. "Is there a way to walk the bank of the river?"

The steps that would lead them to Lenora's wall were just a few shops ahead of them, but it would be sacrilegious to take Miss Keighly there. "There is a nice park on the south side of the bridge with steps that lead to the river's edge," he said. "But we'll need to go back the way we've come."

Hazel frowned and shook her head. "It is getting chilly," she said, stepping closer to him as though for warmth. "And I do not love to be out after dark. Perhaps tomorrow, after services.

I understand they start at eight o'clock. Please fetch me from my rooms at a quarter past seven so that we are sure to be on time."

Aiden agreed, but felt sick. He took Catherine to services at the abbey every Sunday. Though they did not sit with Lenora and Mrs. Simmons, Miss Wilton would see Miss Keighly and feel betrayed all over again. Only a few hours ago, he had all but begged Lenora to give him a second chance, and now, the morning following that exchange, she would watch him walk into services with his fiancée on his arm. She would think that he was exactly what she'd already decided he was—a cad and a flirt without honor or decency. Maybe she was right.

Catherine did not dawdle in her preparations the next morning, clearly eager to see Miss Keighly again. When they fetched Miss Keighly from her rooms, she immediately retied the bow on the back of Catherine's dress and disapproved of Catherine's choice of shoes. They were dance slippers and not meant to be worn on the street. Catherine's mood became more reserved, but she accepted Miss Keighly's comments with far more tact than Aiden expected.

Because they arrived a full thirty minutes before services started, Aiden, Catherine, and Miss Keighly took seats near the front, which meant he would not see Lenora or Mrs. Simmons when they arrived. It was just as well; Aiden was sweating and fidgety enough just knowing they would be there.

He imagined the look on Lenora's face—no, that was no good. She didn't show her emotions on her face. He thought of how she would *feel*, and his heart ached. Maybe he should leave Bath sooner than he'd anticipated, but Catherine was doing much better. She'd told him about the duet she'd learned with Lenora and repeated the French verb conjugations she had memorized. There was no choice but to swallow his pride and regret and accept that Lenora would hate him forever. Maybe knowing that would make it easier to commit himself to Miss Keighly and the bleak future he saw for them.

The sermon was on charity—or maybe repentance—he wasn't listening because he was trying to identify Lenora's presence behind him. Miss Keighly pinched Catherine's arm when she dozed off, causing the girl to jump and Aiden to tense. If Catherine threw one of her fits of temper here . . .

By the time they stood at the conclusion of services, the aisles were a crush, and he could not pick any one person from the crowd of hats and bonnets bobbing ahead of him on their way out of the abbey and into the churchyard. He dared to think that perhaps he had avoided them entirely until he heard Catherine call out.

"Aunt Gwen, over here!" He looked over his shoulder to see the girl waving, quite improperly. Miss Keighly took hold of Catherine's arm and reprimanded her, but Catherine pulled out of her grasp and darted through the parishioners. He pasted a smile on his face and led Miss Keighly after his niece; he may as well get it over with.

Lenora stood in profile to him, listening to another woman recount some travel experience, but he felt sure her attention was attuned to his approach. Her expression was unreadable when he reached the cluster of women, who all turned to face him.

"Good morning," he said, bowing slightly.

"Good morning, Mr. Asher," Mrs. Simmons said, though he could feel her coolness toward the woman on his arm. She gestured to the other women in the group. "You know Mrs. Crawford and Miss Crawford."

Aiden was glad for the reminder; he'd met them once at the Pump Room—an older woman and her middle-aged daughter—but had not remembered their names. "A pleasure to see you again," he said, nodding. "And may I introduce Miss Hazel Keighly."

"His fiancée," Miss Keighly said when he did not supply their connection as he should have.

Mrs. Simmons eyebrows shot upward before her expression became as neutral as Lenora's. Catherine looked smug, as though she'd planned this. She hadn't, had she? Could she? He was suspicious enough of his niece and what she had done thus far that it would be foolish of him not to wonder.

"Wonderful to meet you," Mrs. Simmons said evenly, dipping slightly.

Miss Keighly smiled. "As it is to meet you, Mrs. Simmons." She turned to Lenora, whose face was a mask of polite calm, but Aiden could see the panic in the tightness around her eyes. "And you must be Miss Wilton, Catherine's teacher."

Lenora nodded, but Aiden felt sure she was dying inside, much like he was. "Pleased to meet you, Miss Keighly."

Another woman might have added something like "I've

heard so little about you" or "I had no idea you were coming to Bath" simply to put an edge on the blade, but not Lenora. Her lack of guile made Aiden feel even worse, as though she had crawled as far into her shell as she possibly could, unwilling to reveal any level of feelings she had for him. Unless she truly felt nothing. But if that were the case, she would not push him away so strongly, nor show any pain in her eyes right now.

Miss Keighly beamed. "The pleasure is all mine, I assure you. I was just about to ask Mr. Asher if he might attend me to the parade gardens. Would you care to walk with me instead? I have some questions about Catherine's education that I would very much like to discuss with you."

"We have a visit arranged with my brother this afternoon," Mrs. Crawford said. "If you'll excuse us. Lovely to meet you, Miss Keighly."

Lenora glanced at her aunt during the Crawfords' farewells, the panic in her eyes growing into terror. Mrs. Simmons looked equally trapped.

"Perhaps another time," Aiden said, trying to rescue them. "On a day when the weather is more temperate." Too late, he looked up at the clear blue sky and noted the warmth of the day—rare for October.

"The weather is lovely, Mr. Asher," Miss Keighly said. "There is no reason to put off such an important conversation." She gave him a look of mild reprimand, stepped up to Lenora, and put her arm through hers before expertly turning her toward the promenade.

Aiden looked after them, then at Mrs. Simmons, certain she

could see the misery in his eyes. She seemed to interpret his dilemma, because after only a moment's hesitation, she took his arm. "Catherine, dear. You may walk ahead of us, if you will, so that we might keep you in sight."

"Can we return home, Uncle Aiden?" Catherine whined like a child much younger than her years. "Cook made gingerbread today."

"Catherine," Mrs. Simmons said in a voice a degree lower than usual.

Catherine harrumphed but did as she was told. If not for the stone in his chest, Aiden would have been impressed with the girl's compliance, but he could think of little else but the two women walking ahead of them. He could tell by the way the feathers in Miss Keighly's bonnet bobbed that she was doing all the talking. He ran a finger around his collar, which was tightening like a noose around his neck.

"Please do explain yourself, Mr. Asher," Mrs. Simmons suggested when Catherine was far enough ahead to not overhear. The older woman kept a tight but believable smile on her face. She nodded to an acquaintance as they passed before speaking again. "Perhaps if I better understand your motives, I shall stop thinking of ways to push you into a fountain as soon as the opportunity presents itself."

Yes, push me in, Aiden thought. *Hold me under. Let me drown!*

"She arrived to Bath yesterday without giving me any warning of her coming," he said, equally low.

"I assume your engagement is still intact then?" The accusation in her voice was cutting.

"Yes." He felt Mrs. Simmons's hand tighten on his arm.

They walked in silence. "I had thought your affections were in another quarter."

"They are." He was about to explain that Lenora had put him off yesterday when Catherine ran back to them.

"Could we go for ices today?" she asked, her eyes wide.

"Not on the Sabbath, my dear," Mrs. Simmons said, then shooed the girl forward.

Catherine frowned, but she turned again and moved forward, waving when she spotted a friend from school and hurrying to catch up with her.

When she was far enough ahead, Mrs. Simmons cleared her throat. "Women are supposed to be the more complex sex, Mr. Asher, but you have surpassed every woman I have ever met. I am completely befuddled."

So he explained, or tried to, but it sounded even more ridiculous to say out loud what he had lived these last sixteen hours. He suspected she knew the gist of his conversation with Lenora yesterday since she did not show much reaction. "And so I am left with a niece still in need of stability, a woman still willing to accept my suit despite knowing I'm in love with another, and the woman I love telling me not to break the engagement."

"You will go forward with Miss Keighly?"

"I need to build a future. Hazel is a good woman." He sounded weak-minded settling for a manager instead of love. "And Lenora will not have me."

"Lenora does not trust easily," Mrs. Simmons said. "She was with me for months before she shared personal information with me in conversation, yet I have seen her blossom. Teaching was a great social education for her, ironically. Bath has given her new life, and before these last few weeks, she seemed more at peace than I had ever seen her. I even dared guess you were the reason, though she refused to acknowledge such a thing. Now? Well, she's back to the girl I knew two years ago. She has locked herself away, and I have not succeeded in drawing her out. She's running from the merest hint of gossip and embarrassment and judgment."

"There's been no gossip for her to run away from," Aiden said. "I have been very attentive to that possibility, and, after two weeks, I'm quite sure that Mrs. Henry was true to her word and no scandal has resulted from what happened between us, besides comments that I stole away the best music teacher the school has had in nearly five years."

Mrs. Simmons looked at him. "I agree that there have been no whispers, but that was never what she was truly running from, Mr. Asher. With the engagement in Leagrave, she dared believe in something that was not to be and suffered greatly when it fell apart. She did not love him, which is the only reason I believe she was able to recover."

"Are you saying that she *does* love me?" He could not decide if he wanted her to love him or not. To know his feelings were reciprocated made him want to shout in triumph, but if she *did* love him and still turned him away, there was nothing to rejoice in. Circumstances would remain just as they were.

"She trusted you with something that was not to be, again."

"By her choice, not mine. She told me not to break the—"

"By her *necessity*," Mrs. Simmons cut in. They walked a few steps in silence as she gathered her thoughts. "My late husband was a gambler—not to our ruin, praise the heavens—but when I complained against it, he would tell me that he never risked more than he could afford to lose. Now, he and I would argue about how much that should be, but the sentiment is applicable here. Lenora feels things deeply and wholly, far more than she lets on. If she had not told me herself of your tryst on the riverbank, I'd have *never* believed it. I still can't believe she was walking the streets at night all those months." She shook her head as if remembering her shock. "I believe she feels she risked more than she could afford to lose when she opened her heart to you, Mr. Asher, and it has left her bankrupt. In addition to her difficulties in understanding your feelings for her, and hers for you, for you to break your engagement to Miss Keighly means that she is part of another woman losing more than *she* can afford as well."

Aiden considered that for a moment. "Miss Keighly is not so invested as you think," he said, careful not to sound demeaning. "She believes she is doing me a favor by not allowing me to break the engagement for a temporary infatuation, as she called it. She wants to move forward with our marriage and . . ." He paused, considering carefully whether or not to explain everything about Miss Keighly's investment. What did he have to lose? "She even offered to add a mistress clause to our marriage agreement so that after Lenora is finished teaching Catherine, she might . . ."

He thought Mrs. Simmons might gasp or stop walking, but

she did not, though when he cast a sidelong look at her, he saw that her cheeks were flushed.

"If you do not *already* know that Lenora would never agree to such a thing, we shall put an end to every connection we have this very minute," she said firmly.

"I absolutely know she would never agree, nor would I ever offer such a thing." He could not say the words quickly enough. "I was horrified by the suggestion, and I only tell you now to show you how different Miss Keighly's investment is from what you or Lenora think it is."

"Yet you will still marry her?"

The question sparked his continued frustration. "Lenora has told me I am a man without honor and she wants no part in a shared future. Miss Keighly is still willing to assume the role of mother to Catherine and is not even swayed by knowing my heart is engaged elsewhere. If I knew there was hope in changing Lenora's mind, perhaps I *would* break the engagement, but there would be a scandal, which Lenora would be drawn into." His shoulders slumped. "And Lenora has told me not to do it. I cannot change her mind."

"Unless, of course, you can."

The frustration bubbled up again, and he had to take a calming breath to keep from shouting. "I have explained myself— twice—and she has given absolutely no indication that she has left the door open even a crack for me. How am I to build on that?"

"To start, you have no chance at all to let her see the whole of your good character so long as you are parading your fiancée around town."

Had she not heard him explain the complexity of the situation?

Mrs. Simmons continued. "So Miss Keighly must be the one to break it, therefore avoiding both the scandal of you having to do so and the ridiculousness of you marrying her."

He wanted to throw his arms up in the air. Had Mrs. Simmons heard nothing he'd said? Instead, he took a steadying breath and spoke as calmly as he could, though it still came out through his teeth. "I was very clear with Miss Keighly. She has refused to end the engagement."

Mrs. Simmons gave him a pointed look that he did not understand. Then she smiled and called out, "Catherine, dear."

Catherine turned and came back to them, having already said good-bye to the friend she'd walked with for a time. Mrs. Simmons put a hand on her shoulder. "Your uncle has just told me the most exciting news. He's taking you and Miss Keighly to the opera on Wednesday night. Won't that be wonderful?"

Catherine scrunched up her nose. "I hate the opera."

"Oh, fiddlesticks," Mrs. Simmons said, putting her arm through Catherine's so that she walked between Aiden and his niece. "You have that lovely velvet dress with the French lace your uncle ordered for you, and we shall have Dorothea put up your hair. You can use my ostrich feathers. You will look like a real lady, and won't Miss Keighly be impressed."

Aiden knew what she was doing—hoping that Catherine would be the one to dissuade Miss Keighly, but it would not work. Catherine behaved herself around Miss Keighly and seemed to have already chosen her as the woman she would support as Aiden's future wife. As Catherine was right there, Aiden could not explain this to Mrs. Simmons, nor did he particularly want to. Mrs. Simmons was involving herself in a plan to cause Miss Keighly to cry off the engagement, which gave him just enough hope to . . . hope.

A few minutes later, Miss Keighly was back on Mr. Asher's arm as the groups parted company. Lenora was too tight and tense and overwhelmed to do anything but walk and try to breathe. Aunt Gwen cast furtive glances at Lenora as they headed toward home, but Lenora kept her expression unreadable and gave one-word answers. Finally, Aunt Gwen went silent.

"Did you invite them to dinner?" Lenora asked.

"Invite who?"

"Mr. Asher and Miss Keighly. Did you invite them to dinner?"

"No," Aunt Gwen said.

Lenora relaxed, but only slightly.

"Perhaps you would like to talk about—"

"I would not," Lenora interrupted.

"I think that—"

Lenora stopped and did not speak until their eyes met. "I will not discuss it, Aunt Gwen. And I will not tolerate any interference on your part. Am I clear?" Tears welled up in Lenora's eyes, but she attempted to blink them away.

"Gracious, child," Aunt Gwen said, placing a hand on

Lenora's arm. She'd never seen Lenora cry, and Lenora did not want today to be any different.

"I must have your word that you will not invite them to dinner. If you do," Lenora continued, still blinking, "I will leave Bath forever and never look back. That is how strongly I feel about this." She looked away a moment to compose herself, then back to Aunt Gwen. "Do you understand?"

Aunt Gwen nodded but said nothing.

Lenora extracted her arm and took a step back. "I think I shall skip our walk today, Aunt, and take a shorter route home. I am not fit for company."

"Certainly, my dear. Have Cook make you a tonic and perhaps lie down. I shall check in on you in time for tea."

Lenora nodded and hurried off in the direction of Gay Street. Anger and humiliation and heavy, heavy regret made her feet slow and her chin tremble. She put her head down in hopes no one would stop her and counted her steps until she reached the terrace house where she could finally hide.

Chapter Twenty-Eight

L enora spent Sunday afternoon in her room. After leaving
her aunt and walking home alone, she'd come back to the
terrace house and cried as she had not cried in the weeks since
she'd received Aiden's letter of explanation.

Miss Keighly was confident and composed, interested in
Catherine's education, and as well-mannered as any woman
ever was. Had Lenora not already made her decision about Mr.
Asher's attention—that she would not receive it—meeting his
fiancée would have convinced her that she hadn't a chance. Miss
Keighly was everything Lenora was not, and she would have
everything Lenora never would. Eventually, Lenora fell asleep,
only to be awakened by tapping at her door when it was time
for tea.

"I'm afraid I have a terrible headache," Lenora said, her
head feeling twice its size and pounding like a drum. She had
planned to rest and then drown her sorrows upon the keys of

the pianoforte, perhaps indulging in some obscure Zumsteeg pieces. Instead, she'd indulged in self-pity.

It was not Aunt Gwen at the door; instead, it was Dorthea with some rum, which Lenora drank. She coughed and sputtered, then she burrowed back under the covers and stared at the pattern of stripes and roses on the papered wall, exhausted despite having slept.

The more she tried not to think of Mr. Asher, the more clearly his face showed in her mind. The more she tried to ignore her interview with Miss Keighly—and it was very much an interview—the smaller she felt in comparison to the woman Mr. Asher would marry.

When dinnertime arrived, she begged off again and spent the rest of the evening preparing for her Monday lessons with Catherine. Miss Keighly's questions regarding Lenora's teaching methods made her want to improve her plans, though she could not think of a single reason why she should want to impress this woman. Never mind that this could very well be her last week of teaching—come Friday, her two-week commitment to Aunt Gwen would be fulfilled. She could stop if she chose. Whether or not she would, however, she did not know. There had been undeniable improvement between her and Catherine. The teacher in Lenora was eager to see if this week might show similar improvement. Every other part of her wanted to flee to Mary's house and a new, unknown future as soon as she possibly could.

Lenora took breakfast in the morning room the next day, and then moved to the pianoforte, allowing the music to center her while she waited for Catherine to arrive. When she did, Lenora smiled and nodded, but finished playing through the Playel concerto. She let her hands rest on the keys so that the very last bits of the music would find their way inside of her.

"Shall we remove to the schoolroom?" she asked as she stood.

Catherine shrugged in resignation, but followed Lenora to the second level. They took their respective seats at the desk, and Lenora was grateful for the excitement she felt. The extra time she'd given to planning this week's lessons, and reviewing last week's lessons, had helped her identify which styles of teaching Catherine responded to best and which subjects needed to be taken in smaller portions.

"Today we will address the O-U sound, which is a hard 'oh', an 'oo,' and an 'ow' sound, depending on which word it appears in. Your memorization skills will be an asset with this combination, I think, as the rules don't always apply."

Catherine let out a burdened breath but listened as Lenora explained the lesson. Lenora wiped off the slate so that Catherine could write the words *you, thou, our, out,* and *about,* looking at the list in the primer to make sure she spelled them correctly. She looked back and forth several times, which made Lenora smile because it showed that Catherine wanted to do well. They sounded through the words a few times before Catherine suddenly crossed her arms on the table and gave Lenora a hard look.

"Are you very angry with Uncle Aiden?"

Lenora did not meet her eye. She wiped off the slate and wished her neck hadn't flushed hot at the mention of his name.

"I would like you to write the words again, Catherine, but without looking at the primer this time. I shall say the word, and you write it." She pushed the slate to Catherine, who pushed it back to Lenora.

Lenora held her eyes. "This is your first warning."

Catherine narrowed her eyes. "She's going to be my *mother*—that's what Uncle Aiden says." There was sarcasm in her tone, but what caught Lenora's attention was the part about her uncle having told her.

Lenora had gone over the timeline a hundred times. Miss Keighly had been in Bath Saturday, perhaps at the same time Mr. Asher had been in Aunt Gwen's drawing room making his appeals to Lenora. Did he leave the terrace house and return to Miss Keighly straightaway? Did he take her to the river and kiss her until she could not breathe so as to replace the memory of his kiss with Lenora? Did his fiancée even know about their kiss? What if Lenora had accepted his offer of a second chance instead of putting him off so resolutely? What would he have done then? Flipped a coin, maybe? Kissed them both and chosen his favorite?

Catherine was watching Lenora closely enough that she feared the girl could read her mind. She reminded herself that Mr. Asher was a liar and a cad. She did not want him. Except that some part of her still did. "Every girl should have a mother, Catherine. I wish them happy." That the words did not choke her felt like a victory.

"I used to like her, but now I think she's a cow."

Lenora turned sharp eyes on Catherine. "That is inappropriate, and you are not to talk about anyone in such terms."

"I have met her before, you know," Catherine continued. "We had tea with her and once we went on a carriage ride. She was very nice to me, then, but I do not think I like her anymore, and I do not think she likes me either. Yesterday, she would not let me attend tea with her and Uncle Aiden, and then she dismissed me from supper when I used the wrong fork."

"And I'm sure using the wrong fork was an accident." Lenora massaged her temple, reminding herself to be cautious and not let her thoughts or her tongue run too free.

"I think she is overparticular and dull," Catherine said.

"There are worse attributes," Lenora said, thinking of her nerves and inability to interact with the world around her. Could there be a better word to describe Lenora than *dull*? The thought flattened her already flat mood. She *was* dull. And boring, and anxious, and untrusting. She was not an interesting person who could hope to keep a man's attention. Perhaps that was as much a reason for her putting off Mr. Asher as his own displays of poor character. Who would ever choose Lenora? Evan Glenside hadn't—he'd chosen Cassie's vibrant demeanor and charm. And Mr. Asher hadn't—he'd chosen Miss Keighly, who would make a fine wife and mother.

"I do not think there *are* worse attributes," Catherine said, sounding thoughtful. "He does not love her, you know."

"Love is only one part of the equation, Catherine, and engagements are legal contracts, on the man's part at least. He is doing right by her to continue the engagement, and it is below either of us to question their potential for happiness."

Catherine rested her chin on her hands, but continued to look at Lenora. "My father did not love my mother either."

The confession surprised Lenora and tugged at her continued question as to what caused this girl to be so difficult. Could this be a part of the answer? It was a sad thought. "I'm sure that is not true," Lenora said, her voice sympathetic. "Love grows between husband and wife even when it is not present at the start."

"It *is* true," Catherine said, her voice sad and soft and humble. Lenora had never heard the like of it from this girl. "Aunt Elizabeth told me during one of her rages. She said, 'You are just like your mother. It is no wonder your father couldn't stand her any more than I can stand you!'"

Lenora's heart melted. "Oh, Catherine, please tell me she did not say such a thing."

Catherine did not nod, but the vulnerability in her eyes confirmed the truth. The girl looked away, her finger tracing the wood grain on the desk, her head still resting on one arm. "And then I heard Mrs. Asher—Uncle Aiden's aunt—telling her friends that my mother was the most disagreeable hoyden she had ever met, and that if she hadn't seduced Edwin—that's my father—he would have never shackled himself to such a woman."

Lenora's heart ached, and yet she was aware that Catherine was trusting her with something important. She considered reaching out and placing her hand on Catherine's arm, but it seemed too intimate. What if it broke this moment growing between them? "I'm very sorry those women said such horrible things about your mother, Catherine. It was wrong of them."

Catherine drew her arm closer, so both her elbows rested on

the table, her chin on her overlapping hands. She met Lenora's eyes; whatever openness that had been there was now opaque, but not closed completely. "It is not wrong of them if it is true."

"Cruelty is wrong whether there is any truth in it or not, and they were cruel to say such things." She paused. She was not used to being a confidante or giving advice on important matters. What those women had said had seeped into this girl's belief about herself, and Lenora felt the need to say something that might reverse the recriminations. "Beyond that, you are the person who will define your character, Catherine. Not your mother or these mean-spirited women."

Catherine blinked at her, and then said softly, as though afraid of someone overhearing. "What if I am just like her?"

Another melting sensation in Lenora's chest caused her to finally reach out her hand and place it on Catherine's arm. "*That* is impossible. Every soul is its own, and though we may share attributes with others—especially blood relatives—we are our own selves. God made you who you are, Catherine, and you are unique unto yourself and capable of defining your own measure in this world."

Catherine turned her head so she was laying on one ear and looking out the window. The movement also meant she laid her head on Lenora's hand. With a quick prayer for continued success, Lenora extracted her hand slowly and smoothed Catherine's hair. She was prepared for Catherine to sit up at any moment, throw off her touch, and make some horrid accusation, but she stared at the window for several seconds instead, doing nothing to stop Lenora's tender attentions.

When she spoke, it was in that same whisper, as if telling a secret. "But I'm so bad."

Lenora stilled her hand on Catherine's curls, then gently took hold of her chin and turned the girl's face so she could meet her eye. "You are *not* bad."

"Yes, I am. It is why Aunt Elizabeth and Mrs. Asher got rid of me. It is why I can't go to school anymore and why everyone hates me."

"I do not hate you. Aunt Gwen does not hate you." She paused before finishing. "Your uncle and Miss Keighly do not hate you."

Catherine looked doubtful and so very young and insecure. Lenora removed her hand and mirrored Catherine's position, arms crossed on the desk and her chin on her hands. It put them at eye level across the desk. "Do you know that after Aunt Gwen met you for the first time on the promenade, she said, 'That girl is delightful.' I have to admit I was surprised. I had had nothing but trouble from you." Catherine narrowed her eyes, but Lenora pushed on. "You know that to be true, Catherine, so let us speak as friends."

Catherine nodded as much as she could with her head on her arms, but her defensiveness did not disappear completely.

Lenora chose her words carefully. "Do you know that in the weeks since, I have come to agree with my aunt. Not to say that you and I don't have our troubles and that there aren't times when I want to box your ears, but you are a remarkable girl in many ways."

"Because I can play the pianoforte." She said it as a fact, with a bored tone that Lenora completely understood.

Lenora was often complimented for her musical ability, for which she was grateful, but not without noticing that it was *only* thing she was complimented on. Where her sisters would be complimented on this talent, or that ability, or an accomplishment or clever comment, Lenora only had her music. The result of such singular praise made her sometimes feel as though her abilities were her very identity, that no one saw anything more than her skill.

Perhaps Catherine felt as Lenora did—that the only thing anyone admired in her was her ability to play. Such a belief could make someone feel very small and very scared that if something should happen to that trait, she would find herself without any worth at all. Lenora had once jammed her finger in the door and been unable to play for two weeks; it had felt as though part of herself had disappeared.

"Your skill at the pianoforte is exceptional, but that is not what makes you remarkable. What makes you remarkable is the way you can brighten an entire room when you are of a mind to do so. The way you make Aunt Gwen smile. The way you converse so easily with adults—most girls your age cannot do that. I have seen you act in the role of a leader to other girls your age and show amazing dedication to a topic when it interests you. You have a keen mind and . . ."

Catherine's scowl caused Lenora to trail off. "I cannot even read. A teacher at my last school called me an idiot with a pretty face and a too-sharp tongue. Miss Keighly told me yesterday that I was not fit for proper company."

Lenora winced, angry with all these adults who had been cruel to this child. "I agree on the pretty face and sharp tongue, but not on your being an idiot. You are working harder than most girls would or could, and you are learning." Lenora believed what she said, though she still had concerns.

Catherine struggled with basic words and continued mixing up the order of letters, often without realizing it unless Lenora pointed it out. She would make the same mistakes over and over again, as though she could not remember the correction, and yet she remembered enough to be frustrated. With herself, mostly, though she was proficient at turning that frustration on others.

"Lack of one ability does not minimize the others you possess. You make friends easily, and you . . . understand people. Too much sometimes."

Catherine managed a smile at that.

"Do you know what I think?" Lenora said in a conspiratorial whisper of her own. "I think there is so much going on in that amazing mind of yours that it left out reading to make room. I think that because circumstances were hard for you when you were young, you developed some habits. Some good—like reading peoples' gestures to determine their thoughts and expectations—and some bad—like knowing how to upset people and take control of a situation if things are not working in your favor.

"The challenge for all of us, myself included, is to use our strengths as a way of overcoming our weaknesses. To be able to look back from every place we find ourselves in life and see that we are better now than we were before. I look at the Catherine of today and the Catherine of two weeks ago and see improvement. Because of that, I can only imagine what I shall see in a few months' time." No sooner had she said it then she wished she could take it back. Her two-week trial was over this Friday, and though she had not made a plan, it seemed she'd just committed herself to another two weeks at least.

Catherine held her eyes, and Lenora sensed she was weighing what Lenora had said and trying to decide if she could trust it. This was something else they had in common—neither of them trusted easily but had learned to read the people around them and act in a way that protected them. For Lenora, she kept herself apart. For Catherine, she drew attention away from whatever made her uncomfortable. Two remedies for the same problem—fear of being rejected by the people around them.

"I'm sorry I wrote that letter to Mrs. Henry," Catherine said, surprising Lenora yet again. "Or rather, forced the maid to write it. I am sorry you had to leave the school." Catherine had never apologized to Lenora for the letter that had changed everything, and yet, not changed anything, really. Mr. Asher had been engaged all along, letter or no letter, which meant Lenora's heart would have been broken one way or another.

Lenora managed a smile, though it was not entirely genuine due to the reminder of how painful it had all been, and still was. "I forgive you, Catherine. Thank you for the apology." She sat back up and busied herself with the primer, then thought of something and looked at Catherine. "How did you know we would be at the river that night?"

There was a glint in Catherine's eye, an involuntary display of the pleasure she found in mischief. "I can tell what people are saying even if I cannot hear them."

Lenora furrowed her eyebrows. "What?"

"A person's lips move to form words," Catherine explained. "When we came to dinner, you left to show those old people to the door, and when you came back, Uncle Aiden talked to you about going to the river. You told him no, but then when we were leaving, you nodded at him and he smiled back."

"That's remarkable," Lenora said, careful to keep any judgment from her voice. "But that does not explain how you knew we were there three weeks later."

Catherine just smiled, lifted her head, and pulled the slate back to herself, the familiar arrogance back in her demeanor. She picked up her chalk pencil. "O-U makes an 'oh' sound and an 'oo' sound and an 'ow' sound. Which sound shall we start with today, Miss Wilton?"

Lenora gave in, certain she would get nothing more from Catherine, but grateful for the insight she'd gained today. It was a welcome mercy. "Let us start with the 'ow' sound this time. *Our, out, about, thou, shout . . .*"

Chapter Twenty-Nine

Aiden attended Miss Keighly to the Pump Room Monday morning, grateful when she ran into an acquaintance who was staying in Bath for the winter. After a polite amount of time, he excused himself from their company, claiming correspondence he needed to address. Miss Keighly frowned, but agreed when her friend expressed how lovely it would be to spend the morning together.

Aiden hoped that her friend was excessively lonely and would seek as much of Miss Keighly's attention as possible. He did have a great deal of correspondence to attend to, as well as the continued study of several documents regarding the estate.

He had been communicating with the family's solicitor, the estate steward, and any number of professionals engaged in past management. There was much to learn, but he was dedicated and determined to do his best. Catherine would inherit the entire estate one day, and he wanted the transition to be as smooth as possible. Within the next few weeks, he would need to visit Cheshire; there was only so much he could learn from a distance. He had hoped that Catherine would be established enough that his leaving for a fortnight would be possible, but he was not sure whether or not that was a viable plan now. It seemed a terrible imposition to ask Mrs. Simmons to take the girl for weekends too after she was already doing him such a favor. Perhaps he could put the estate visit off until the Christmas holiday when Catherine could come with him—Lenora's tutoring kept the same calendar as Mrs. Henry's school.

Miss Keighly sent around a note later that afternoon inviting him to escort her to dinner, and he steeled himself as he chose his evening dress for the occasion. He needed to learn to enjoy her company. The rest of his life would be miserable if he did not, but then, if Mrs. Simmons's plan was successful, perhaps he still had an alternative.

As he buttoned up his waistcoat—the plain black silk Miss Keighly had suggested—he paused and began undoing the buttons instead. Miss Keighly was excessively attentive to etiquette, which dictated that a gentleman was to wear a plain waistcoat, preferably white or black, for formal dinners. Only the eccentric and the dandies would wear a colored or patterned garment, which sent Aiden to his wardrobe, where he fingered through the half dozen waistcoats he owned. That his own tastes were rather simple irritated him slightly; he did not own anything that would be considered boisterous. But he did have a silver waistcoat with purple birds sewed into the pattern. It would have to do. Mrs. Simmons was doing her part—though he was unsure what exactly her plan was—the least he could do was play his part. Even if he ended up marrying Miss Keighly—something he dared not hope for or against anymore—he would not allow her to dictate his clothing choices.

Miss Keighly's eyes were drawn immediately to his waistcoat as soon as he entered the foyer of the White Hart. She scowled sharply, and as soon as they were seated in the dining room, she remarked on his choice. "Did I not specify that you wear a black waistcoat?"

"Do you not like this one?" Aiden said, straightening his back as though to help her get a better view.

"No, actually, I do not. It does not suit you. It makes you look, at best, to be a man who shrugs off societal expectations, and at worst, a rake."

He had to smile at the distaste in her tone. "A rake? Truly?" Lenora had accused him of the same, but he'd found no humor in it then.

Miss Keighly's mood did not lighten. She scowled and took a sip of her wine. When she lowered the glass, her expression had recovered. "I would like to discuss the plantation in Jamaica. Please do remind me of the acreage, tenants, and crops."

Aiden was relieved. This was a topic he quite enjoyed, and they spent the rest of the evening discussing the details of the plantation, which was his sole holding. He hoped to purchase something in England before Catherine inherited the Cheshire estate once she either married or turned twenty-nine years of age. He couldn't help but admire Miss Keighly's interest and questions, but he also couldn't help but wonder if Lenora would be equally interested.

Wednesday was the night of the opera, and Aiden's heart was in his throat. Catherine had attended the opera with him during a trip to London before and proclaimed it the most boring evening of her life. She'd kept tapping her feet and sighing loudly, distracting the people around them. When intermission came, she darted through the crowd, and it took him ten full minutes before he found her in the coffee room with a plate of biscuits and a cup of tea, quite at her leisure, sitting on a chair that did not allow her feet to touch the ground.

They had left rather than staying for the second half, and Catherine had been quite pleased with the change of plans. Aiden knew Mrs. Simmons was expecting Catherine's bad behavior to be on display in hopes it would cause Miss Keighly to reconsider their arrangement. He was hopeful the goal would be reached, but anxious about the discomfort ahead. He also worried about the lack of consistency for Catherine. It felt wrong to encourage disobedience when they had worked so hard to improve her behavior, which meant he would have to discourage it while secretly hoping she would misbehave enough to put Miss Keighly off. He hated the complexity, but if Miss Keighly broke the engagement, he could have another chance with Lenora.

He shook his head as he tied his own cravat—he'd become self-sufficient during his time in Jamaica, where it was difficult to find a decent valet. He wondered for the hundredth time why

Lenora was so invigorating to him. He knew little of her family or childhood, her politics, or her preferences in literature. That he liked everything he *did* know about her was the biggest attraction, and yet that there was more to her than the traditional gentlewoman was also appealing. When they were together, the air became rich, and his senses were keen.

He had chosen Miss Keighly months ago because she was everything he'd come to expect in a gentlewoman, and she had been accepting of his situation. He *wanted* Lenora, however, because there was more to her than met the eye, and he longed to discover what lay beneath. He smoothed his cravat and thought only of the evening ahead—he must not get distracted. As long as Miss Keighly was engaged to him, Lenora was out of reach.

He had rented a carriage for the evening, though most of the patrons would walk, and drew up in front of Mrs. Simmons's terrace house to collect Catherine. Jacobson let him in, and he waited in the entryway.

When Catherine descended the stairs with Mrs. Simmons, he couldn't help but grin. Catherine fairly glowed with confidence, and in the moment, she was not a twelve-year-old girl who drove the adults around her mad, but rather she was a young lady on the brink of womanhood. Her hair was curled about her face and pinned up in the back, complete with Mrs. Simmons's promised ostrich feathers. The blue velvet of her dress was lovely, and silver slippers peeked out from the hem as she walked.

When she reached the bottom of the stairs, Aiden put one hand behind his back and the other across his waist before bowing deeply. "Might I be the lucky man to have the honor of escorting you to tonight's performance, Miss Manch? You are an absolute vision."

Catherine giggled, then immediately put a hand over her mouth, eyes wide. Mrs. Simmons and Aiden exchanged a look before both of them burst out laughing. Catherine *never* giggled.

"Stop funning me," Catherine said as she put both hands on her hips—a much more familiar reaction.

"Yes, m'lady," Aiden said, pinching his lips together and winking at Mrs. Simmons, who showed equal difficulty in hiding her own mirth. Jacobson helped Catherine don a fur-lined cloak while Aiden glanced up the stairs, wishing Lenora had come to see them off. When he looked away, he caught Mrs. Simmons watching him with a sympathetic smile. He turned his attention to Catherine and put out his arm. Catherine took it as though she were the very lady he hoped to raise her into one day. "I shall return her after the performance, Mrs. Simmons."

"I shall wait up so that I might hear all about it." She walked them to the door and gave Catherine a quick kiss on the forehead. Catherine attempted to pull away, but the smile on her face showed that she was pleased by the attention.

"You really do look lovely, Catherine," Aiden said as they walked down the steps toward the carriage where Miss Keighly waited.

"Thank you, Uncle Aiden." She sounded almost shy about the compliment, and Aiden filed away the reaction. Perhaps he should find more reasons to compliment her in the future.

He handed her into the carriage and then sat beside her,

across from Miss Keighly, who smiled at Catherine. "Good evening, Catherine."

"Good evening, Hazel."

She scowled. "You are to call me Miss Keighly."

Catherine scowled back. "Sorry, I forgot."

"See that you remember in the future, my dear. You look very nice."

Catherine brightened and adjusted her skirts. "Thank you."

Miss Keighly looked at her expectantly. "When someone compliments you, it is good manners to return the compliment."

Catherine scrunched up her face with a calculating look Aiden knew well. "What if you cannot think of a compliment in return? Lying is a sin after all."

Miss Keighly's smile did not falter. "You can always find *something* nice to say about someone."

Catherine looked doubtful and began fiddling with the latches on the window in order to lower the glass.

"It is too cold for that," Aiden told her, reaching over to remove her hands from the latch. "And the wind might dislodge your feathers."

Catherine slumped in her seat and crossed her arms over her chest with a harrumph.

"Young ladies do not pout, Catherine," Miss Keighly said.

Catherine glared at her.

Miss Keighly turned her eyes to him and lifted her eyebrows. Did she want him to reprimand Catherine? Aiden began to sweat.

"Shall we practice sitting up straight?" Aiden said. "We will be to the theater soon, and we are all to be on our best behavior while we are there."

Catherine sighed dramatically but sat up with her back straight. She placed her hands in her lap with exaggerated emphasis and put on a completely polite, and utterly false, smile. "How is this?" she said, batting her eyes. Miss Keighly frowned.

"Better," Aiden said, because it *was* better, and Miss Keighly must learn to acknowledge any improvement.

"I have been thinking," Miss Keighly said, "that we ought to develop a reward system for you, Catherine."

Catherine was immediately suspicious, and Aiden tried to keep his reaction in check. Miss Keighly had said nothing of this to him, and he didn't like feeling as though she were usurping him.

Miss Keighly continued. "For most children, pleasing their caretakers and seeing their own success is incentive enough for good behavior, however, I understand that your raising was . . . incomplete in this regard. Therefore, I thought of creating another incentive. I understand you like the ices at Hoopers."

Catherine considered her answer for some time before she answered. "Uncle Aiden takes me every Saturday."

Miss Keighly turned her disapproving eyes to Aiden. "Without earning the privilege?"

"It is an occasion where we can enjoy one another's company. She does not need to earn it."

"I see," Miss Keighly said, though her disapproval was obvious. "Then something else, perhaps."

"A reward for what?" Catherine asked.

"Behaving appropriately," Miss Keighly said.

Catherine rolled her eyes and slumped again, but Miss Keighly's idea struck a chord in Aiden.

"That is an excellent idea," he said, thinking quickly. "Do you remember the white gloves you admired at the shops a few weeks ago?"

Catherine eyed him with suspicious curiosity. "You said I would get them dirty."

"White gloves are inappropriate for a girl her age, Mr. Asher."

He held up a hand to Miss Keighly but spoke to Catherine. "You would certainly have to be careful with them, but I think a young lady who attends the opera and behaves as she should could care for those gloves."

She regarded him a few seconds, still distrustful. "You will buy me those gloves if I behave well tonight?"

"Yes. If tonight is a success, I shall bring them to Mrs. Simmons's tomorrow."

Miss Keighly cleared her throat, but Aiden spoke first. "What do you think, my dear? Can you manage your best behavior for the evening in exchange for those lovely gloves?"

She looked between him and Miss Keighly and then back again. "Miss Wilton gives me two warnings during our lessons. I am only twelve, after all, and I don't always know that what I am doing is inappropriate."

The little minx knew very well what was appropriate and what wasn't, but he did not disagree with her suggestion. "I think we could keep to those same rules," Aiden said, liking how this made him feel as though he and Lenora were working together. He looked at Miss Keighly and smiled innocently. "Excellent idea, Miss Keighly. Thank you for suggesting it."

Miss Keighly was not pleased, but because the reward system had been her idea, she was loathe to argue. She nodded and then raised her eyebrows at Catherine. The girl correctly interpreted the gesture and sat up straight again—without overdoing it this time. She looked at Miss Keighly for several seconds. "I very much like your . . . necklace, Miss Keighly."

Aiden inhaled slowly. Miss Keighly's dress was ornate and splendid in every way. She wore an elaborate headdress and satin gloves, yet Catherine had complimented the simple string of pearls at her neck. No one missed the point Catherine was making, and yet no one could fault her for it either. The girl was frighteningly clever.

"Thank you, Catherine," Miss Keighly said tightly.

"I would prefer you address me as Miss Manch, if you do not mind. It is only proper."

Chapter Thirty

Did you have a nice evening?" Lenora asked the next morning when Catherine joined her in the school parlor, as it had come to be known. They had delayed lessons until eleven so that Catherine might get enough rest after her late night. She had not returned until almost midnight; Lenora knew because she had been sitting by her window without a candle so as not to reveal her silhouette.

Lenora had watched Mr. Asher alight from the carriage first, then help Catherine step out. A short time later, he returned and climbed back into the rented carriage, but not before looking up at Lenora's window. She was certain he could not see her in the dark, but his attention left her flushed all the same. He had gone to the opera with Miss Keighly. It could have been her by his side, if she had allowed it, and yet she couldn't imagine simply *deciding* to trust Mr. Asher. Trust what he said he felt for her. How could he feel that way, after all? It was misplaced guilt and gratitude and . . . perhaps attraction. Not enough to change one's life over, and better they both accept it now rather than later.

"The evening was nice enough," Catherine said with a shrug. "I still do not much care for the opera, a great caterwauling if you ask me, but I thought the costumes were interesting. A man wore a ruffled collar that seemed to stretch his neck out the whole night. His jowls bounced against the folds when he sang with his shaky voice."

Lenora held back a smile at the girl's assessment. "I think you mean vibrato. It's a great skill for a vocalist."

Catherine shrugged.

Lenora had been to the opera only twice, both times in Bath, and claimed to like it more than she did for Aunt Gwen's sake. She found the orchestration more interesting than the vocals, though she could appreciate them for the sake of proficiency. "I am glad you found some portion of the night to enjoy. That is an important skill in life—holding to the good of every situation." Lenora would be wise to follow her own advice, but sometimes it was difficult.

"Uncle Aiden is buying me gloves because he only had to issue me two warnings, though he likely could have failed me when I accidentally stepped on the back of Miss Keighly's dress." She frowned. "It was not good of me to do that, was it?"

"No, it was not," Lenora said, giving Catherine a knowing look. "Especially if it was not actually an accident."

Catherine pulled her eyebrows together and cocked her head to the side. "Sometimes I cannot tell the difference. I had thought it would be funny if I stepped on the back of her dress, possibly causing her to stumble, but then I told myself not to do it, and then suddenly her hem was beneath my shoe. I *was* sincere in my apology, though."

Oh, this girl. "Perhaps next time, if you think of such a thing, you should make sure there is enough distance between you and the hem so that you don't accidentally act on such a thought."

"That is a good idea," Catherine said with a nod.

"I would like to start today with the 'th' sound." She opened the primer just as Jacobson entered the room.

"A package for Miss Catherine and a letter for you, Miss Wilton."

Catherine was out of her seat like a shot and met Jacobson halfway across the room. She pulled both items from his hand and spun back toward Lenora, then paused and turned back. "I am sorry for grabbing these from you, Jacobson." She held them out to the footman, and Lenora tried for the third time in ten minutes not to laugh. "You may give them to me properly this time."

Jacobson bowed slightly but put his hands behind him rather than taking the items he would only hand right back to her. "It is very good, Miss Catherine."

He left the room, and Catherine ran back to her seat. She practically threw the letter at Lenora before attacking the paper-wrapped parcel.

Lenora recognized her name written in Mr. Asher's handwriting across the front of the letter and took a breath before reluctantly breaking the seal. She had not seen him since the churchyard on Sunday, if she did not count her view of him from her window last night. Would he try, again, to explain himself? Did she want him to?

"Oh, they are lovely!"

Lenora looked up to see Catherine putting on a pair of white leather gloves—finer than anything Lenora had ever owned, though she was not jealous. Rather, she was genuinely happy for Catherine and pleased at the brightness of the girl's face. Once Catherine had the gloves on, she practiced waves and flourishes, stretching out her fingers and smoothing first one glove and then the other. She put her elbows on the desk, laced her fingers, and propped her chin on her hands. "How do I look?" she asked, casting her eyes at the ceiling as though she were a cherub gazing toward her heavenly home.

Lenora did laugh this time, and the joy that washed through every part of her felt good. "You look perfectly elegant," she said. "Like a proper young lady."

Catherine grinned and settled back in her chair, lifting her hands to admire the gloves a few more moments. "Could I show Aunt Gwen?" she asked eagerly. "It will take but a minute."

"I am not certain she has returned from the Pump Room." Aunt Gwen tended to leave them to their studies until tea so as not to distract Catherine.

"Might I check? I told her I would be receiving the gloves today, and she wanted to see them, I'm certain of it."

Lenora glanced at the letter in her hand and decided she would prefer to read it in private. "Go on, then, but no more than five minutes. Come right back if Aunt Gwen is not yet returned."

Catherine spun on her heel and was gone before Lenora unfolded the half page sheet.

> *Dear Miss Wilton,*
>
> *I hope you do not mind my adoption of your warning techniques with Catherine. As it proved to be a great success at the opera, I would like to further implement the methods into her studies, if you would support it.*
>
> *I would like to offer rewards to be given at the end of each week dependent on her behavior during your lessons. If she can go the entire week without you ending lessons early, I shall plan an activity of some kind. If she can go the whole week without warnings of any kind, I shall have a more tangible reward in addition. I feel this will help her see you and I as a team in regard to her education as well as provide opportunities for her enjoyment.*
>
> *Please let me know if this is acceptable to you. I look forward to your reply.*
>
> > *Sincerely,*
> >
> > *A. Asher*

Lenora hated that she was disappointed by his purely professional manner, even though she told herself that was exactly what she wanted. She was his niece's teacher, and that was all she would ever be.

Catherine seemed to be improving without the additional

rewards, and Lenora worried about spoiling the girl, but she could appreciate Mr. Asher's desire to be a part of her education and could not help but admire his continued devotion to his niece. He was making so many sacrifices on Catherine's behalf, not the least of which was marrying a woman he did not love. The thought shot a bitter dart through Lenora's heart, but keeping his agreement was still the right thing for him to do.

She thought back to how confident he had been that Miss Keighly would cry off and allow him to pursue his heart—pursue Lenora—and she wondered what she would have done if things *had* happened that way. She had been certain of her decision when she denounced him in the drawing room last week, and yet now she was not sure. The uncertainty made her uncomfortable, and she pushed the matter aside.

Lenora was penning her acceptance of his terms in her mind when Catherine returned, removing her gloves as she crossed the room. When she reached the desk, she placed the gloves carefully back in the box and then put the box beneath her chair. "Aunt Gwen told me to be extra careful with them and that the best place to store them would be in the original box. She says they are of the finest quality and therefore will require my finest attention."

Lenora smiled, her feelings warmer toward Catherine than they had ever been before. "I am sure you will take excellent care of them. Now, shall we begin?"

Chapter Thirty-One

L enora and Catherine were finishing their lessons on Friday afternoon when Jacobson brought them two letters on a silver tray. Both were addressed to Catherine but included different postscripts written on the back. On the first it said, "To be opened if warnings were issued throughout the week. Burn immediately if no warnings were given." The second said, "To be opened if there were NO warnings issued throughout the week. Burn immediately if warnings were given."

Lenora read the instructions of both aloud and then looked across the desk to her pupil. "You had no warnings this week, Catherine." She handed over the appropriate letter, and Catherine took it, but looked at the letter Lenora was holding.

"I wonder what that one says," she said, curiously. The forbidden was always so enticing.

Lenora smiled, then stood and made her way to the fire. "No!"

Lenora tossed the letter into the fire and watched the edges catch, the wax seal melt, and the words disappear into black smoke as the fire bloomed, then reduced again.

Catherine was beside her. "Now we will never know what it said."

Lenora put an arm around the girl's shoulders and gave her a squeeze, only then realizing that she'd actually initiated a physical display of affection. Did that mean she felt affection for Catherine? If so, did that mean she had forgiven her? "I would hate for your uncle to rescind his generous rewards due to our not following the rules he set out, wouldn't you?"

Catherine was not convinced, but she looked at the letter in her hand and her face lit up with excitement as she broke the seal and unfolded the paper.

"Dear Catherine," she read, though Lenora knew that those two words were ones she had memorized by sight.

"As a roo-way, roowayd foor . . ."

Lenora kept her teeth clamped together so as not to rescue the girl. Catherine had to learn to decipher words, even if they danced away from her on the page. "Hay-vie—oh, having. As a reward for having." She stopped to grin at Lenora, who gave her an encouraging nod. It was a few minutes before Catherine had read the entire letter.

As a reward for having behaved so well this week, we shall take a horseback ride tomorrow after-noon. You may bring one friend to accompany you. Instruct them to be at Hilltop Stables at two o'clock

in the afternoon. I am very proud of your accom-
plishment.

Sincerely,
Uncle Aiden

"I get to bring a friend," Catherine said, her eyes dancing.

"We must send an invitation right away." Lenora returned to the desk and extracted a sheet of paper. Catherine's handwriting was abominable, but they had been practicing correspondence, and the girl was improving. Even still, she had a bit of a scowl on her face as she took her seat and glared at the paper.

"Who would you like to invite?" Lenora said, moving the paper across the desk and readying the pen for Catherine to use. "I had thought of Mary from school." She was a day student whose family lived near the Parade, and Catherine had gone to tea at her house a few times.

"Mary Cranston?" Catherine frowned. "I do not know if she rides."

"Hmm, that is an excellent point to consider. Well done. Are there any girls at the school you *know* ride? Perhaps those raised in the country."

"Martha Rumby rides, but we are not very good friends, and she is three years older."

Lenora knew Martha. Not only was she three years older, but she was often impatient with the younger girls, and Lenora was unsure she would accept the invitation. Lenora would hate for whomever Catherine invited to refuse. "Anyone else?"

Lenora positioned the slate in front of her. "We can make a list and consider each girl in turn."

She led Catherine through the process of writing Martha's name on the list, then added Mary as well since it was good practice. Catherine looked between the two words on her slate. "Their names start the same, but *Martha* is a soft *A* and *Mary* is an 'eh' sound."

"Very good," Lenora said. "Who else should we put on the list?"

Catherine thought for a moment, then scrunched her face and began writing, angling the slate so Lenora could not see. Catherine's lips moved as she wrote each letter, often stopping and going back and then stopping again. After some time, she smiled and turned the slate to show Lenora.

MISS MILTON

Lenora was surprised enough that she did not correct the mistakes. "Me?"

Catherine nodded, obviously pleased. "You were raised in the country, so you ride, do you not?"

"I do ride," Lenora said slowly. "But I believe your uncle intended one of your school friends to be invited."

"You are my school friend in addition to being my teacher," Catherine said as though it were the most natural thing in the world.

The part of her that wanted to see Mr. Asher warred with the part of her that did not dare, and at the same time she understood the level of compliment she'd been given. Even as a young girl, Lenora had not been invited out by other girls her age. She was too shy and anxious. If she did go on an outing, it was with one of her brothers or sisters, which suited her just fine.

"I will still write the invitation," Catherine said, trading the chalk pencil for the pen and moving the paper in front of her. "D-e-a-r M-i-s W-i— Oh, there are two S's in 'miss.'" She scratched out the letters and looked up at Lenora. "This will be my first draft, then I will write it without mistakes. I would never send an invitation that showed mistakes."

How could Lenora talk her out of her enthusiasm, even if her own chest fluttered with anxiety? Each time Catherine looked up, Lenora smiled encouragingly, and by the time Catherine finished the final—perfect—invitation, Lenora had accepted that she could not refuse. This was the first time Catherine had not attempted to get out of a writing assignment.

"Now we must seal it," Lenora said, removing the wax and stamp from her drawer. "Then it will be official."

Catherine insisted she do it herself. They had written a few letters before, and the wax was Catherine's favorite part. After she'd stamped the seal into the hot wax and wriggled it free without pulling the wax away from the paper, she smiled and handed the invitation across the table.

"Why, thank you, Catherine," Lenora said, then broke open the still-soft wax and read the invitation out loud. When she finished, she removed another sheet of paper, thinking for a moment how rare paper had been in her home growing up and yet now she could use it for little more than a game.

She penned her reply, then let Catherine seal the letter by herself again and handed it across the table. Catherine was waving the letter, insisting that the wax be dry so that it would snap in that satisfying way, when there was a tapping on the doorway of the parlor.

Lenora looked past Catherine and the flapping letter and saw Mr. Asher standing in the doorway. She stood up too fast, pushing the chair back so that it crashed into the wall behind her and fell on its side. Face flaming, she righted the chair as quickly as possible, then faced him again. "Mr. Asher," she said, then looked at the clock on the mantel to verify that it was four o'clock—the time he had said he would fetch Catherine for the weekend. "I had not realized it was so late." But she and Catherine had been at the end of their lessons when they'd received Mr. Asher's note, and then had spent more than an hour working on the responses.

"I can come back if you are still engaged."

Engaged. Had he used that word on purpose?

Catherine spoke up. "Miss Wilton is going to ride with me tomorrow."

Mr. Asher raised his eyebrows and avoided looking at Lenora. "Miss Wilton?"

Catherine crossed the room to him and passed Lenora's acceptance letter to him as proof. "You said I could invite a friend, but you did not say it could only be a friend from Mrs. Henry's school." She put her hands on her hips while her uncle skimmed the words of Lenora's letter of acceptance.

Lenora's face was burning so hot she would not have been

surprised if it burst into flame. She could no longer remember why she had not insisted that Catherine invite a friend from school. What had she been thinking?

"And Miss Wilton rides, so you cannot go back on it now."

"Certainly not," Mr. Asher said, shaking his head. "Only . . ."

"What?" Catherine demanded.

"Only I had planned for Miss Keighly and I to attend you and your friend."

"That is all right." Catherine's answer was surprisingly quick. She turned to Lenora. "You do not mind, do you?"

"I do not mind, but perhaps Miss Keighly would." It was a lie. Lenora *did* mind; she did not want to be around Miss Keighly. Especially not Mr. Asher *and* Miss Keighly together.

Catherine turned back to her uncle, who looked a bit flushed. Lenora frowned at him, hoping he would see the expression as an apology. She wished she knew how to get out of this situation.

"Miss Keighly will not mind," Catherine said as though that were obvious. "But you and she must ride behind us, Uncle Aiden, otherwise she will say things like"—her voice went suddenly high and squeaky—"'Catherine, do not bounce so much' and 'Catherine, do not laugh so loud' and 'Catherine, do not have *so* much fun.'"

Lenora noticed that Mr. Asher's jaw clenched, but he did not reprimand Catherine or defend Miss Keighly.

"Perhaps it would be better for you to ride with Miss Keighly and your uncle alone tomorrow," Lenora said. "It could be an opportunity to—"

"Uncle Aiden said I could bring a friend!" Catherine stomped her foot and clenched her fists at her sides—the prelude to one of her fits.

Lenora and Mr. Asher shared a look, and Lenora could see in his expression that Mr. Asher was not going to uninvite her.

"And I wrote that letter—twice, if you count the first draft—and gave it to you." She seemed to remember Lenora's response now in her uncle's hand and quickly snatched it back and held it in front of her, her eyes moving faster across the page than she could possibly read. "And it says, 'Dear Catherine. I wow-led, wowled—would—'" She glanced up triumphantly, but two deep spots of color had flooded her cheeks. "'I would be'—that's easy—'puleez-ed—pleased to.'" She paused and then began reading fluently, or looking as though she were reading fluently. "'I would be pleased to go riding with you as it is sure to be a day as lovely as this one, and I have very much missed riding since it has been some time since I have been to the country and do not have my own horse here in Bath. I look forward to spending the afternoon with you as your particular friend and am very grateful to have been asked. You are an excellent student and have earned this reward due to your excellent behavior, and I will do all in my power to make it as fun an adventure as possible.'"

Lenora covered her mouth with her hand to keep from laughing, but Catherine's eyes were fierce when she raised them from the paper. Her eager and clever determination convinced Lenora to concede the fight. This would have to be the first step in the professional relationship she had claimed she would have with Mr. Asher. Surely after this first interaction, it would be easier to be in his company. She would not think of her hand on the back of his neck, the smoky sweet taste of tobacco on his tongue, the way . . .

"Miss Wilton?" Catherine said.

Lenora shook herself back to the present. "That *is* what I said. More or less."

Mr. Asher lifted his eyebrows, equally disinclined to call her out. When Catherine looked at her uncle, Lenora shrugged. He nodded. Her stomach began to knot. She would not be able to eat until after tomorrow's ride for the butterflies that would undoubtedly fill her stomach.

"I think it shall be a lovely afternoon," Mr. Asher said. "And Miss Keighly and I will stay back so as not to interfere."

Catherine grinned the smile of a child who had bested all the adults in the room. She moved back to the desk and began clearing the implements they had used as part of their lessons— something Lenora usually had to remind her to do.

"I can put everything away since we ran late today," Lenora said.

"All right," Catherine said, putting down the slate and looking even more pleased with herself. "And you'll meet us at Hilltop Stables at two o'clock?"

Lenora kept her eyes on Catherine so she would not see the discomfort on the face of her uncle. "Yes, I will."

Chapter Thirty-Two

Lenora had hoped it would rain, therefore canceling the riding excursion. So, of course she woke up to bright blue skies and crisp autumn sunshine. She walked to Hilltop Stables, but had been so nervous that she'd left earlier than necessary and arrived at 1:30. She walked around the corrals as she waited, petting the muzzles of a few horses that approached her and then feeding them some small apples the groom provided her.

She'd had little opportunity to interact with any type of livestock since leaving Leagrave and was filled with nostalgia for home. She missed the simple country life; if she were perfectly honest, she missed the chance to hide. Though she was glad to have grown so much here in Bath, it was difficult not to long for the protection of her former life. She stroked the muzzle of a beautiful butter-colored mare, the same color of the famous Bath stone used for so many buildings in this part of the country.

"Miss Wilton."

Lenora startled and spun around, upsetting the horse, which ran to the other side of the corral. Mr. Asher stood a few feet away from her, looking handsome in his buff-colored riding breaches and short coat. "You've had a haircut," she said without thinking, then colored. Where had such a comment come from? Except that he *had* received a haircut since she'd seen him yesterday. It was cut closer to his head, and, though she missed the devil-may-care of the longer hair, this style looked more distinguished.

He smiled. "You are the first to notice, but, yes. When I found myself tucking it into my collar, I decided I ought to have a trim."

They were silent, and Lenora realized it was her turn to speak. "It looks well on you, Mr. Asher." She looked past him for Catherine and Miss Keighly.

Mr. Asher seemed to interpret her glance. "The groom led them to the east corral to choose their mounts." He nodded to the corral behind her. "He directed me to this one; apparently, these horses are better appointed for a grown man." He shrugged, as though hesitant to accept such a distinction. It was quite adorable, but she refused to let herself dwell on the thought.

"Well, then, perhaps I should get direction from a groom on my own mount."

"He said to have you go to the east corral as well. He'll wait on you and saddle the mount."

"Very good," she said, lowering her head and stepping to go around him. It was difficult to be close to him. As she passed beside him, he reached out and touched her arm. The merest feather-light touch, but enough to stop her and fill her with warmth. She looked at his hand, resting gently at her elbow, and then up to his face. *Close enough to steal a kiss,* she thought, but of course she wouldn't. She'd done that once before, and it had ended in disaster.

"Thank you for accompanying Catherine today. It shows your devotion to her, and I appreciate it very much."

She could not speak for the lump that rose in her throat at his sincerity.

"Of course," she said, then gently stepped forward and out of reach. She did not want to throw off his hand, but she could not abide his touch for much longer. Already her heart was racing in her chest.

He nodded and stepped back. She took a breath and let it out slowly as she made her way to the east corrals.

Catherine was already on her mount, a concentrated expression on her face as the groom adjusted the single stirrup for the sidesaddle. Lenora was comfortable on both a sidesaddle and gentleman's saddle, but she had first learned to ride bareback and preferred it whenever possible—which wasn't often since she was now a grown woman. Today would be a sidesaddle, of course.

Miss Keighly and Catherine were both dressed in beautiful riding habits. Miss Keighly's was a light gold color with black trim and matching bonnet. Catherine's was lavender with silver military trim down the front and at the cuffs. Lenora lamented that she only had her striped day dress—she'd never owned a riding habit—but she had worn additional petticoats to cover her ankles for the ride. She approached the others with a smile she hoped looked more natural than it felt.

"Miss Wilton!" Catherine said, and her excitement to see Lenora helped to ease Lenora's rising anxiety even as she touched the corral fence, petted the horse that approached her, and pressed one hand against the side of her leg to help calm her. She hated how often she had to resort to her tricks, and yet it was getting better. This was the first time in nearly a week that she'd needed to ground herself.

"Good afternoon, Catherine. You look lovely in your riding habit."

Catherine straightened in her saddle and grinned. Her horse sidestepped, and as she turned her mount, Miss Keighly clicked her horse to turn toward Lenora. "I am pleased to see you again, Miss Wilton."

"As am I to see you," Lenora said with a nod, chastising herself for disliking this woman. There was no reason not to like her other than Lenora's envy, which did her no credit. If she were determined to be better for the whole of this experience, she needed to dispose of such petty feelings.

Miss Keighly opened her mouth to say something more, but the groom approached at that moment, holding the reins of two horses. He introduced the butter-colored mare Lenora had petted earlier, as well as a dark chocolate-colored gelding—a truly magnificent animal, likely retired from racing but still a solid animal for riding.

"The gentleman said you were an experienced rider, miss. I recommend one of these two animals—either Miss Devonshire or Tartan."

Lenora looked between them, and although part of her

wanted to choose the striking thoroughbred, her heart had been captured by Miss Devonshire. She moved to take the reins from him, and though the groom looked momentarily perplexed, he nodded and led the thoroughbred away. He returned a short time later with a sidesaddle, putting it on remarkably fast, giving the girth an extra tightening before holding out the whip. Lenora took the whip, thanked him, and turned to the saddle.

"Might I assist you, miss?"

"No, thank you," Lenora said, feeling the need to prove herself capable. It was a benefit not to have the heavy riding habit when mounting a sidesaddle without assistance. She moved the whip to her left hand, steadying the stirrup iron, and hoisted herself up with her left foot. Despite not having ridden for months, maybe years, she expertly found her seat and adjusted the stirrup before spreading her skirts over her legs as best she could. An inch or two of ankle was left uncovered, but she'd done the best she could.

She looked up to see Miss Keighly watching, but she looked away quickly and patted her mount on the head. The flash of disapproval or envy or maybe just surprise was oddly satisfying.

Catherine was walking her horse in a circle, and Lenora clicked her horse to move closer to her. She was determined to keep herself in Catherine's company. Though she'd arrived at the stables wondering how she would possibly get through the afternoon, between Miss Keighly's reaction to her mounting without help and the freedom of being on horseback, she was feeling much more comfortable. At least until Mr. Asher joined the three women, then every one of her senses was honed and on alert.

Lenora kept herself on the other side of Catherine as the groom pointed out the various trails and gave basic instructions.

Mr. Asher and Miss Keighly led out. Lenora purposely allowed her horse to fall behind, and Catherine stayed with her. Lenora asked Catherine about when she'd learned to ride, and as Catherine told her the story, Lenora realized it was the first time she'd learned of something from Catherine's childhood that was not sad. After a time, Catherine asked Lenora about her childhood, and Lenora was surprisingly comfortable relaying her own story.

"Five sisters and two brothers?" Catherine said with awe. "I cannot imagine it. Did you enjoy having so many sisters?"

"They were my best friends," Lenora said wistfully. She really did miss her family, especially lately. "My only friends, really."

Catherine considered this. "I think I would have liked to have brothers and sisters."

Lenora felt a pang of sadness at the thought of Catherine being so alone in the world. Orphaned and unwanted, not even siblings to belong to. Lenora could not imagine such loneliness. They rode in silence until Catherine pointed out a rabbit hiding in the brush, changing the subject.

They rode another half an hour before Miss Keighly and Mr. Asher came back toward them on the path. Catherine and Lenora moved their mounts to the side to allow the others to pass, then turned and followed them back to the stables, once again allowing the engaged couple to take the lead.

By the end of the ride, Lenora was pleased with how things

had unfolded. Mr. Asher had been polite, he had not sought her out, and she'd gotten to know Catherine better. Quite a lovely afternoon. They dismounted—Lenora by herself again, feeling very accomplished by her self-sufficiency. She felt Mr. Asher's eyes on her.

"Miss Wilton, I've a carriage coming in"—he checked his watch—"quarter of an hour. Would you like to join us for the ride back to the city?"

"No, thank you, Mr. Asher," she said, still holding the bridle of her horse as she stroked the mare's neck. "I appreciate the invitation, but the day is fine enough." She looked up, only then noticing the sky was no longer the bright blue it had been when she'd first set out for the stables. Clouds had set in throughout the afternoon, and some darker ones lay in wait to the west. Still, she would rather walk in the rain than be in a carriage with Miss Keighly and Mr. Asher.

Mr. Asher did not leave. She did not acknowledge him and, instead, led her horse to the groom who was unsaddling the first of the other horses.

"Might I curry Miss Devonshire?"

"Certainly. I can untack her first."

"No, I shall do it, if that is all right."

"Yes, miss." He left the other three horses long enough to show Lenora the equipment, then attached a lead rope to Miss Devonshire's bridle before turning the mare over to Lenora.

Lenora thanked him, excited to be busy with a task she had enjoyed back in Leagrave.

She led Miss Devonshire to the bucket of water hung on a

post the groom had pointed out, then spoke soothingly to her as she began removing the tack. She was struggling to lift the saddle when a pair of hands reached from the side to help her. The saddle wasn't particularly heavy, but the horse's height made it awkward. She turned to smile at who she assumed was the groom, then froze to see Mr. Asher instead. He moved the saddle to the rail, and Lenora watched him until he looked back at her, then she proceeded to remove the blanket. "Thank you," she said.

"You know your way around a stable."

"I am horribly self-sufficient, I'm afraid. We did a great deal of the care when I was growing up." She wondered where Miss Keighly and Catherine were but did not want to ask. The pleasantness of the afternoon still lingered about her, persuading her to allow him to stay, even though she should dismiss him.

Mr. Asher took the blanket from her, and she reached around him for the currycomb. She started with a light touch, but when Miss Devonshire made no protest, she increased the pressure, moving the comb in small circles as she moved across the horse's flank. Mr. Asher remained in place, watching her. It did not make her feel as uncomfortable as she thought it ought to.

"I am glad you came out with us today, Miss Wilton."

She glanced at him before focusing on her work again. "I am glad I came as well."

"I do hope that we can be friends and that . . . I hope that you know I am trying to do the best-right that I can within the circumstances."

She looked at him, her hand stilling. "Best-right?"

He nodded. "If doing the right thing were black and white,

it would be a far simpler choice, but it seems I have put myself in the middle of a gray area that proves difficult to navigate. But I am trying, and it is important to me that you know that—or for me to say it, at least."

"I believe it is right for people to honor their commitments."

"Yes, I know that you do." He kicked at the ground at his feet.

"You do not agree?"

Mr. Asher put his hands in the pockets of his coat and rocked back slightly on his heels, an unexpected hardness or maybe frustration showing in the lines around his eyes. "I know you will interpret my answer as further evidence against my character, but I believe each person should be committed to their own happiness."

Lenora was immediately uncomfortable and went back to currying Miss Devonshire. "I'm sure Miss Keighly will make you happy, Mr. Asher. Was that not your expectation at the time of your proposal?"

"Certainly I believed that once," he said, nodding thoughtfully but looking at the ground. "And then I found someone who could make me happy now *and* later, but she will not have me, and so I must settle for the second choice—the best-right."

Second choice. The words reminded Lenora of how she'd felt as Evan Glenside's second choice, and then learning she was Mr. Asher's second choice as well. And yet, he was saying that wasn't the case, that Lenora was his *first* choice, if she would allow him to make it, which she could not. She could not risk the life she felt she was holding on to by a thread on the words of a man she could not trust. She heard him step toward her, and she looked up, certain her contrasting emotions showed on her face.

"Do not worry for me, Miss Wilton. I will make the best of my marriage to Miss Keighly, and I am certain we shall find accord. She is a good woman—I have never said otherwise—and is willing to take me and my situation with Catherine as is."

He was close enough to reach out and touch her face as he had once before, close enough that one step would bring them near enough to kiss. She had been the one to step forward for their first kiss. She was the one who had gone up on her toes. It would not be difficult to repeat it, and she sensed that he wanted her to, just as the traitorous parts of her own body and mind wanted to comply with that wish. But back then, she had not known he was engaged. It had been a mistake, but not a sin. To kiss him again, now, with full understanding, she would have no defense. And it would unravel what she knew she must do, which was forget everything he'd made her feel.

They stared at one another across the short distance between them. When he spoke, his voice was barely a whisper, and it was as if she could hear the soft movements of the river behind her. "In my heart, I believe you and I would have found far more happiness together than I ever shall with her."

He held her eyes, which she could not move away from his face, then turned to the stable door and left her to her solitude. She faced the horse again, who shifted impatiently. Lenora began the circles again, slower than before, her mind elsewhere.

Chapter Thirty-Three

L enora was reading aloud on Friday afternoon while Catherine followed along in her own copy of the book of nursery rhymes when she looked up to see Jacobson standing in the doorway of the second-level parlor. Lenora glanced at the clock. Was it three o'clock already?

"Mr. Asher awaits you downstairs, Miss Catherine," Jacobson said.

His name shot a shiver through Lenora's chest, transporting her back to the stables, the last time she'd seen him, when he had confessed his love to her . . . again. She'd relived that moment a hundred times, sometimes disbelieving it had happened and reminding herself what a fool she would be to trust his words. Other times believing everything he'd said to be sincere and genuine. Why had she not confessed her own feelings? Why could she not admit her heart and have faith in his?

Because he was engaged to Miss Keighly, of course.

Catherine sprang from her chair, her eyes dancing as she closed the book and tossed it on her chair. Mr. Asher had sent his standard two letters that morning, and Lenora had tossed the one to be opened if Catherine had received warnings into the fire. His plan of rewarding her behavior was working very well. The letter Catherine had earned had simply said that he had a surprise in store and would meet her in Aunt Gwen's drawing room at three o'clock.

Catherine was hoping for a set of paints, as she had decided she wanted to be a watercolorist after Lenora had shown her some of the paintings her sister Cassie had done; they'd arrived yesterday by post and sparked a bit more homesickness. Lenora did not tell Catherine that her uncle had no idea of her newfound passion and therefore would not know she wanted paints.

"Where do the books go, Catherine?" Lenora called out when the girl was halfway across the room.

Catherine stopped but dropped her shoulders with a dramatic sigh. "But it's Friday!"

"And I can still give you a warning for not taking proper care of the book, which still needs to be shelved even on a Friday."

Catherine groaned but returned to her chair and picked up the book. She crossed to the bookshelves and put it where it belonged, or at least on the same shelf. Lenora nodded that it was good enough. "I shall see you Monday, Catherine. Enjoy the weekend."

"Are you not coming to see my reward? It could be downstairs this very minute."

"I was not invited, Catherine."

Catherine frowned, and Lenora hurried to remedy what might have sounded like a complaint. "Which is just as well because I have some music to copy before I return it to Mrs. Grovesford tomorrow morning. You should not keep your uncle waiting. I shall see you next week and look forward to hearing all about your reward. I am very proud of your behavior this week."

Catherine seemed to consider arguing, but then nodded and left the room.

Lenora shelved her book and gathered up papers from the desk. Once there was no evidence of the school day, she retrieved the sheet music Mrs. Grovesford had loaned her and the crisp parchment she'd purchased upon which to copy. She'd used the last of her lesser-quality paper copying the school's sheets. She had sent the music sheets back to Mrs. Henry last week, along with a note of apology for keeping them so long and for causing such difficulty for the school. Mrs. Henry had not written back, though Lenora hadn't expected she would.

This finer paper was an extravagance for a woman with such modest income, but not nearly as dear as purchasing printed music sheets. It was a blessing that musicians with better-lined pockets than her own were generous. Lenora was trimming her pen when she heard the pianoforte from the first-level parlor.

Aunt Gwen was out, so it must be Catherine playing, and yet the song was not one she had ever played for Lenora. Catherine's repertoire was rather small and limited to common pieces. Lenora put the pen back in the stock and walked to the doorway to listen, then to the top of the stairs, and finally down the hallway until she could peek through the doorway of parlor. She could not see the pianoforte, but she could see the green-striped skirt of the dress Catherine had worn that day. She was sitting in one of the chairs rather than at the pianoforte.

Miss Keighly, Lenora told herself, the realization crushing her curiosity. Miss Keighly had once said she was accomplished on both the harp and the pianoforte and must have decided to perform.

Lenora turned back to the second level, not interested in staying for the rest of the piece she did not recognize and mildly offended on behalf of her aunt that the woman had taken liberty with her parlor and her pianoforte without permission—though she was sure Aunt Gwen would not mind. Neither would Lenora if it were not Miss Keighly who had taken the liberty. Lenora rolled her eyes at her own pettiness.

As she made her retreat, Lenora wondered if Miss Keighly's playing was Catherine's reward for the week. If it were, she did not want to overhear Catherine's protest, though a small and wicked part of her took some inappropriate satisfaction in it.

Lenora was at the top of the stairs when the playing stopped, and two sets of hands applauded the performance. "Uncle Aiden, that was lovely. I had no idea you could play so well!"

Lenora stopped. *Uncle Aiden?*

"I've had little opportunity to play for some time, but I told you I could play and felt it was time I proved it. The Bath Hotel allowed me to use their pianoforte to practice."

Catherine laughed. "We should play the duet Miss Wilton and I learned! Do you remember I told you about it? Could you play her part, do you think? I could ask her for the sheet music. She has an entire collection, you know."

"I'm afraid I do not read music, Catherine."

"Then she can teach you the part as she taught me mine!"

Everything went silent.

There was a feminine clearing of the throat, and then Miss Keighly's voice spoke, "Perhaps another time. We've tickets to a musicale tonight as your weekly reward and shall need to be ready in two hours' time. Your uncle has rented a carriage so that we do not need to walk."

"*That* is my surprise?"

The petulant tone reminded Lenora that she was eavesdropping. She did not wait to hear the reprimand Miss Keighly would deliver, which Catherine deserved for being ungracious, and returned to the schoolroom parlor, where she closed the door so that she would not be tempted to overhear anything else.

It was good that the three of them were going to be a family, she told herself. Catherine needed a firm hand and Miss Keighly was that.

"It is what you wanted," she said out loud, but the lump in her throat was difficult to swallow as she turned her attention back to the sheet music waiting for her to copy. The copy must be perfect, nothing scratched out or vague in its transcription. It took meticulous attention and focus, which is why Lenora never attempted the work when Catherine was there.

An hour passed before Lenora decided to take a break. Her hand was beginning to cramp, but she had made her way through a perfect copy of the first half of the piece. It would be lovely to have this piece in her collection. Catherine would not be ready for it yet, but it was a fun Irish jig the girl would likely enjoy once she improved enough.

Lenora took the completed sheets to the downstairs sitting room so she could play them through, but regarded the pianoforte with a bit of trepidation from the doorway. The last person to play the instrument had been Mr. Asher, which gave it an aura of intimacy. *It is just an instrument*, she told herself as she forced herself across the room and settled on the piano stool.

She went to put her copied sheets on the music rack, only to see a stack of sheets already there and held together with a gilded clip. Carefully, she set aside her copied sheets and picked up the unfamiliar papers—printed music by Schubert, one of her favorite modern composers. The song was unfamiliar to her, and she quickly turned to the last page to see that the year of composition was 1817, which meant this was brand-new music. Perhaps the very first public printing of it available for purchase, which sent an invigorated shiver through her chest.

Then she noticed her name printed in the upper corner. A slower perusal of the pages showed "Lenora Wilton" written on every page, which marked these sheets as her own. The hand that had written her name was the same from the letters she and Mr. Asher had exchanged.

Lenora blinked back the tears, wishing she could disregard or dislike such a thoughtful gift. But she couldn't. She removed the clip and spread out the music before settling her hands on the keys. It only took a few measures to realize that it was the same song Mr. Asher had been playing earlier, but since he did not read music, and it was a new composition, he must have had someone help him learn it. Miss Keighly, perhaps?

She thought back to the sound of his playing, wishing they were in such a place that she could compliment his skill—she'd known very few men who were so proficient and now better understood his support of Catherine learning to read notes. Lenora would have to write a thank you letter, but as the idea made her stomach feel tight, she pushed it aside and let herself simply explore the notes and measures for now.

Chapter Thirty-Four

A iden returned Catherine to the terrace house on Monday, more than a week after the horseback ride. He did not go inside for fear he would see Lenora. The less he saw of her after having confessed himself again—and too openly—the better. He could only hope that in time he would not *want* to see her, *wish* to see her, plan his day according to the possibility that he *might* see her.

He walked through the drizzly morning to the White Hart to collect Miss Keighly, whom he escorted to the Pump Room each morning. She had melded into Bath society as easily as butter on hot bread. He admired her ability to make friends and feel comfortable in a new environment, and yet he did not enjoy the sociality as much as she did. Though it did mean he was becoming accustomed to her company.

The hope he'd had that Catherine might give Miss Keighly reason to cry off had not come to fruition. She handled Catherine's misbehaviors with grace and acceptance, and Catherine was becoming more compliant in the process. It was exactly what Aiden had hoped would happen when he'd made his offer to Miss Keighly. He should be pleased. But instead, he was resigned.

He had said everything he could say that day in the stables, and Lenora had remained unaffected. At church yesterday, he'd seen her across the yard but had not approached her. At one point, he thought that he and Lenora had caught one another's eye, but Catherine had pulled on his sleeve just then, and the moment had broken, leaving him unsure if he'd imagined it or not.

He hoped she'd enjoyed the sheet music he'd left for her on Friday—a reward for her patience and excellent teaching of his niece. He could push all his personal feelings for Lenora aside and would still feel overwhelming gratitude for what she was doing for Catherine. The success and security he'd tried so hard to find for Catherine seemed to have been achieved, and yet he was unsatisfied with how his future would now move forward.

"Good morning, Miss Keighly," Aiden said when she descended the stairs of the White Hart to the foyer. As always, she was perfectly coiffed and dressed and presented.

"Good morning, Mr. Asher," she said as she slid her delicate hand around his elbow. "I do hope you brought an umbrella."

"Of course," he said, waving toward the door where he had stored his large black umbrella, big enough for four people if necessary.

"Very good," she said.

They made small talk on their way to the Pump Room.

"I expect to receive our contract from my solicitor this afternoon," Miss Keighly said as they walked across the Pultney Bridge to the east side of Bath. "I shall look it over and then give it to you, if you're agreeable."

Looking at the water of the river beneath them drew him to other memories, which he pushed away. "Certainly," Aiden said, though his stomach tightened.

"We should talk about a date for the wedding, now that the paperwork is nearly in order," Miss Keighly said, nodding to one of her new acquaintances as they passed. "I was thinking January would be well enough, perhaps the twentieth."

"So soon," Aiden said, his mouth going dry in an instant.

"It is nearly three months from now, and will be just over a year since our engagement."

Unofficial engagement, he wanted to say, although he seemed to be the only person who saw it as such. Everyone else acted as though the agreement had been signed and sealed months ago. "We had discussed next summer, after Catherine had completed a full year of school."

"And yet she is not even *in* school, is she? If the contract is finished, then there is no need for delay."

There *wasn't* any need for delay—other than the hope he had not yet completely released from his heart. *You must give it up,* he told himself. *This is your future, embrace it.* He reminded himself that twice he had laid his heart at Lenora's feet, and twice she had pushed it away, like a piece of driftwood blocking her path. He had nothing left to give her. It was time to accept that she did not want him, and he would never have her.

"Very well," Aiden said, making sure he didn't sound petulant.

They reached the Pump Room and took the waters—dreadful. He told Miss Keighly about drilling a well in Jamaica, a surprisingly difficult job, and she was attentive and asked thoughtful questions. She would make a good wife. He needed to remember that.

They began walking the perimeter of the room, talking to acquaintances and remarking about the week ahead. Bath was a small enough city that the entertainments were limited; most people saw the same plays and the same operas. There was another musicale on Saturday afternoon in the lower rooms, a traveling orchestra from Scotland that was causing excitement since they would be a change from the typical classical music.

"Miss Keighly. Mr. Asher."

Aiden inclined his head in greeting to Mrs. Warner, a new acquaintance of Miss Keighly's. The women had shopped and dined together a few times—women made friends so quickly. He imagined that after he married Miss Keighly, she would entertain quite often. He would need to make his peace with that.

"I heard back from my sister and gained the address," Mrs. Warner said. "There are three spots open for winter term." She handed over a folded notecard, then leaned in as though to hide what she said next, although she had to know Aiden would overhear. "She agreed it would be just the place for your ward. They have . . . considerations."

Aiden felt a flare of suspicion but kept his expression

neutral. Miss Keighly thanked Mrs. Warner and tucked the note into her reticule. They moved forward again.

"What was that about?" Aiden asked.

"Mrs. Warner's sister once taught at a school for girls in Wales. She's found the address so that we might inquire about Catherine's possible enrollment."

"We?"

She looked at him, smiled, and then tapped his arm. "Of course *we*. We would make the decision together, Mr. Asher. I only wanted to gather some referrals, much as I did for Mrs. Henry's school here in Bath."

Aiden felt himself tightening like a rope.

"I have no interest in sending Catherine to Wales or any other distant school, Miss Keighly. She will remain near me throughout the duration of her school years." He had to speak through a smile as they continued to nod greetings at the people they passed.

"But that decision was made before— Good morning, Mrs. Simmons."

Aiden met Mrs. Simmons's eyes and wished he could talk to her right now instead of Miss Keighly. She had given him good counsel in the past; perhaps she could help him out of this muddle.

"Good morning," Mrs. Simmons said.

"And how is Catherine today?" Miss Keighly said as though she were not at that moment orchestrating the removal of the girl.

"Very well," Mrs. Simmons said, inclining her head politely. "She and Lenora were working on a puzzle when I left."

"A puzzle?" Miss Keighly sounded surprised, her eyebrows drawn together.

"Catherine responds very well to games, so Lenora has found a way to combine letters and puzzle pieces. I do not really understand it myself, but Catherine enjoys it."

"I'm sure she does," Miss Keighly said. "I would have adored doing puzzles instead of composition."

"I'm glad to hear she is well," Aiden interjected before Miss Keighly could add anything else. "Please give her our regards."

"And Miss Wilton too," Miss Keighly said.

"Certainly," Mrs. Simmons said before she moved on. She caught Aiden's eye long enough to raise an eyebrow.

He hoped she saw the desperation in his eye, but Miss Keighly continued forward, and he was forced to walk with her. He tried twice more to return to the topic of Catherine's schooling, but they were interrupted both times. He decided to wait until they had finished the morning promenade.

The rain had not slackened in the least during their turns about the room, and they huddled under the umbrella as they made their way through the puddled streets toward the White Hart. Delaying the conversation had only encouraged more boldness on Aiden's part. He spoke at the first opportunity he could.

"I will not send Catherine to Wales, Miss Keighly."

"Of course we will, if it is the best place for her." As ever, she was calm and perfectly composed.

"The best course for her is to remain connected to what is left of her family. I only agreed to Mrs. Henry's school because I could stay nearby and support her through it. I will not send her across the country to a school I know nothing about."

"Which is why I will send for some literature about what they have to offer. We would certainly not send her somewhere we had not properly investigated. You know I am in full support of her education, Mr. Asher, but you cannot believe that she is getting what she needs in Bath." She gave him a rueful look. "Puzzles? Games? Surely you are as disappointed to hear of that as I am. She needs a proper education if she is ever to succeed in this world, and knowing that her day is filled with games, in addition to the prizes you insist to continue rewarding her with, surely helps you realize that she needs something more than this."

"Miss Wilton is making good progress with her."

Miss Keighly scoffed. "She coddles the girl."

The tension Aiden felt returned full-force, like a frayed rope near to splitting. "Once Catherine has caught up, she will return to Mrs. Henry's school."

"Catherine will never catch up if she is not taught proper fundamentals. The school in Wales is for girls who have the very difficulties Catherine has exhibited. The teachers are trained to address her struggles, not bend to her will."

She meant physical punishment, demerits, restraints, and confinement designed to break their students like horses. *Like the school in Germany*, Aiden thought.

"I will not send her away, Miss Keighly. I am pleased with the current arrangement and have full confidence that her situation will continue to improve. I appreciate your interest, but I ask you not to pursue this further."

"You act as though I made a commitment of some sort, when we have not even received the literature. Surely you agree that we should make an informed choice."

"I will not send her away, therefore there is no reason to send for information. I will ask again—do not pursue this course." The tightness he'd been feeling had seeped into his tone, and he did not attempt to disguise it.

They walked in silence until they reached the White Hart. A footman opened the door and took Aiden's umbrella. Miss Keighly turned toward one of the sitting rooms set off the entryway, and he followed her. She turned to face him in the empty room.

"I understood that we would make decisions together," Miss Keighly said, her eyes showing the first sign of anger he'd ever seen from her, which only fortified his refusal to retreat. "As your wife, I expect to be your helpmeet and fulfill my role as Catherine's mother."

"I had thought we were of the same mind in regards to Catherine—that she needed a family, a home, and support. She is improving at a steady rate here in Bath, and I will not abandon her or send her away as everyone else has done."

The determination in Miss Keighly's eyes showed her to be a formidable opponent. "I was of the same mind after her last failure, Mr. Asher. Bath seemed to be the solution, but she has failed here as well. You are being selfish in your decision by choosing what is best for *you* rather than what is best for her—or, rather, us."

"Selfish?" he repeated. "I have turned my life upside down to help her." He'd said as much to Catherine several times, but never to anyone else.

"Yes, to assuage your guilt of the treatment she received in your absence. You have already done more for her than anyone could expect." She stepped toward him and he tensed. Would she attempt to appeal to some other part of him? Quick on the heels of that thought was the realization that he had nothing to fear. He did not respond to Miss Keighly physically, so there was no risk that her feminine wiles might blind him to his goals.

She placed a hand on his arm—he felt no warmth, no invigoration. For a moment, Lenora flashed into his mind. His body responded to her memory a hundred times stronger than it did to Miss Keighly, who was so close to him.

Her expression softened, but he could feel the calculation of it. "I admire your devotion, Mr. Asher, but we shall be a family of our own come January and cannot allow Catherine to be the deciding factor in our life together. You have done all that is required, but this slipshod effort to maintain the facade of education is too much to bear." She trailed her fingers down the sleeve of his coat. He felt nothing but frustration as he tried to keep his temper in check. "I must warn you that I am devoted to convincing you that this is the right course, the best course. For all of us." She smiled, as coy as he'd ever seen her.

He lifted her hand from his sleeve and stepped away from her. She frowned.

"It is not *guilt* that motivates my devotion to Catherine. I care for her because she is my family and a priority in my life. My motivation in proposing to you was to give Catherine a family—you know this. Sending her away is at complete odds with my hopes for her. For us."

Miss Keighly's expression changed. "Is Catherine a higher priority than your wife?" She folded her arms over her chest.

"Yes," he said without hesitation. "I came back to England, for her. I proposed to you, for her. I came to Bath, for her. She has been my motivation for everything; I thought you understood that. If you are unable to accept that, then perhaps you should reconsider your decision regarding our engagement."

Her expression turned thoughtful, and she cocked her head to the side. "It is Miss Wilton, isn't it?" There was the hint of a laugh in her voice, as though she had suddenly discovered a hidden meaning and now understood the joke. "You want to keep Catherine under Miss Wilton's tutelage so that you might remain close to her. Is that what you discussed with her in the stables last week?"

Aiden felt his neck heat up but stared at her coldly. "Miss Wilton has nothing to do with my commitment to Catherine, aside from the progress she is making under her teaching." In fact, getting away from Lenora would be a relief. Perhaps then he could forget about her completely. Keeping Catherine under her care kept him in a state of constant discomfort. "And you will not insinuate such ideas again. I have no prospects with Miss Wilton."

Miss Keighly adopted a neutral expression. "We will talk

about the school situation later, when you are not so . . . invigorated."

She thought he would change his mind. She believed that by stowing the topic for later, he would be more reasonable. She expected to get her way.

Aiden kept his voice level when he spoke again. "Catherine is, and will continue to be, my first priority, Miss Keighly, above even you, and then with shared commitment when I have children of my own. Can you abide that?"

She held his eyes for a few seconds. "And if I am the mother of those future children, I still shall not rise in rank on your scale of priorities?"

"Not to the point that you will ever make decisions regarding Catherine's care."

"You would shut me out of such things completely?" She scoffed, as though she still did not believe he was being serious.

"On this matter, yes, I will. It is obvious that you have disregarded my commitment to her, therefore I can only trust my own instincts."

Miss Keighly took a breath, then unfolded her crossed arms and straightened the cuff of her pelisse. "As I said, I believe we should discuss this another time." She turned toward the door, dismissing him, and pounding the last nail into a coffin he had wanted to bury for some time. It was clear that, should they marry, this would be a continued argument. She did not believe his determination and felt she could sway him.

"You have twenty-four hours to cry off from our engagement, Miss Keighly."

She turned to face him, her eyes wide. "What did you say?"

"It has become clear to me that we have irreconcilable differences that will not allow for a happy or companionate marriage between us. I had hoped—" He stopped. No, he had not hoped. "I had *thought* that we might make our arrangement work, but it was always for Catherine's sake, and yet your interests for her are not what I thought them to be. Rather than put ourselves in a situation where we would be on opposing sides of such a long-term and important issue, it would be better that we end our connection now and move on separately with our lives."

Miss Keighly narrowed her eyes. "It is Miss Wilton again. You have been looking for—"

"It is not Miss Wilton," he said with a growl of frustration. He tempered it before he spoke again. "It is Catherine. And the fact that we are not compatible. Have your solicitor send me a settlement request, and please accept my apology for wasting your time. I shall always be grateful for your initial acceptance, and regret that we did not better understand one another's motivations. You have twenty-four hours to cry off through a letter addressed to me, preserving both our reputations in the process, or I shall do it, come what may."

He strode past her and left her standing in the middle of the room. He grabbed his umbrella on his way out the front doors but did not open it. He welcomed the cold rain on his face, hoping it would cool his temper and slow his racing heart. For an instant, he felt exultation—he was free of Miss Keighly, or would be soon. Lenora had told him not to break the engagement, and he had broken it anyway—regardless of whether Miss

Keighly decided to take the responsibility of it publicly. Would he crawl back to Lenora and beg, again, for her consideration? The thought made him angry, and he stomped in a puddle for the satisfaction of watching the water explode—much of it landing on his pants and dripping into his boots. These women were making him completely mad!

If Lenora had wanted him, she could have had him weeks ago. He'd given her every opportunity to do so, fairly throwing himself at her feet and at her mercy. She had slapped away every attempt in the name of honor and commitment—which was exactly why he'd told Miss Keighly the engagement was over. His honor and commitment was to Catherine first, and yet Lenora had never managed to see that. Perhaps he could not trust his heart's choice of Lenora any more than he could trust his mind's choice of Miss Keighly.

Perhaps he needed to accept that it was more important for Catherine to know of his love and devotion to her than it was to give her the family she'd never had.

Chapter Thirty-Five

A unt Gwen invited Lenora to join her card party on Friday
night. She and a few friends took turns holding the
ladies-only games of whist, and while Lenora was not much
for cards, she agreed to join them. Mr. Asher had collected
Catherine that afternoon, and playing cards would be a good
way to distract her from the quiet of the house.

Lenora also accepted Aunt Gwen's offer of sherry and, as the
night wore on, felt herself softening in response. The women got
louder, the laughter more effusive, and the game much harder
to win. After changing tables following the third round, Lenora
was seated next to Mrs. Warner, a woman she'd met only once
before; she'd come as the companion to one of Aunt Gwen's
closer friends. Partway through the round, Mrs. Warner asked
whether or not Lenora would be returning to Mrs. Henry's
school in time for the winter term in January.

Lenora felt herself tense, hating to be reminded of her

dismissal, or resignation, or whatever it had been. "I am quite comfortable in the work I am doing now with Miss Manch. I don't foresee a change anytime soon."

"I meant after Miss Manch goes on to Wales. As I've heard it, Mrs. Henry is rather bereft without you."

Lenora had to repeat what she'd heard before she responded, wondering if the sherry had made her confused. She faced Mrs. Warner. "Wales?"

Mrs. Warner lifted her penciled eyebrows. "Yes, to that school for troubled girls." She leaned closer and lowered her voice. "I'm sure it is such a relief for Mr. Asher to have her established in an appropriate school. He's done too much for that girl already, if you ask me." She straightened and played her hand.

Lenora's mouth was dry. A school for troubled girls? In Wales? Yes, Lenora had once deemed Catherine a good candidate for such a school, but that was before she understood the girl's past and her challenges. In the weeks since Lenora had been working with her on a regular basis, she'd come to realize that the difficulties Catherine faced in learning may never be remedied. The way the letters changed in her mind had not improved, but she was improving in so many other ways. She could memorize anything and was progressing in her ability to read music. Lenora was more and more encouraged every week that with a few considerations, Catherine could rejoin the girls at Mrs. Henry's school come spring, though she may always need help with written work. To send her away to a school for troubled girls now would be devastating.

Lenora kept her composure throughout the rest of the

round, asking a few well disguised questions to glean more information. Mrs. Warner was only too happy to comply. According to Mrs. Warner, Miss Keighly had always planned to send Catherine to a school as far away as possible. She did not understand Mr. Asher's devotion to the girl even if she saw the kindness behind it. The wedding was planned for January, not summer as Mr. Asher had told Lenora in his letter of explanation.

"I'm sure that's why she's left Bath so suddenly. She only has three months to plan the wedding. I think it will be a relief to everyone once Catherine is properly settled. Some children are truly incorrigible, pity that it is, and the sooner she is put away the better."

Put away.

It was all Lenora could do to respond with a polite smile and a nod. Her hands shook as they held the cards, and her stomach twisted in knots, but she managed to keep her composure until the party ended and the last of the guests were shown out. When Lenora returned to the parlor, Aunt Gwen was enjoying her whiskey.

"Remind me not to invite Lady Barbara again," Aunt Gwen said with a shake of her head. "She has all the sportsmanship of a three-year-old. I've never seen such whining from a grown woman." She finished her glass before holding it out for the footman standing near the door.

Lenora waited to speak until the footman had exited. "Did you know that Mr. Asher is sending Catherine to a school in Wales for troubled girls?"

Aunt Gwen raised her eyebrows. "Whoever told you that?"

Lenora recounted her conversation with Mrs. Warner.

"Mr. Asher would have told us if that were the case."

"He has made no mention to you of other plans?" Lenora confirmed. The angry heat in her chest had not gone away, and it made her suspicious of everyone, even Aunt Gwen. Maybe she was hiding the information from Lenora for some reason, thinking Lenora would quit if she knew that Catherine would be shipped to Wales.

Wales! Lenora clenched her fists at her sides.

"I'd have told you if he discussed anything with me," Aunt Gwen said, her jaw tight. "And I'd have a pretty bit to say to him about what I thought about it, too."

Lenora began pacing. "Perhaps he made the plan without us because he knew we would object to it."

"I can't imagine it is his idea," Aunt Gwen said.

Lenora was in no mood to absolve Mr. Asher. Yes, Miss Keighly might have been involved, but Mr. Asher had been clear—in word and deed—that he was the one who took responsibility for Catherine's care. But he was to marry in January, not the summer, so perhaps he was already turning the decisions over to Miss Keighly.

"Mrs. Warner said she gave the address to both Miss Keighly *and* Mr. Asher earlier this week. At the very least, he is in agreement. It is exactly as I thought. He is a man of low character with little regard for the commitments he makes."

"Now, Lenora—"

Lenora turned toward her aunt and did not let her finish.

"He blackmailed me into helping Catherine at Mrs. Henry's school."

Aunt Gwen's eyes went wide, and Lenora had to look away, already regretting having blurted out such a sensitive thing. Now that it was out there like feathers from a pillow, she had to explain. "He'd caught me at the river one night and then recognized me at the parents' tea. He said if I did not help Catherine, he would reveal me."

"Goodness," Aunt Gwen breathed, setting down her glass.

"I know you thought me pious and unforgiving in my measure of him when I learned of his engagement, but I did not make that decision lightly. It was not only that he would so easily break his commitment to Miss Keighly, but also that he would stoop to such levels of using my actions against me in the first place. He is opportunistic, and now, after convincing us of his good graces toward his niece, he is ready to send her off as surely as his other relatives did. She will be caned and threatened and . . . not loved at all."

She tried to hold back her tears but was unsuccessful and brushed at her cheeks. She faced the window so her aunt would not see her crying. She thought back on all the years she had lived in fear of making a mistake and how she'd seen that same fear in Catherine. She thought of the progress Catherine had made, and the confidences she had shared with Lenora. The idea of bringing all of that to an end was staggering. And Mr. Asher was supporting it? Any warmth of compassion she had ever felt for him was extinguished, leaving behind only rage—an emotion she had never felt in her life.

"I think we need to have a conference with Mr. Asher," Aunt Gwen said, standing from her chair and moving toward her writing desk. "I shall ask him to come first thing tomorrow morning."

Lenora shook her head. "I cannot sleep with this spinning through my mind." She clenched her fists. What if her anger continued to build through the night? What might she do when Mr. Asher arrived tomorrow? She imagined pushing him down the stairs while calling him every vile name she had ever heard, which wasn't very many, truth be told.

"It is too late to ask him to come tonight," Aunt Gwen said.

Lenora looked at the clock. It was nearly ten. Definitely too late, not to mention that Catherine was with him for the weekend. But to wait until morning . . . Lenora took a deep breath. Another idea stepped out of the shadows of her thoughts

"Unless . . ." Aunt Gwen said, drawing Lenora's attention back to her. "Do you still have those trousers?"

Chapter Thirty-Six

It was nearly midnight when Aiden arrived at the river. Lenora was already there. He hated that she'd come without an escort. Anything could have happened to her.

He paused halfway down the stairs. Even from a distance, he could see her breath clouding in front of her face. It was cold tonight—would likely snow before morning—and yet he hadn't hesitated. He'd made sure Catherine was settled for the night, of course, and told Paulette to watch her door to make sure she didn't follow.

Miss Keighly had left Bath on Wednesday, after sending him a note officially breaking their engagement due to an inability to settle on mutually agreeable terms. She asked for a settlement of one thousand pounds as compensation for the last ten months. He agreed and sent a letter saying as much to both her solicitor and his. He hoped that one day they might be friends again, since both their families were in Cheshire, but he was content to wait a year or two before he attempted any reconciliation.

The relief he felt at no longer being tied to Miss Keighly was tempered by the fact that he was unsure how things might progress from here. With Miss Keighly gone, would Lenora be open to him? Could he disregard how much she'd put him off these last weeks? He still felt wounded by her rejection and still questioned if she cared for him as much as he cared for her. However, his hopes were high upon receipt of her request to meet him at the river. This is where they'd met. This is where they'd shared their first—and to date, only—kiss. A fitting place for them to start anew.

Lenora did not seem to hear him until he reached the bottom of the steps, then she spun toward him and stood very still. She wore that cap pulled down to her forehead and those man's clothes that hid her figure, but her eyes were bright and her lips were soft and . . .

She did not look happy to see him. Was she angry that he'd called off the engagement? She'd told him not to, and yet he'd hoped . . .

"Good evening, Miss Wilton," he said carefully.

"Are you sending Catherine to Wales?"

He studied her while considering his answer. Gone were his hopes that this was a different sort of reunion. There would be no repeat of their riverside kiss, no rekindling of the feelings between them. She was as set against him as she had ever been, and he shored up his defenses, since hers were so well in place. "No."

She looked confused and let silence hang between them for a few moments. "You are *not* sending her to a school for troubled girls?"

He lifted his chin, irritated at himself for expecting something different than this. "No, I am not."

"There is gossip that Miss Keighly found a school for troubled girls that would accept Catherine in December. I had to know if you were in fact planning on such a thing."

Just how much gossip had she heard? He decided to proceed cautiously. "Catherine is my niece, and I will make decisions regarding her education and future interests. I am content with the situation you have helped me develop for her here in Bath. I have no plans to send her elsewhere, and if for some reason I were considering such a thing, the first people I would speak to about it would be yourself and Mrs. Simmons, who have made so many sacrifices on our account." His words were cold and crisp. He did not allow any of his feelings for this woman to show since she seemed to have no feelings toward him but negative ones.

"Oh." Lenora looked at the ground, nervousness seeming to replace her anger in an instant. "Well, I am glad to hear it. I should return to my aunt, then."

She made to walk past him, but he reached out and took her arm, not so tightly that she couldn't easily shake off his grip, though she didn't. She looked at his hand on the sleeve of her coat, and then at his face. A very similar action had happened at the stables almost two weeks ago. But he'd felt softer then. Tonight, he was tired and heavy and hopeless. She'd only called on him to berate him. She had nothing else to give him. Did she

know of the broken engagement and had not changed her opinion of him? Or did she not know? Should he tell her? He chose
not to—he wanted her to *choose* him. In spite of Miss Keighly.
How else could he know Lenora's actual feelings? Unless this *was*
how she felt—him being engaged to Miss Keighly or not.

"I am not a man of such low character as you have determined me to be, Miss Wilton. I hope one day you can truly
believe it."

He held her eyes until she looked away. He released her
arm and watched her go but did not follow until she reached
the top of the stairs. When he came through the space between
the shops and turned toward Gay Street instead of his own, she
stopped and turned.

"I do not need an escort," she said from across the distance.

"I shall escort you all the same."

"I do not *want* an escort," she said in clipped words.

"But I am a gentleman and shall escort you all the same."

She shook her head and moved forward, apparently convinced he would not give in—which he wouldn't. As he walked
ten paces behind her, he allowed his disappointment to settle
upon his weary shoulders.

She believed that he would go against all he'd said regarding his devotion to Catherine and change his niece's situation
without discussing it with her or Mrs. Simmons. It seemed that
she was determined to see the worst of him in every situation.
That, above all other thoughts and difficulties, fueled his growing hopelessness. She'd made her decision about him and could
only see his flaws.

When he turned the corner of Gay Street, she was waiting for him. He came to a quick stop, only a few feet separating them. She had her hands deep in the pockets of a thin coat that could not be keeping her warm.

She looked at his shoes as she spoke. "I am sorry that I jumped to conclusions. I was just . . . incensed at the idea and—"

"You fight for what is important to you." He said it as a statement, not a question.

She looked up and drew her eyebrows together as though she didn't understand.

"I am gratified to see that Catherine is worthy of your defense," he said in that same even voice. "We should all be so lucky."

He watched as understanding widened her eyes slightly before she turned and hurried toward the terrace house. He did not follow as he could see Mrs. Simmons's house from where he stood. She did not look back as she went through the front door. The lights were still on in the drawing room, which likely meant her aunt had waited up for her. He watched the lighted window for a few minutes, then turned and walked slowly home. Did she know? Did she not? Either way, she wasn't willing to fight for him. And he wasn't going to beg.

Chapter Thirty-Seven

Well, I am relieved to hear it," Aunt Gwen said.

Lenora was pacing again—her cap off but her hair still pinned up—trying to sort out her thoughts after recounting the exchange to Aunt Gwen. She should not be feeling unsettled, but she was. Mr. Asher had told her exactly what she'd wanted to hear—that Catherine was not being sent to Wales—and yet she was as anxious now as she'd been angry before. Finally, she stopped and turned to her aunt.

"He said . . . he said that he was pleased I was willing to fight for what was important to me."

"Catherine?" Aunt Gwen supplied.

Lenora nodded and stared at a spot on the rug while trying to remember his exact words. "He meant something more," she said aloud.

"What do you think he meant?"

Lenora shook her head. "I don't know."

Aunt Gwen stood and crossed the room. She took Lenora's face in her hands and looked at her deeply, unblinking. "Don't you?"

They stood that way for a few moments, then Aunt Gwen guided Lenora's head down so she could kiss her forehead. "Good night, my dear."

Lenora did not sleep well, but by morning, she believed she had sorted out Mr. Asher's words. She should fight for him. When she first deciphered the meaning, she'd been angry all over again—fight for an engaged, blackmailing cad! He was a man without honor . . . except that he had devoted himself to his niece's care whatever the cost. Except that he had honored his engagement to Miss Keighly even though he did not love her. Except that he had apparently defied Miss Keighly, who wanted to send Catherine away.

He'd said last night at the river that he would make the decisions for Catherine's care. Had he told Miss Keighly the same thing? Putting Catherine above the opinions of his fiancée—was that right? Shouldn't the woman he marry have an opinion? But if her opinion was to ship Catherine off to Wales, should her opinion be honored? And hadn't he blackmailed Lenora because, in his heart, he was simply desperate for Catherine to succeed? Did his motives make his actions right?

Her head felt near to exploding as she went back and forth between what was right and what was wrong and whether or not sometimes the wrong thing was actually right and the right thing was actually wrong. Sneaking out at night was wrong because it broke social protocol and put her at risk, to say nothing of the risk that could damage the reputation of the school and her aunt in the process. But it was right in that the night walks settled her mind and made her feel capable and confident and part of this city.

Allowing herself to be blackmailed into giving Catherine special consideration was wrong because her motivation was completely self-centered, but it was right because her attention actually helped to uncover Catherine's difficulties and eventually led to a situation where the girl could succeed. Lenora had grown to care deeply for the girl she had originally hated. She'd found healing just as Aunt Gwen had hoped

Kissing Mr. Asher at the river that night had seemed so right, and yet it had also been wrong because he was engaged. And for him to jilt Miss Keighly would be wrong. But Miss Keighly wanted to send Catherine away, which was also wrong.

Lenora finally sat up in bed, put a pillow in front of her face, and screamed in frustration. *I know what is right. I know what is right*, she thought, remembering all the moral lessons she'd been taught as a child. Right was right and wrong was wrong, yet it had somehow turned into a mash of confusing circumstances.

Mr. Asher's words came back in an instant, as clear now as they had been the night before—*"You fight for what is important to you."* And yet, Lenora could think of few things she had ever fought for.

After being jilted by Mr. Glenside, she had fought to go to Bath as Aunt Gwen's summer companion because she'd had to get away from Leagrave and the gossip and pity and stares. When she'd returned to Leagrave a few weeks later and realized how sincere Cassie and Evan's feelings were for one another, she'd fought for her father to reconsider his decision forbidding Cassie and Evan from finding happiness together. And last night, she'd gone to the river prepared to fight for Catherine.

"You fight for what is important to you."

Do I? She hadn't fought to stay at Mrs. Henry's school. She hadn't fought to be more than "the musical Wilton girl." She hadn't fought to make a match or learn to waltz or to even leave Bath after learning Mr. Asher was engaged.

She fell back on the bed with her pillow still on her face, sick to her stomach and her head throbbing. Mr. Asher had been important to her, and yet she had turned him away. She could argue that she had done the right thing because of his commitment to Miss Keighly, but was that truly her motivation? Or had she been afraid? Afraid of how he'd hurt her by not telling her of the engagement, afraid of ever feeling such pain should he disappoint her again.

He had told her that he would marry his second choice because Lenora would not have him and that he would always do what was best for Catherine. Did that not put his character in a different light than she had chosen to see? Did that not make him the honorable man she had already judged him not to be?

Avoiding pain was not the same thing as healing. Being safe was not the same as being right.

Lenora missed church and did not come downstairs on Sunday until nearly noon, settling for toast and tea rather than anything resembling an actual meal. When she finished, she went into the parlor and sat down at the pianoforte. The Schubert piece Mr. Asher had left for her was still on the music rack. She'd not yet accepted that it belonged to her. She spread out the sheets and began to play, slow but perfect. That was how Mr. Thompson had taught her: take her time, but execute each note perfectly. It was what she'd tried to do all her life, and yet the most important victories she'd ever made had come when she had been bold and strong.

She wasn't sure when Aunt Gwen came into the room, but at some point, she looked up, and her aunt was sitting on the settee, listening with her eyes closed. Lenora finished the piece, then let her hands still on the keys, and Aunt Gwen opened her eyes.

"You play like an absolute angel, Lenora. That is a lovely piece."

"Mr. Asher gave it to me," Lenora said, looking at her name printed in his hand upon the page.

"What a thoughtful gift."

Lenora stared at the sheet music until tears blurred her vision. She felt her aunt's hands on her shoulders a moment before Aunt Gwen kissed the top of her head. Lenora reached up and took hold of her aunt's hands. "I don't know what to do," she whispered, tears streaming down her cheeks. "I don't know what is right anymore."

"The very hardest thing a person can do is be brave. Brave enough to trust someone, brave enough to forgive the wrongs done, and brave enough to trust what their heart tells them. I do not believe Mr. Asher's intention was ever to hurt you, Lenora, not for an instant."

"But he did," Lenora said. "And I do not think I could bear it if he hurt me again."

"*If*," Gwen repeated. "Will you base your entire future happiness on one word? Will you let fear rule your future?"

Lenora was terrified she would do exactly that. Although she'd had bursts of courage and moments when she had acted with faith, she had never risked much. Loving Aiden gave him the power to break her heart. Loving Aiden meant accepting that Miss Keighly would feel the same rejection Lenora had felt. The choice felt selfish, and Lenora had never been selfish. She was the daughter who always lent her clothes and jewelry to her sisters. She gave the bigger portion when a tart was cut in half. She did extra work, asked for little, and took the smaller bedroom even when it was only she and Cassie living at home. She'd taken pride in her unselfishness, but wasn't pride a sin too?

Aunt Gwen wrapped her arms around her niece, embracing her from behind and speaking softly. "Life never comes with guarantees, Lenora, and there *is* security in never taking a chance. But if you do not take hold of the opportunities of happiness that come your way, you will only find empty tomorrows. Life is both too long and too short to allow fear to guide your ship."

Chapter Thirty-Eight

Monday morning, Aiden delivered Catherine to Mrs. Simmons's terrace house. He had decided to visit the estate in Cheshire. He hadn't been there since August, Bath was uncomfortable, and Catherine was doing well. He would make his arrangements and then ask if Catherine could stay with Mrs. Simmons for the two weekends he would be gone. If she was unable, he would look into hiring a temporary governess. How Catherine would *love* that.

First, he needed to send letters to his steward and his solicitor and see about purchasing a horse. He didn't mind taking the journey on horseback, except he'd left all the horses in Cheshire, having rented a carriage when they came to Bath. It was a relief to have details to fill his mind, preventing his thoughts from going back over to the too-familiar regrets and "I wish that . . ." and "If only I had . . ." He needed distraction and distance.

Aiden was shrugging out of his coat when Martin cleared his throat.

"There is a woman waiting for you in the visitor's parlor, Mr. Asher."

Aiden experienced a moment of déjà vu and looked at the parlor in trepidation. Had Miss Keighly returned? Was she not finished with him after all? "Miss Keighly?"

"No, sir," Martin said, shaking his head. "Miss Wilton. She said she is Miss Catherine's teacher."

Aiden turned toward the parlor without delay, quickly handing off his coat and hat. Miss Wilton, here? He'd only left Catherine at Mrs. Simmons's house half an hour ago. He had assumed Miss Wilton had been there, waiting for him to leave before she began the day's lessons. He entered the parlor, and Miss Wilton came to her feet, a nervous smile on her face—but a *smile*. He had not seen one from her in such a long time.

She was not in her schoolteacher costume of the severe hair and dull dress, but she was not dressed so elaborately as she was for social events, either. Instead, she wore a blue linen dress with white flowers sewn throughout and lace trim around the bodice. Her hair was down, a great blonde cascade, though the front portions were pulled back from her face and pinned up as a cluster of curls. The style made her look both young and confident, and entirely beautiful.

They held one another's eyes, and he braced himself, not knowing what to expect. Then he feared he *did* know what to expect. If she'd heard Miss Keighly had broken the engagement, did she now deem him not so low of character as she'd previously determined? He waited for her to speak, for her to set the tone of this interview.

"Mr. Asher," she said, nodding her head.

"Miss Wilton," he replied, not dropping her gaze.

She licked her lips and began fidgeting with the folds of her skirt. "It is completely inappropriate for me to be here, and I fear you will find me a hypocrite for saying what I have come to say, but . . ." She paused, swallowed, took a breath, and then let it out.

She doesn't know Miss Keighly has broken the engagement. He could tell in the blush of her cheeks, the nervous sway of her skirt, and the way her gaze would flit to him and then away. He considered rescuing her, but then decided against it. He wanted to know what she'd come to say without her knowing that he was no longer an engaged man.

"I told you not to break your engagement to Miss Keighly." Her voice shook, but she was able to lift her regretful eyes to meet his again. "I told you that doing so would make you a man without honor. A man I could never . . . love." Tears rose in her eyes, and he resisted the impulse to cross the room and take her in his arms.

She paused to swipe quickly at her eyes. "I am so sorry," she said. "I am so sorry that I let fear rule me, that I put you in such a difficult situation, and that I did not fight for what I wanted."

Aiden kept his expression neutral. "And what is it you want?"

She swallowed. "You." It was barely a whisper.

He took a few steps toward her and put his hand behind his ear. "I'm afraid I couldn't hear that."

She managed a teary smile and shook her head at his teasing. "I want you to break your engagement to Miss Keighly. I'm sorry for running away."

He didn't say anything, but the weight he'd been carrying in his chest was suddenly light as a feather and bright as the sun. He simply took her face in his hands and kissed her.

She startled the moment his lips met hers, but when she didn't pull away, he let his hands slide to her shoulders. Then her arms came around his back, and she stepped closer. He deepened the kiss, and she welcomed it just as she had on the river, just as he'd dreamed she would every night since then.

Finally, he lifted his head and stepped back so he could look into her eyes. He smiled at her, relishing being able to say the next words. "Miss Keighly broke our engagement a week ago."

Lenora's eyebrows flew upward, her eyes wide and her surprise genuine. She opened her mouth as though to speak, but Aiden kissed her again. Lenora melted into the kiss as she had with the others they'd shared, then pushed him away.

"Wait," she said, slightly breathless. "Miss Keighly broke your engagement? Why? How? Are you terribly upset?"

"Do I look terribly upset?"

She quirked a smile. "No, you do not."

"I learned that she was executing plans to send Catherine to that school in Wales. Apparently, *that* portion hit the gossip lines of Bath, but the fact that I drew a line did not. She did cry off, but I gave her the option of doing so herself or else I would break the engagement. If you must judge my character harshly for that, so be it."

"I have been too judgmental already." She reached out her hand, and he took it, giving it a squeeze before lifting it to his lips. She watched him kiss her hand, her eyes bright. "I have wanted to avoid pain and do what is right, but nothing in my life has been as painful as these last weeks have been. Please forgive me for letting fear blind me to the man you are, and what I want to be to you."

He let his fingers stroke the lock of hair draped over her shoulder. "You understand that Catherine will be a part of my life and a part of the family I hope very much to create. I fear she will never be easy to manage, but I am committed to her, regardless."

"Any woman would be lucky to earn the love and respect of such an honorable man. I am committed to her also."

He cocked his head. "She is difficult."

Lenora's bright smile lit the room. "Yes, I know. But she is also a delight."

He pulled her hand, causing her to step forward until she hit up against his chest. She let out a small gasp that sent warm shivers down his spine. Clasping one hand against his chest, he used his other hand to tip her chin up. "I will not lie and say your words that day in your aunt's parlor did not wound me deeply."

"I know," she said in a whisper.

"But I happen to be a very forgiving and reasonable man."

She smiled.

"Only . . ."

"What?" she asked.

"It might take some time, maybe even a lifetime, for me to be sure that you are and ever will be the woman who will make me the happiest of men. I fear it will take hard work on your part—loving my niece, making a family, proving your devotion in every way a woman can prove such to a man."

Lenora laughed, then tried to school her expression. For perhaps the first time, he could read every thought and feeling on her face, and that, more than even her being here and the words she had spoken, assured him that they would find every happiness together. "So my punishment for letting fear rule me is to be a life sentence, then."

He lowered his face and barely brushed her lips with his own. "Precisely."

Epilogue

Five years later

Aiden and Lenora Asher stood at the entryway to the ballroom, welcoming guests to Catherine's debut ball at the estate in Cheshire and smiling until they felt sure their faces would never return to normal. They only stopped receiving when they heard the orchestra strike up the first dance. The grandson of one of Aunt Gwen's friends was escorting Catherine in her first dance—a waltz. Catherine had insisted upon it, even though it was completely improper. There was always a great deal of bartering and negotiating when it came to Catherine's compliance in any given situation.

Aiden and Lenora reached the edge of the dance floor, and Lenora sighed as she saw Catherine's presentation up close. She and Catherine had argued for days about what was appropriate for her to wear for her debut ball. White, of course, but Catherine had wanted red slippers. Lenora had forbidden it, a choice that Aunt Gwen had supported, thank goodness.

Aunt Gwen was still the most steadying influence for the headstrong girl, so it was a blessing that she didn't mind visiting them in the country a few times a year and was diligent in returning correspondence when she was residing in Bath.

Lenora had thought the topic was finished, but sometime between the receiving line and the dance, Catherine had procured a huge bow in bright red satin and pinned it directly to the back of her head. From the front, it looked as though she'd sprouted wings.

"That girl," Lenora said under her breath, swallowing the residual embarrassment. Perhaps she should have agreed to the shoes.

"Is delightful," Aiden finished for her. They repeated the mantra half a dozen times a day sometimes. And Catherine *was* delightful, sometimes, and petulant, obstinate, irritating, and defiant at other times. But as she got older, she was getting better at controlling her moods and understanding the effect her actions had on other people.

She adored Lenora and Aiden's daughters as though they were her sisters, not cousins. Hannah would be three in April, and Gwendoline was just six months old. So far, their personalities were much more like their mother than their older cousin. For that, Lenora was grateful. She could not handle more than one Catherine in her life, but she had to admit she had learned to handle Catherine rather well. Lenora's natural calmness had become an asset, just as Aiden's dogged devotion had convinced her that she was truly loved.

"Now," Catherine said loudly as she and Mr. Kindershod

waltzed in front of where Aiden and Lenora stood. She had wanted to dance a few measures as the only couple on the floor, then have the others join them.

"I believe we have our orders," Aiden said, standing before Lenora as he put out his hand. Lenora took it and remembered their first dance—countless waltzes ago—and how breathless she'd been in his company that night. She took his hand and allowed him to lead her into the first steps.

"Do you remember our first waltz?" Aiden asked.

Lenora laughed. "I was just thinking about it." She made the mistake of looking past him, at the eyes that watched them on the floor, and tensed beneath the scrutiny. She was still never quite comfortable in a crowd, let alone being the center of attention. She hoped everyone was too distracted by Catherine's silly big bow to notice.

Aiden let go of her waist in order to turn her chin back to face him. "Watch my eyes, don't think too much, move with me."

She immediately softened in his arms, as she always did when he looked at her like that.

"You look lovely tonight, my dear," he said.

"Thank you. I was surprised the dress would fit." After two children, the youthful slimness she'd taken for granted had given way to a plumpness she found uncomfortable.

"Better than ever," he said, pulling her closer.

They were all but pressed together. Lenora shook her head and felt her cheeks heat up. "You're going to spur gossip," she said, trying to pull back, but that only encouraged him more.

He winked at her. "What is a little scandal among friends?"

She couldn't help but smile as she looked into those eyes she loved so dearly. Eyes that had seen through the different personas she'd worn and found the whole of her. Eyes that had stared in wonder at their first child, and then their second. Eyes that had held back their fury when Catherine vexed him to the limit, and eyes that had teared up when his niece performed to a standing ovation at the music hall a few months ago—performing a musical piece she had *read*. This husband of hers was a man of feeling, a man of goodness, and a man to whom she had entrusted her heart, body, and soul.

She caught sight of Cassie and Evan, who had traveled from Leagrave for Catherine's debut, and felt the connectedness of so many people she loved so well.

"What are you thinking of?" Aiden asked, watching her face as they executed a turn between two other couples—the floor was quite full now.

"That I am the luckiest woman in the world," Lenora said.

"That's only because you married the luckiest man." They danced a few more steps. "What do you say about taking a trip to the river tonight?"

He was not referring to the Avon River in Bath, but the Meresy, which ran through the south end of their Cheshire estate. For her birthday last year, Aiden had commissioned a set of stone steps leading from the top of the embankment to a small section of riverbank, complete with a stone bench perfect for reading or kissing or watching the river.

It was somewhere Lenora escaped to when life became overwhelming—which it often did, and always had. The rippling water seemed to move through her thoughts like music, clearing and cleansing her from the anxiety and stress. Sometimes Aiden came with her. When he did, the goal was not to relax but to remember the feelings that had started them on the course of their lives together.

"After the ball?" Lenora asked, allowing her acceptance of his offer to show on her face.

Aiden smiled that dashing smile. "Oh, how I adore you, Mrs. Asher." He turned her more sharply than necessary, leaving her breathless.

Watch my eyes. Don't think too much. Move with me.

Acknowledgments

I wrote the first 41,000 words of this book over a four-day writing retreat. It took me four months to write the rest. I struggled to pinpoint Lenora's story, but really, really wanted to make it work. Thank you to my beta readers, Margot Hovely (*Glimmering Light*, Covenant 2014) and Jennifer Moore (*Miss Leslie's Secret*, Covenant 2017). And to my editor, Lisa Mangum, for her patience with my pushing the deadlines and then her being so spot on with feedback.

Additional thanks to my product manager at Shadow Mountain, Heidi Taylor Gordon, to Rachael Ward for the typesetting, and to Heather Ward and Kimberly Durtschi for the cover, as well as all the other hands that helped push this book along.

Big thanks to my agent, Lane Heymont, for being so positive, savvy, and kind.

I am greatly blessed with friends, faith, and my family. Thank you to everyone who lifts me up and makes it possible for me to do what I love and love what I do. God bless.

Discussion Questions

1. What do you feel Lenora's role was in her family? Can you recognize your "role" in your family growing up? How has your role changed over the years?

2. Lenora struggles with anxiety but learns some coping mechanisms to help her live a different life once she comes to Bath. Do you have any experience with ways to mitigate anxiety? What are your favorite ways to relax or find balance in your life?

3. Though Lenora is musically gifted, that strength is also a weakness because it allowed her to avoid developing other skills. Do you have strengths that have also sometimes been stumbling blocks? Have you been able to turn a weakness into a strength? How have you been able to find that balance?

4. What are your feelings regarding natural ability versus acquired talent? How does one affect the other?

5. Was there a character in this story to whom you related better than the others? What qualities of that person drew you to that character?

6. Catherine struggles with dyslexia, which makes certain tasks more difficult for her. How was she able to hide her dyslexia, and what made her finally willing to ask for help? Have you ever found it difficult to ask for help?

7. Should Aiden have told Lenora about the broken engagement when she confronted him about the rumors she'd heard regarding Catherine being sent to Wales? Did you understand or agree with his decision?

8. Is there a particular scene or moment that stood out to you in this story?

9. Lenora finds peace and comfort by sitting alongside the river. Is there a special place you like to go to find peace?

10. The waltz that Lenora shares with Aidan is a turning point in her life and in their relationship. Do you remember your first dance?

About the Author

© Sha-Retree Photography. Used by permission.

Josi is the author of twenty-five novels and one cookbook and a participant in several co-authored projects and anthologies. She is a four-time Whitney award winner—*Sheep's Clothing* (2007), *Wedding Cake* (2014), and *Lord Fenton's Folly* (2015) for Best Romance and Best Novel of the Year—and the Utah Best in State winner for fiction in 2012. She and her husband, Lee, are the parents of four children.

You can find more information about Josi and her writing at josiskilpack.com.

FALL IN LOVE WITH A

PROPER ROMANCE

BY

JOSI S. KILPACK

Available wherever books are sold

SHADOW
MOUNTAIN